Every Family Has One

All Things D

Joanna Warrington

http://www.joannawarringtonauthor-allthingsd.co.uk

All rights reserved
The moral right of the author has been asserted
Copyright 2015 Joanna Warrington

ISBN: 1512092029
ISBN 13: 9781512092028
Library of Congress Control Number: 2015907600
CreateSpace Independent Publishing Platform
North Charleston, South Carolina

Disclaimer and background to the story

This story is a work of fiction. Names, characters, businesses, places, events, incidents and the human experiences are either the product of my imagination or are used in a fictitious manner. Any resemblance to actual persons, living or dead, or actual events is purely coincidental.

This story is in two parts: 'A Catholic Woman's Dying Wish' focuses on the search for Kathleen across several continents. 'Every Family Has One' focuses on her life in a Magdalene laundry and beyond. They can be read together or as stand-alone stories.

This story was inspired by my interest in the Magdalene Laundries: institutions that existed in Ireland until 1996 - maintained by religious orders in the Roman Catholic Church these homes were run by nuns for women labeled as 'fallen' by their families or society. There has been a great deal of interest in these institutions over the past 15 years; immortalized in films like The Magdalene Sisters and Philomena and documentaries such as Sex in a Cold Climate.

Through my work as a funeral celebrant I had the privilege of meeting the family of a Magdalene survivor and some of my information about the long-term impact of incarceration has come from this family. I would like to thank the families for helping me with this project and for their information about Liverpool. I would also like to thank Liverpool historian and academic Ken Pye and the Liverpool Central library and Steven Culshaw – Liverpool man born and bred and to Jacq Molloy, Eastbourne writer who edited the book for me.

'The Weeping Lady' Magdalene Laundry is a fictional institution and does not necessarily represent what happened within the laundries across Ireland at this time. However it may provide a glimpse into the life of the laundries that some people might identify with. Experiences varied.

My heart goes out to all the women who passed through these institutions; their fight for justice, the search for missing relatives and loved ones and the long-term consequences of their incarceration. Kathleen's life is fictional but it follows an emotional pattern that many women might identify with.

The story was also inspired by recent and widespread media coverage of historical sex abuse cases by people in positions of power and authority and explores some of the emotional and physical consequences of child abuse through the characters of Darius and Kathleen as well as touching on the recovery process. The story includes a violent scene that some might find distressing. There is also strong language.

The opinions and views expressed in the book are the opinions and views of the characters and not mine, the author or any living person.

Please note that legal advice has been taken prior to publication of this book.

Every Family Has One

Please visit my website which is a blog about
all issues beginning with the letter D.
http://www.joannawarringtonauthor-allthingsd.co.uk

Joanna Warrington 2015

The story begins in Liverpool, England, January 12th 1974

Kathleen

1
Kathleen

January 1974

Her first concert: a coming of age. A rite of passage. And like any rite of passage it was going to be a night to remember... but just not in the way she was imagining.

Hawkwind. Liverpool Stadium. 1974. It sounded grand. She rolled the words on her tongue. She could see the t-shirt. She'd buy it and wear it proudly.

But if Kathleen had known what was going to happen that evening she would have missed the band she'd longed to see and willingly stayed in with her mother to play Ludo under candlelight. But without the aid of a crystal ball how could she have possibly known?

She fizzed with excitement as she climbed the rickety stairs to her attic bedroom to get ready for the evening ahead. Her mother stood at the bottom, hands on hips, a face of thunder.

'That music is filling your head with sin but emptying your heart of God.' Kathleen inched further up the stairs ignoring the ridiculous statement, wondering where she had pulled it from. Her mother wasn't going to stop her going out. Not tonight. She'd waited months to see her favourite band, Hawkwind – dreaming of nothing else, thinking of nothing else. Had saved her birthday money to go. Yet knew she would be dragged to confession. Maybe her mother was right. Her conscience pricked. She knew she was a seeker of pleasure and God was sure to disapprove. She would pay her currency for the evening in Hail Mary's and Our Father's.

'There's no point in going out tonight. We're expecting another power cut. It'll be too dark to walk back and you'll trip over the rubbish stacked along the pavements.' Her mother's voice was icy, lacking in the cookie cutter sincerity that other mothers seemed to have.

'I'm warning you Kathleen...' Her tone was now deeper as she tried to sound menacing, but Kathleen - knowing that she was struggling to perform the role of two parents rolled into one - ignored her. *All mothers are slightly insane* she had read in a book by JD Salinger - a quote she found reassuring.

Kathleen knew her game. Her mother wasn't good at being alone; not even wrapped in the big electric blanket of her faith; scared of her own shadow; every creak in the darkness and howl of the wind outside.

'I forbid you..'

There was a tremour to her voice now, maybe realizing, Kathleen thought that her power was crumbling.

Kathleen stood at the top of the stairs looking down on her archetypal 1950s mother scowling in her pinny, her cleavage under wrap. What an oddity she was. It was hard to believe that she had lived through the sixties and she wondered how on earth she'd ever opened her legs to have sex. Twice in fact, unless there were miscarriages she didn't know about.

Mary Quant could have made your life so much better she wanted to shout down.

'Forbid me? What sort of a word is that mam?' She sniggered, her feisty spirit rising and slammed her bedroom door. Her mother's exasperated groans floated up and she knew she would be returning to the warmth of the fire and her crutch – the Bible. Her faith had become a soft blanket ever since the fateful day her father had been in the wrong place at the wrong time, caught up in the Troubles visiting his sister on Belfast's Falls Road.

In her bedroom Kathleen peered in the cracked mirror and smiled guiltily at her reflection. Her skin glowed in the pool of light from a table lamp. Her radiant, dark curls cascaded around her shoulders, complimenting the white of her cheesecloth top. Her friends told her she looked and sounded like Nerys Hughes in the comedy The Liver Birds but she liked to imagine she was Farah Fawcett Major starring in a blockbuster movie; a thought that she tried to quell because it led her into a dark and lonely place – where they punished the vain and the proud; vices that enveloped her soul in a plethora of guilt and self loathing.

When she was ready she put the pot of rouge back into the crack she'd chiseled out under her bedroom windowsill remembering how pretty it had looked on her friend Sandra's dressing table sitting on a dainty doilie. The pot was nearly empty. She didn't know where the next pot would come from. Gathering new supplies was always a challenge, but Kathleen tried to see the funny side of her situation. *My house is like the bleedin' Soviet Union* she laughed to friends.

Standing up she peered out of the tiny misty window that looked out over the Liverpool docks. A breeze was gently rattling the pane. She closed her eyes remembering the long walks by the Mersey with her dad; looking up at the liver birds nestled on top of the Royal Liver Building, his hand squeezing hers. *One bird is watching the football, the other the shipping so it is Kathleen.* The memory still made her glow inside even though it was now three years on.

She loved to watch the view out of her window. How she longed to skip down to the Docks one early morning and meet a sailor dressed in white and blue from a faraway place who'd whisk her away on his ship to a sandy beach thousands of miles away. But that was the stuff of fairytales or a story in Mills and Boon. The only men she ever saw at the docks were grubby balding men with missing teeth and sweat patches under their arms going about their work at the quayside. But

3

these days there wasn't so much activity down at the docks as there had been when she was little. Dominating the scenery now were stacks of brightly coloured containers, like Lego bricks and huge cranes lifting those Lego pieces onto ships. Like the sentiment within the song 'American Pie' her dream had curdled too.

She lifted her mattress and put the crusty mascara in the centre, next to the latest Jackie Magazine. She flicked through the magazine and could hear her mother's voice in her head.

That magazine is filling your head with romantic clap trap. Get rid of it.

But it was nice, warming clap trap. Preferable to reading long, turgid passages of the Bible. Her mother reminded her of Mary Whitehouse; a tight lipped, cold hearted killjoy. She picked up the Bible, sitting on her bedside table, pride of place and in a moment of defiance flung it into the air and watched it come crashing down. When it landed it was a heavy thud: the type of thud that would have sent her father scuttling down to the lav' at the bottom of the garden to play his banjo. She could see her mother downstairs, probably bowing in silent prayer, bearing the daily cross of grief.

Kathleen wondered what her mother would say next to stop her going out but in the kitchen she found her hugging the picture of her dad holding an enormous trout, dressed in his fishing gear. She was rocking back and forth next to the fire, silent tears trickling down her face. A faint smile flickered across her face. Kathleen knew she was remembering the time he had dressed in his rubber suit with every piece of tackle and rod he owned dangling over his shoulders and had fallen down the muddy bank, clawing his way back up. In her mind's eye she could still see the muddy claw marks on the bank and everyone laughing hysterically.

But as quick as the memory flashed both their minds her mother looked up; brushed the tears from her sleeve and placed the photo frame back on the mantel.

'Mum we could revive the musical spaghetti nights. Fill the house with music and laughter again. Invite Auntie Hilda to clatter her tuna can? We could even invite Cilla Black's dad, John White and maybe he'd invite Cilla if she's not too busy singing somewhere else.' John White, father of the famous singer had become good friends with Kathleen's father when they worked on the docks together and he was still a regular visitor to their house. 'She could sing You're my World. She'd soon cheer us up.'

Her mother's face looked as if she had suggested a walk in a storm. She turned back to the photo; probably remembering how Paddy used to bulk the spaghetti out with porridge oats and invite the whole street round.

This is Liverpool, Kathleen thought to herself. *Every house in the city where modern music was born should be making its' own music and singing all the hits that made this city great.* Suddenly she could see herself walking down to the Cavern with her dad. They were the Saturdays she had looked forward to as a child.

'Father Joseph might drop over later for a cuppa.' Maria's face relaxed as she spoke of the priest.

Kathleen studied her mother's face. She was still pretty. Had the type of legs any man would desire. But she knew it wasn't going to happen. She thought of the priest, bible tucked under his arm clutching his collection box appealing for more money to save the church roof. There were better ways to spend a Saturday evening.

'You've not had your pudding' Maria snapped, the memories now a million miles away. Kathleen watched her move to the counter more sluggishly than normal to dish the slop - her body showing the strain. Life seemed to be slipping out from under her.

She banged the bowl onto the table in front of Kathleen in an unloving way as if it were a great effort. Kathleen looked at the runny mess. Any minute now she expected Marlon Brando to blast in to complete the 1950s scene. It would be so nice, she thought, to be offered butterscotch Angel Delight for a change and a glass of refreshing Rise and Shine: sunshine in a glass.

As she ate the slop she could feel herself buckle under her mother's cold stare and waited for the negative comments to fly.

'You look ridiculous in all that makeup and that skirt is too short. You're asking for trouble.' She suddenly shouted. 'You girls these days. It would pain God to see you so it would.'

'I won't be late. Don't wait up.' Not giving Maria another chance to break her spirit she got up and headed into the hall to put her coat on, calling her goodbye from the front door; her spirit strong and determined.

But unfortunately her feisty spirit was to be to her peril.

2
Kathleen

January 1974

After the concert the street outside was drab and grey compared to the feverish excitement of seeing Hawkwind. All around them lights were flickering and within moments the city was cloaked in darkness. Bracing herself against the artic gust Kathleen pulled her duffel coat around her thin clothing and linked arms with her two friends. After the intense heat of the Liverpool stadium the chill was a shock.

'Fuck. Another power cut. Me mam did warn me.' Kathleen staggered to the wall in the sudden darkness, avoiding a brick she was about to stumble on.

'That was explosive. Incredible.' Sandra gushed.

'I loved the space effects.' Lois said.

'They remind me a bit of Pink Floyd.' Kathleen added.

Kathleen fumbled in her pocket for the torch she was now used to carrying and the three carefully picked their way along the pavement in the ribbon of light.

'Bloody minded greedy fuckers. When are these strikes going to end?' Kathleen moaned.

'God only knows. Soon I hope.' Lois replied.

Turning a corner in Tithebarn Street her friend stumbled over some bags of rubbish on the pavement.

'Fuck. The dustmen haven't been either.' And then they all yelped as they looked down to see a couple of rats scuttling away beneath the rubbish.

The girls began to sing some of the lyrics they'd heard during the evening.

"I'm an urban guerrilla
I make bombs in my cellar
I'm a derelict dweller
I'm a potential killer
I'm a street fighting dancer."

'Me mam hates me singing that song. She says it's disrespectful to me daddy, killed in the Troubles. She says I'm tempting more IRA bombs.' Kathleen said.

Lois and Sandra stopped walking, silenced by Kathleen's words. Sandra put her arm round Kathleen and rubbed her neck.

'I bet you really miss him. Nobody round here will forget what happened to him. Bastard IRA.' Lois spat; her voice a mix of sadness and anger.

'Anyone got a ciggie? I need to warm up like.' Kathleen said, taking a deep breath and trying to be strong.

The conversation moved on and they chatted about music, school and the boys they fancied.

Kathleen said goodbye to her friends at a fork in the road, the flicker of light from her torch guiding her path ahead and she fought now a howling icy wind slapping her cheeks and whipping through her hair. With both hands she pinned her duffel collar hard against her frozen ears and battled on, eyes to the ground, desperate to get home but knowing that a cold house would be her welcome.

She turned into a side street, a short cut from home. The red sandstone church with its' fish scale slate roof loomed ahead; the landmark indicating she was nearly home and ready to crash into bed. Its' imposing Neo Gothic Victorian structure and neat iron railings, flanking the scruffy grass verges made her feel strangely safe and secure, conjuring happy memories of Sunday school and church parties when she was much younger with jelly and ice cream and party games in the back hall. This was where she had met so many lovely, kind and caring people over the years and although she had started to challenge the rules of the church and found her mother's ways oppressive, the Church still offered a sense of comfort and stability for it was the one certain thing in her life and was linked to family tradition that went back centuries.

The Church would never change. It was like the Queen; there to eternity. It wasn't going to go away, or let her down, not like her dad, now dead and unlike her brother who was planning to leave Liverpool, to seek his fortune in the south.

She planned to cut the walk home by ten minutes, following the path between the cedar trees, through the back of the church to the alley way that led to her street. If she walked fast and tried to think of something cheerful she wouldn't be scared of the gravestones lurking in the darkness. And the spirit of her grandparents - buried there - would protect her.

As she crossed the road and looked up, the watery moon was nudging through the pewter sky above the church roof, trailing shimmery white streaks across the clouds, illuminating the straggly dead vines above the porch, reminding her of an old black and white Christopher Lee horror movie. Suddenly she didn't feel so comforted by the church. As she reached the railings, about to walk up the steps she noticed a dark figure in the shadows struggling with a key. His hands seemed to be shaking; maybe unable to grip the key in the cold. Under the shelter of the porch she recognized him immediately and felt a sense of relief. Father Joseph would be able to walk her home.

'Father. Can I help you?' she called up, joining him at the door.

'Kathleen. What are you doing out after dark? It's not safe to be out during a power cut.' From behind his glasses his gentle eyes were lit with concern.

'Tell me about it. I've just been to a concert at the stadium. It was great.'

'The stadium?' Disapproval showed in his frown. But she hadn't expected him to say *nice one*. He dropped the key. Kathleen bent down to pick it up and as she stood up he met her eyes and smiled.

'Stiff knuckles. I can't get a grip. I've got carpal tunnel syndrome in the hands. They go all tingly and painful. I tried to dig a grave this week.'

'What on earth for? You can't do that on your own.' She said with alarm.

'There's been talk of the gravediggers going out on strike.' He sighed.

'Seems everyone wants to strike.' Kathleen said.

'What a fool I was. There was no way I could dig a hole that deep.' He started to flex his fingers and shake the pain from his hands.

'That's madness, so it is.' They both laughed.

'It's given me big muscles though. Actually I'm glad I've bumped into you Kathleen, so I am.' His tone was warm and casual and he beamed down at her through soft grey eyes, pearlescent in the light of the moon. She studied his features. He was very handsome, in his 40's with a fresh olive complexion and high sculptured cheekbones. She had always loved the lilt of his southern Irish accent. She wondered why such a good looking man would want to become a priest, condemned to a life of chastity and thought of the happiness denied to a good woman, missing out on love in order to serve God.

'Oh?'

'I've got a C.S Lewis book in the vestry your mother wanted to borrow. May take me a moment to find it. Nip in for a moment would you.' He beckoned her in giving her little choice, closing the heavy door behind him. Kathleen followed on as he chatted enthusiastically

Every Family Has One

about how the book was going to be a great inspiration to her mother as he led the way up the red -carpeted aisle towards the altar and into the small musty room at the back where choir robes along the left wall covered the primrose walls like heavy curtains and a desk groaned with Father Joseph's paperwork and books on the right hand wall. She looked at the little wall heater next to his desk and instantly went to pull the cord in the dim torchlight but remembered the power cut and shivered in the dank air.

'Now let's see. Where did I put it?' He glanced across his shelves and it seemed he had no idea where to begin the search. There were so many books, all rammed in haphazardly over the years. He began pulling books out, one by one at random. Dust rose and swirled, illuminated by the thin moonlight from a small window above the desk.

Kathleen sighed. Looked at her watch hoping he would register the hint. Her mother would be worried but she didn't want to be rude.

He stopped, swiveled to face her, balancing precariously on a step ladder.

'I wonder if another member of the congregation has it.'

'Don't worry I'll pick it up another time Father. I better go now. It's late.'

'Sorry. Yes it is. I'll walk you back.'

But he didn't step down; frozen to the spot it seemed his mind was miles away. He was looking at her now in an unnerving way, his eyes shifting to her cleavage. She shifted further into the room as he stepped down, his eyes still anchored to her breasts. Kathleen pulled her coat around her, shutting away his wandering gaze and inched backwards into the robes, her shoulders now nestled among the cloth.

'Hey Father.' She waved him away with a nervous giggle, her cheeks burning. She started to shiver frantically against the cold air and the unnerving feeling she now had.

'I bet your mother doesn't approve of the way you dress. Low cut tops revealing your tender young breasts and short skirts to flaunt

11

those lovely long legs. Some men find it hard... to keep their hands to themselves. You know what I'm saying?' His voice was deep and wintery as he cast his eyes over her body.

'Mothers will always criticize. I really must go Father.' She said waving him away.

'You can always come to me with any questions about boys.'

Why would she go to the priest about boys and sex when she had friends and magazines, she thought to herself. Stepping further back, now hugging the wall with fear as the shock of his statement hit. She didn't like where this was going and struggled to find a light hearted reply.

'I've got Jackie magazine to answer all my burning questions.' She giggled nervously, hoping he'd join in the joke. 'It's what every girl reads. Make up, hair, boyfriends, kissing, tampons...' She stopped, realizing she'd gone too far.

'How to grow into a little slut you mean.' His eyes had narrowed.

Kathleen froze. She hadn't expected that.

'Steady on Father. It's full of stories too and cartoons.'

'And I suppose that magazine has made you into the girl who've become. Your mother complained to me about how you dress.'

Kathleen shrugged. 'It's not up to her what I do.'

'You're offending God in the way you dress.' He looked down at her bare legs. Do you understand what it means to be a disciple of Jesus?' He asked, his eyes predatory.

He slowly inched forward trapping her against the choir robes. She could feel his breath upon her, hot and acrid and was desperate more than ever to go. The wind outside rattled against the loose window pane. She could be home now, tucked up in bed she thought. If only she hadn't stopped.

'I'll come back for the book.' It was a good fob off and added 'Mammy will be wondering where I am.' She tried to sound casual.

'I think you need a lesson. The eighth sacrament...'

What the hell was that? She wondered.

There was a sneer in his tone. Their faces were close. She wondered if he'd been drinking wine. Tiny ruby veins coursed across his lips. His teeth were blotted red.

Her legs were giving way as she sank deeper into the folds of the robes lining the wall, working out her escape.

She struggled free of the robes threatening to drown her and regaining her composure made a dash for the door, but she wasn't quick enough. He was blocking the only exit, his hand on the iron latch.

'I need to go home Father.' She pleaded, knowing her voice sounded weak. He grabbed her arm, opened the door and pulled her in the direction of the altar. She hadn't expected him to stop her leaving. He was the family priest she kept reminding herself. And she certainly didn't anticipate what was about to happen next. A searing pain burned up her arm as he pushed her hard against the cold, stone wall pressing his mouth clumsily against hers, forcing his way inside her mouth, devouring and biting her lip so that she screeched in agony. Pinned to the dank wall with one hand he pressed her neck so that she couldn't move and the other cold reptilian hand snaked inside her top, finding her breast, clawing and pulling the nipple. Terror washed over her. She screamed as he bit into her nipple and soon he was pushing her down towards the altar and the life size stone statutes of the Virgin Mary and Jesus. In his wake a pile of hymnbooks thudded to the floor, several loose leaves escaping and a brass candlestick clattered across the flagstones, the candle cracking in two. From the corner of her eye she registered the meek shy smile of the Virgin Mary, exuding an air of calm innocence that made Kathleen angry, as if she were a by stander unwilling to come to her aid. She wondered if there was a special place in hell for women who didn't help other women.

'You need to atone for your sins Kathleen.' His voice echoed around the church. With one hand grabbing her hair he reached for a half empty bottle of communion wine sitting on the altar. The cork popped and he sloshed the sweet nectar into a silver chalice in which all her family had drunk from over many years and forced her head down, tipping it into her mouth. The cold metal hit against her teeth, the edges knifing into the sides of her mouth causing more pain. She coughed and spluttered, then wiped her mouth with her sleeve. But this wasn't the end. It was just the start.

'I don't like the way you dress Kathleen. It's offensive. It's not how women are supposed to dress.' He ordered. There was venom in his voice, spittal at his mouth. He began to yank her skirt above her waist. Her muscles tightened as she gripped her legs together. She was determined he wouldn't lever them apart. But as she refused access he grew stronger, more confident. She couldn't predict his next move. He was too quick. Too clever. She didn't expect her knickers to be torn from her body but they were made of cheap cotton and with one swift hand they were off.

He hastily untied the heavy buckle around his waist, tugged the zipper of his flies, frantically withdrawing his hardened penis and in the painful moments that followed he violated her body with such force that she thought her insides would tear apart.

The kind man she had known over several years had transformed into a crazed and wild beast and her faith in him, the person to whom everyone in her family went to for help and support lay shattered as his grip over her intensified.

Paralysed with fear, drained of all strength all she could manage was a faintly audible whisper for him to stop. Her bravado had long melted away, revealing a vulnerable and deeply distressed child.

Issuing each hard and deep thrust he wailed a catechism over and over again for her to receive the Holy Spirit. 'You will receive the Holy Spirit, you will receive the Holy Spirit.'

Hard though it was she tried to blot out the vision of him pounding on top of her. With her eyes shut tight she silently prayed over and over but through her closed eyes she could see the image of the statute of Jesus inches away; his eyes became those of Father Joseph, a deep and foreboding pewter, narrow, snake like and menacing.

Every Family Has One

As he thrusted deep inside the intense pain turned to a dull throb and the more she tightened her muscles the more she could tell he was enjoying it. His body was hot, clammy and sticky and she felt sick as she breathed in the woody aroma of his skin. While he shafted his hand grabbed and clawed at her nipples, the pain intense. It was as if he were a bird of prey swooping down upon a road kill, pecking and plucking at raw and fresh flesh, a frenzied consumption before other predators descended.

∽⃝

As she ran through the graveyard after the ordeal, her abuser's last words echoing through her mind *you're now dismissed* she didn't know that the agony she had just endured marked the start -not the end - of a nightmare that was to get worse.

Pausing on her doorstep she straightened herself up, buttoned her coat so that her mother couldn't see her torn clothes, smoothed her hair down, wiped the mascara from under her eyes with a used tissue in her pocket.

She flew through the door and her mother - hearing the key in the lock was already waiting; hands on hips, a face of thunder. She collapsed in a crumpled heap to the floor, drawing her knees tight to her chest wailing and shaking, bile rising in her throat. The power was back on and the kettle was bubbling but she wasn't registering anything as she sobbed and shivered, vaguely aware now of her mother's towering figure standing over her.

Her mother stooped in concern asking what had happened. Kneeling on the floor she lifted Kathleen up from under her arm to rest her head on her lap. She waited, gently rocking her back and forth as if she were a small child disturbed by teething pain, until the sobs subsided and the gulps turned to hick ups.

'Are you going to tell me what's happened?' She asked, in a gentle caressing voice as she stroked Kathleen's hair.

Kathleen gulped.

'Your face is streaked with that black eye liner I said looked ridiculous. Do you have to apply so much?' She couldn't resist a dig even in Kathleen's hour of need.

'Don't start mam.'

Her mother sighed. Kathleen knew it had been hard bringing up two children virtually alone; not a day going by when her mother didn't think about her husband, Paddy and mourn his loss.

'Well?' She tried again. The gentle tone had now disappeared, replaced by a sharp zest of impatience.

Kathleen choked back her gulps, stopping mid sentence after blurting 'I've been atta... Father J...' And for the first time since the attack she wondered what her story was going to be. Was it safe for her to tell the truth? Would it be easier to blame it on a stranger in a dark alley? If she told her the truth she'd accuse her of blasphemy, slap her hard across the face and send her to her room for a week and tell her she had turned mad. In any case she wouldn't believe. No one would believe. She was struggling to comprehend it all herself, finding it desperately hard to digest the reality of what the priest had just done.

Father Joseph could do nothing wrong in her mother's eyes. Did she want to shatter that illusion? Despite everything - her mother needed his support and knowing what he had done to her would destroy her and destroy the faith that she relied on as a crutch. It would only make matters worse. And who was she? She had no power. She was nothing more than a schoolgirl, who knew nothing of life, sitting in her room drawing information from Jackie Magazine. She wondered when she would stop feeling like a child.

Her fragile watery eyes met her mother's and she said 'a man in an alley knocked me to the ground. He hurt me mammy.' She didn't like lying but what choice did she have?

In the next few moments Kathleen felt her faith rise up inside her like a burning flame and then the lash of cold water as it was extinguished.

Her mother gasped and clapped her hand to her mouth, her eyes widening in shock. Kathleen could see tears forming in her mother's eyes, but it was a short lived concern.

'Jesus, Mary and Joseph why were you in a dark alley and dressed for trouble? Whatever would the priest say if he knew one of his young flock were behaving like that?'

And then her mother's hardness melted again. She was clearly struggling with mixed emotions, not knowing which way to swing.

She wrapped her arms tight around her daughter, nuzzling into her neck and for a few moments neither spoke as her mother started to sing in a quiet voice the lullaby she used to sing when Kathleen and Darius were babies crying in their cots at night.

'Hush little baby don't you cry mumma's gunna sing you a lullaby.'

And then her mother's body stiffened. It was as if she needed to regain control over her daughter and reaffirm her belief in the Church and what it stood for, once again.

'You went out this evening asking for trouble.'

Kathleen took immediate umbrage.

'Mam that's not fair.'

'Hard though it is for you to accept – and I've been around for a lot longer than you – there will always be some men who will look at a girl in a short skirt and low top and think to themselves *now there's an invitation*. It's just the way of nature. It's best to protect yourself. Safer to dress modestly, darling. You've learned a hard lesson. Now just forget the evening. Tomorrow is a new day to thank the Lord for.'

Kathleen had no energy to go through a repeat of the arguments she always had with her mother. It was easier to stay crumpled on the floor and just listen. Engulfed by tiredness and lethargy all she wanted now was to sleep. Amnesia, a coma would be welcome. Anything to erase what had happened, and clear her head of all the muddled thoughts she had.

Maria pulled a greying hanky from her sleeve, spat on it and pulling Kathleen's chin towards her she began to rub the black smears from under her eyes.

'Worse things happens at sea.' Her mother smiled but there was no warmth in her eyes of the kind Kathleen imagined other mothers had. And as she smiled back her insides were burning in fury. Stabbing pains were shooting up and down and she was sure she felt a trickle of blood seeping between her legs. She carefully stretched and stood up, shaking like a newborn foul taking its' first steps of life and headed for the toilet and with every tentative step she made she dreaded the burning sensation that would surely follow as soon as she sat down on the toilet.

But the pain was only temporary – maybe – or was the pain just the beginning she wondered.

3
Kathleen

March 1974

In the weeks that followed the rape Kathleen slowly found herself withdrawing into herself. Chatting to friends became an effort and she couldn't face doing all the things she used to enjoy doing – going to gigs and clubs, playing netball and hockey and making clothes on her Grandma's old Singer sewing machine. Simple things like walking home from school and being alone in the house frightened her and she found she was always looking over her shoulder to see if anyone was following her. She didn't like these new fears. It was like being a small child again; not the normal behaviour of a fourteen year old.

Gradually she started to spend more time locked away in her attic room where her brother used to sleep until he left home to follow his teaching career and where she could stand at the window and look out over the roofs of the houses and the building work around the docks. Sometimes she spent whole weekends under her bedding.

Kathleen had avoided mass for the first fortnight, feigning a headache, then toothache which her mother surprisingly accepted and booked a dentist's appointment. But on the third Sunday she couldn't excuse herself again. Suspicion would be aroused and questions might be asked. Deep down she knew paranoia was setting in. Her thoughts were absurd. Why would the parishioners be interested in her? She was an insignificant fourteen - year old schoolgirl, who merged into the congregation; somebody who hadn't made an impression on anyone. But much to her relief when she entered the church, her stomach churning with nerves a different priest was taking the service and on each subsequent occasion. She melted into the back row every Sunday, blotting out the words of this new priest and the faith she now questioned.

The small pleasure in her week was to curl up on the settee with her slippers and a pillow to watch the latest episode of The Little House on The Prairie; a series that her mother didn't object to her watching. And when her mother went out, which wasn't often she occasionally caught an episode of The Rockford Files, drawling over James Garner.

Kathleen's mother didn't question her new lifestyle. At first Kathleen found this odd but then she realized that it suited her to have her daughter nearby, out of mischief, not doing all the things that displeased God. She constantly grumbled though about the amount of food Kathleen ate and how much she was costing her.

'You have no idea about bills. I don't suppose you've been listening to the news. Of course the oil crisis means nothing to you. Jesus Mary and Joseph. The price of food, the price of coal. It's all going through the roof while you just sit up there in your attic room. I can't afford to heat the whole house anymore. Come and sit down here where you'll cost me less.' She shouted.

Thankfully she hadn't seen Father Joseph since the evening of the attack. His visits to their house had stopped. A different Father had visited; a priest that used to visit when she was very young who seemed to know her mother well. Maybe Father Joseph had asked for a transfer, afraid of what she might say or do. She didn't like to ask her mother for fear of arousing suspicion.

It was a morning in late April when she woke with a strange taste of metal in her mouth, a painful stabbing in her breasts – as if a knife was slicing into her - and a dull ache in her abdomen. She went to sit on the toilet expecting it to be the first day of her period but it wasn't. She cleaned her teeth, hoping the nasty taste would disappear.

And then it dawned on her that she hadn't had a period in several months.

She sat on her bed pulling her legs up, wrapping her arms around them. Panic tightened in her stomach and coiled around her like a noose. Now she was thinking about it she definitely felt different. She had been very tired lately. She propped the pillow up behind her back, nursing her sore tummy with a fresh hot water bottle and wracked her brain trying to work out what was wrong. She recalled an aunt talking about a metallic taste in the mouth being an early indication of pregnancy. Surely she couldn't be pregnant? She picked up a hankie, coiled it into a tight cigar. She got up, still clutching the hot water bottle to her stomach, went to look out of the attic window across the roofs to the Mersey, over and over telling herself that no she couldn't be pregnant: nobody got pregnant first time and you had to enjoy sex to get pregnant and besides she was too young to get pregnant; had only been having periods for a year. It would take a year or two for her body to get used to producing eggs. It was impossible. This wasn't happening. But all the time a faint bell tinkled in the back of her head. *What if I am?*

With growing unease she lifted the mattress and took all the copies of Jackie Magazine out, fanning them on the bed and then she began searching through every copy for an article about pregnancy. There was nothing. *Don't bottle it up and suffer in silence, tell us all about it* the Cathy and Claire page begged. But as she read and scanned there were no problems as big as hers. *My glasses get in the way when I kiss. Are love bites dangerous? My new shoes are an embarrassment. He says he loves me but how can I be sure? What's the best way to kiss?* These were a few of the problems appearing.

And then she turned to the doctor's page – a recent addition to the magazine which offered answers to the *below the waist issues*. There were a few questions related to late periods but no mention of the signs of pregnancy and all offering reassurance that late periods were perfectly normal and probably linked to stress or some upset like an argument with a friend or boyfriend or loss of weight. She wondered about writing to the doctor but she wouldn't put it past her mother to open the reply.

She stared at the tiny purple flowers on her Laura Ashley wallpaper, tracing the creases and the joins absentmindedly, her mind frozen and in denial. Suddenly she felt filthy, ashamed and hated herself more than ever. *Why did I go into the church with him? How could I be so foolish? But he is a man of God. I thought I could trust him.* Silent tears fell from her eyes as she asked herself those questions over and over. The tears found her mouth, warm and salty. Part of her wanted to pretend, to blot it all out and just get on with day- to- day living in blissful ignorance but she knew that wouldn't solve anything. The problem wasn't going to go away. If she was pregnant it was going to grow inside, eventually have to come out. She had to get hold of one of the new home pregnancy kits she'd seen advertised but she'd heard they were complicated, taking hours to do and required the mixing of urine with solutions using test tubes and that they weren't always accurate. It sounded a messy business. She knew nothing about chemistry.

At school she messed around in Chemistry lessons, hated the subject and her teacher, Dr. Rogerson who always banished her to the cupboard for misbehavior; where she played pranks by mixing different chemicals together then pouring them into vials, always poking her head around the corner of the cupboard to give cheek. *What's this Doc?* She'd ask holding up some precarious concoction then watching in glee as thunder hit his face.

Soon it would be Monday's Biology lesson. She hated the teacher; a scowling nun from Southern Ireland but now felt desperate to get to the lesson to flick through the Longman Human Biology textbook. Next to Jackie A.E Vines had become her bible of answers to a whole gamut of physical problems from ulcers to verrucas.

The fear of what might happen gripped her with a terror she hadn't experienced since the attack. She knew that whatever her mother said her reaction would be to hand the problem over to the Church. Every problem her mother had ever had was handed over to the Church. But what that would actually mean in reality – beyond prayer and confession – she had no idea. In the past she knew that things had been much tougher for Catholic women. Her mother had grown up in Ireland and she remembered her telling the story of a cousin falling pregnant at 16, labeled a 'fallen woman;' sent off to an asylum or hotel where she'd worked as a skivvy and slept in a cockroach infested basement, then had the baby adopted. But that was all in the past. Or so she thought... *This is the seventies, attitudes are different*, she kept reminding herself.

As a child Kathleen often visualized with great embarrassment standing at the altar as a bride kissing her new husband in front of the gaze of her mother and everyone else. She had vowed not to kiss her husband in public. But now she laughed at that former innocence and shuddered as she imagined her mother's reaction if she were pregnant; knowing that a man had entered her body.

She sat on a tall wooden stall in the lab in Monday's Biology class. The class was busy writing notes from the board on receptors and the only noises in the room were the swish of the nun's robe and the scrape of her chalk on the board and the occasional cough or sneeze. Kathleen paused to flick through A.E Vines, staring at diagrams of the female reproductive system. There was a small paragraph about amenorrhea, which talked about hormone disruption and the reasons for this but it was all very matter of fact and no discussion around those facts.

On the way home she sat at the back of the bus with her friends and wondered whether to confide in them. Every so often she flinched as another stab pierced her nipples. It was noisy on the bus. Somebody had let off a stink bomb. Somebody else was throwing a roll of toilet paper and it cascaded across several rows, like a trail of white ribbon. A couple of boys at the back were sniffing glue in a plastic bag. She turned away, disgusted, not wanting to watch the ghastly habit. The driver had stopped the bus; turning round to warn everyone to behave - otherwise they would be walking. He was at his wit's end. Had been like it for weeks. But this was the party bus; that's how the kids described it.

Her friends were giggling and one friend was talking about snogging behind the bike shed. Snogging behind the bike shed and fingering in bedrooms at parties was the extent of their knowledge about sex. Kathleen laughed, inwardly at the irony of the way she used to feel disgusted by fingering. Boys said that fingering was like *doing time* but what they really dreamt of was the real thing. If a couple were upstairs at a party nobody ever suspected them of going the whole way. Word would go round: *he's having a good finger* and then everyone would start singing the advert for Fudge: *a finger of fudge is just enough to give your kids a treat* collapsing in laughter.

It was early one Monday evening, now four months after the attack and they were eating prunes and custard, yet again. A.E Vines had given her no answers to her questions.

Her mother put her spoon down and smiled across the table but it was a smile etched with strain. Her mother's pale eyes mirrored her own anxiety and in a flash she wondered if her mother suspected what was wrong and had known all along. An uneasy silence lay heavy between them.

'Tell me what's wrong?' The question made Kathleen flinch. She hadn't been expecting this. Her mother's eyes were cold and her face wasn't lit with the concern and warmth she craved. A frown was carving a treacherous path across her forehead.

'I'm worried I might be pregnant.' The words were out, unplanned, splatted like ink, hovering, ponderous in the air but the statement felt surreal: as if someone else had said them.

'I did wonder... the man in the alley after the concert?' She whispered, staring into the bowl of sludge before her. She pushed the bowl away, as if pushing the problem away. Kathleen couldn't read her thoughts. Her face was now blank. She was astonished that her mother had nothing more to say.

'Yeah.' She waited, not wanting to say anymore, hoping her period would return in the morning so that she could get on with her life and try to forget what the priest had done.

'I'll book a doctor's appointment. He'll do a test.' She said in a matter of fact tone. Then she inched her chair back, wiped her hands on her apron and with an arctic look on her face stood up, went to turn on the news and pretended for the next ten minutes to be deeply concerned about the events in Vietnam.

'You've brought great shame on this family Kathleen. And I won't be telling our Darius. Lord only knows what he'd say.' It was a week after the doctor had taken her blood for testing and she was now in a state of shock. Kathleen had hardly slept while she had waited for the results; crying into the pillow each night, fear coiling its' way around her.

Her mother's voice was slow and heavy with the burden of what was happening. They were eating their Friday fish meal in the tiny kitchen. The doctor had rung during the afternoon to confirm the results. The news was gradually sinking in.

'Every family has one.' Maria slowly said, as if beginning a well-rehearsed speech.

25

'Has what mammy?'

'A fallen one. One who falls from grace, stumbles, makes a fool of themselves. One who embarrasses their family at every opportunity. One who doesn't quite fit in.' She stretched the words out, peering at Kathleen through icy eyes.

' And in this family ... Kathleen... that's you.' She added in a sharp lemon tone.

Silence sat between them. Kathleen watched the myriad of changing expressions on her mother's face: a frown, a raised eyebrow, a twist of the mouth. It was as if her mother was wheeling back in time, calculating regrets, dwelling on past events; an internal battle going on that she couldn't resolve.

'I read a passage in the Bible once that said *don't find fault with the man who limps, or stumbles along the road unless you have worn the shoes he wears or struggled beneath his load.*' Kathleen felt proud of herself for remembering the passage.

Neither spoke for a time and into the gap between the conversation they finished their dinner.

'I can't accept the sin or the shame. To every woman it's the biggest sin of all. That's just the way it is.' Maria said placing her knife and fork on the plate.

'Only in the Catholic Church. I keep saying I'm sorry mammy. But it wasn't my fault. I didn't plan to get pregnant.' She pleaded, batting away the shame her mother was throwing at her.

'No woman does.' Kathleen noticed a cruel look in her mother's eyes but then it was gone and she stared down at her food. Her mother's appetite gone, Kathleen watched her push the plate away.

'Mammy this isn't the 1950s anymore. Times are changing. That's how it was when you were growing up in Ireland. This is England. We're not a backward country anymore. We've had women burning their bras, marching for their rights. And we've got contraception even though you probably don't agree with using it.'

'Sex is sex. Times haven't changed that much. What are you saying?'

'I can raise the child.' Kathleen eyes widened as she considered the leaden weight of this idea for the first time.

Shock registered across her mother's face.

'You? But you're a child yourself. How will you support it?' She mocked. 'God forbid. Please Mary Mother of God help this child see the error of her ways.' Maria closed her eyes, looked to the ceiling, hands folded in prayer.

'Well what do you suggest I do? I'm four, nearly five months gone. It's too late for an abortion. And you'd never agree to one.'

'God would never agree. Dear Lord. You need to show repentance. I'm taking you to confession where you'll examine your conscience, show contrition and God will determine what you must do to repair the damage. Sin weakens us Kathleen. We need to acknowledge our true sins before the priest. And he'll bless you with God's grace. Father Joseph has been away in a different parish for a while. He's back. I want you to go and see him. Offer your forgiveness and he'll impart absolution. It will take a lot of prayer Kathleen and this problem isn't going to go away. Maybe I'll ask Father Joseph to come over this evening and see what can be done. You can't stay here, so you can't. You'll bring shame upon the whole community and we've no room for a baby.' Her mother was in full rant now. Kathleen stared down at the tuna, imagining her mother with a placard on the street corner spouting God's word. But just then she registered what her mother had just told her. And then she tried to filter the shock. *Father Joseph is back.* Her mother was closing in on her. And the church was closing in too. And she could hear God's voice punishing her.

She tried to suppress the tremour in her voice as she composed her words carefully.

'I'd rather see a nurse. The priest can't do anything. He's hardly a midwife mammy.' Kathleen said. A feeling of panic coiled around her like a hangman's noose. If she told the truth she wouldn't be believed and Father Joseph was a figure of power that couldn't be challenged.

'No arguing. We've had enough of that. Arguing gets us nowhere. We're going as soon as you've eaten your tea, so we are. Hurry up and finish. I'll be wanting to get back for 'Some Mothers Do 'Ave 'Em.'

Kathleen shook her head in disbelief but smiled inwardly at the irony of the TV show title. Her mother had a TV programme to watch. The feeling of defeat was suddenly overwhelming. Why was it always one rule for her, another for everybody else?

4
Kathleen

April 1974

Kathleen's heart was pounding hard when she entered the confessional that she wondered if Father Joseph would be able to hear it and enjoy the smell of her fear. The confessional always reminded her of a large wardrobe rather like the wardrobe that led into Narnia. She knelt at the screen and bowed her head, aware of his shadow at the grated window that divided the box. At least that way she didn't have to look her abuser in the eyes and see the triumph on his face. In the confined space she felt claustrophobic. It felt as if the wooden walls of the box were breathing, all knowing, moving in on her - threatening to suffocate.

With a shaking hand she began with the sign of the cross and said the familiar words:

'In the name of the Father, and of the Son, and of the Holy Spirit. My last confession was five months ago.'

She waited and then she heard the familiar cold voice of her attacker.

'If we confess our sins, he is faithful and just, and will forgive our sins and cleanse us from all unrighteousness. 1 John 1:9. What are the sins that bring you here?'

Kathleen felt every muscle in her body shrivel to jelly. Taking a deep breath, knowing her mother was waiting outside the church for her, she chanced her next words.

'I'm pregnant Father. I'm pregnant after what you did to me.' She sat up willing herself to be strong.

There was a brief pause but he carried on as if he hadn't heard her.

'You are to say the following words. *Father I am sorry for these and all the sins of my past life.*'

He was refusing to listen.

Like a robot Kathleen spoke the familiar text.

'I am sorry for these and all the sins of my past life.' And then with anger starting to mount she felt the stirrings of courage begin to send warm ripples across her body.

'But you aren't listening Father. You raped me. You defiled my body.' Her voice was shaky. She knew she was in danger of losing control. She had to stay calm, composed.

'Are you ready to receive the absolution?'

His voice of steel, authoritative as ever hid an unmistakable sneer. He carried on.

'God the Father of mercies, through the death and resurrection of his Son has reconciled the world to himself and sent the Holy Spirit among us for the forgiveness of sins; through the ministry of the Church. May God give you pardon and peace, and I absolve you from your sins in the name of the Father, and of the Son and of the Holy Spirit.'

Anger bubbled and boiled as she listened to his sickening voice. What gave him the right to represent God? Suddenly she had a burning desire to punch his face. And then she remembered her mother outside, waiting by the steps.

'Father. You aren't listening. You raped me.' Her plea came again.

Silence descended. She couldn't run - her mother would wonder what it was all about. She could sense her mother pacing up and down the church aisle. She regretted her words. What if her mother had heard her? She feared a beating from her mother. She didn't know what to do. She felt pummeled from every direction, there was nowhere to turn, no one to turn to. All she could do was wait for his next words or next move.

But then the silence was broken. 'That was part of your penance giving thanks to the Lord. In a moment I'll invite you to complete your penance.'

Kathleen was shaking. Bile rose in her throat as he ordered her to repeat the words after him:

'Give thanks to the Lord, for he is good. May the Passion of our Lord Jesus Christ, the intercession of the Blessed Virgin Mary, and of all the saints, whatever good you do and suffering you endure, heal your sins, help you to grow in holiness, and reward you with eternal life.' His voice was calm, unchanged, as if nothing at all had happened and all the time she was screaming inside but more than anything wanted to fling the door open and scream all the way home. But all she could do was fight the tears and maintain her composure.

'You will now say these words:

O my God, I am heartily sorry for having offended you and I detest all my sins, because I dread the loss of heaven and the pains of hell. But most of all because I have offended you, my God, who are all good and deserving of all my love. I firmly resolve with the help of your grace, to confess my sins, to do penance and to amend my life. Amen.'

In a matter of fact and professional manner he ended the confessional, bold as brass, confirming that he would be visiting her house later to discuss her fate.

'Father Joseph thank you so much for coming.' Kathleen's mother welcomed him into the hallway, ushering him through to the kitchen. It was early evening.

Kathleen loathed the sycophantic way her mother spoke to the priest and wished she could scream the truth at the top of her voice. It felt like being trapped on the tracks of a railway, the train fast approaching yet being unable to get up in time.

'Kathleen turn Coronation Street off would you? You know how much I dislike that programme. Watching the breakdown of Ken and Janet Barlow's marriage is a really bad influence on the nation's morals. Father cup of tea? There's a fresh one in the pot.' Maria asked.

She began to open and shut the mustard yellow cupboard doors of their brand new Hygena kitchen - installed by her mother's friend on the cheap because he worked at their Liverpool headquarters. Her actions were speeded up, clearly desperate not to keep the priest waiting for his tea.

Yes sir no sir three bags fucking full sir, Kathleen screamed in her head, her hands making fists in the pockets of the maternity dress she had made on her Grandma's Singer sewing machine. Her mother had kept her off school for the past couple of weeks telling the headmaster that she was on long- term sick leave for asthma. And she had told Kathleen that she had to stay in the house for fear of being seen in the state she was in.

Kathleen had felt the first flutters of the baby moving. She didn't know what to feel. Something was growing inside her. Was that possible she wondered? Sometimes her stomach moved when she splashed water over it in the bath and she'd sit there for ages sprinkling water over her swollen belly from a plastic jug, till the water turned cold, amused and excited yet at the same time terrified and alone.

Kathleen stood in the doorway as her mother guided him to a chair with his cup of tea and fresh piece of fruit cake. She didn't see why she had to sit at the table with him. Having him in the house was cruel enough – her mother; in blissful ignorance was aware of nothing – but having to engage in false pleasantries was more than she could bear.

Every Family Has One

'Nice bit of fruit cake Maria.' He said, smiling at Kathleen's mother while Kathleen seethed inside and dreamt of rubbing the cake into his face.

'Kathleen don't be rude. Come and sit down.' Her mother pulled out a chair opposite Father Joseph but he didn't turn to say hello. She felt a sudden surge of teeth grinding irritation. He had the audacity not to even acknowledge her presence, thinking he could just walk right into her kitchen as if nothing had happened. *How dare the fucking bastard* she screamed inside.

She walked slowly towards the table, tempted to kick his briefcase across the kitchen floor. Too busy stooping to sit down she didn't miss his flinch as though she'd slapped him. She picked her tea up, with shaking hands, wishing it were a strong tot of her father's homemade wine. The air between them was icy and she did her best to avoid eye contact. Her mother joined her at the table tucking into her tea and cake.

Although seated around the table together Kathleen was excluded from the conversation and after a while she switched his voice off in her head and stared out of the window to the derelict warehouse opposite the road, only vaguely aware of his evil presence, his hands making steeples on the table in front of him, deep in thought as to how he could help with the problem he had caused.

Kathleen instinctively stroked her belly as if protecting it from its' evil father.

'You can get your bags packed by morning can't you Kathleen?' He asked.

Kathleen had not heard a word of the conversation but the words *pack your bags* penetrated her consciousness, snapping her back to the table and the plans they were busy forming without her consent.

Her life seemed to be sliding from under her at an alarming speed and she had no control over the fate that awaited her.

'Tomorrow you'll be going away for a while. It's for the best. It's a home in Southern Ireland where you'll meet other mothers and in return for your keep you'll be doing some light chores, peeling potatoes, polishing furniture, washing laundry, that sort of thing and the baby will be adopted.' Her mother said all this in a careful and hesitant voice as if negotiating the release of a hostage.

Kathleen was speechless. Trapped in a deep dark well she didn't know how to claw her way out or what to say or do. She felt drugged and light headed; unable to snap out of the state they had injected her with. In a splinter of time her future - it seemed - had been decided and there was nothing she could do. Her mother refused for her to have the baby. It was too late for an abortion and even if it hadn't have been that wouldn't have been an option. Abortion was murder and life began at conception. Despite the baby's father being an evil man Kathleen believed with all her heart in the sanctity of human life.

She was about to go on a journey with her baby and she would make the best of that time. And maybe her mother would visit and after seeing the baby her heart would melt. Kathleen knew that becoming a Grandma was a very special and privileged role. Her own Grandma had been very special indeed. *Yes*, she thought to herself with certainty *her mother would welcome them back*. She was after all the matriarchal figure in the family; a role of some considerable importance. The house wasn't crowded. *Mammy is still coping with the shock* she told herself. She'd get used to a baby being around and in time be proud to take her grandchild for walks in its' pram and push it on the swings in the park.

Everything would work out in the end, her inner positive voice told her.

5
Kathleen

May 1974

As the bus clattered and jolted along the winding lanes following a grey patchwork stone wall on each side of the road, Kathleen enjoyed the lush blanket of green all around her. The bus came to a sudden halt as the driver waited for a farmer and his herd of cows to pass allowing her to look around and to appreciate her new surroundings. She thought of the variety of greens on a Fad's colour chart; every green seemed to be represented in the trees, the bushes and the rolling hills folding across the landscape.

Suddenly her excitement rose and everything took on a new shape. This was an adventure. Perhaps Father Joseph was trying to make amends for what he'd done. Maybe this was his way of taking the strain from her mother. He knew about the tensions and arguments she'd had with her mother. She had heard her mother complain to him several times. *Our Kathleen has a troublesome mind.*

Kathleen knew she hadn't been an easy teenager and that her skimpy outfits and music had scared her mother. This break would give them some breathing space. Her head started to fill with different images of how she would spend her time. She imagined walks over the fields in the fresh bracing air and milking cows in the diary - if there was one - and collecting eggs from a farm. And she visualized late night feasts with the other teenage mums.

And at last she would be able to talk to other girls who were going through the same thing. She had felt so alone and frightened ever since finding out about the pregnancy. She had spent every day, every hour wondering how she was going to cope yet all the time unable to talk to her mother or friends. She didn't know anything about babies. And what would the birth be like? But above all one question had steamed around her head over and over. *What was going to happen after the birth? How would she cope with a baby? And if she gave it away how would she cope with the loss?*

But now, looking around at the landscape she felt positive vibes surge through her body and all her questions melted away leaving a warm glow. She looked down and patted her belly with a smile. *It's ok little Windysella things are going to work out.*

⁂

The bus rattled to a stop at the end of a long avenue and the driver caught her glance in the mirror above his seat nodding an indication that this was her stop. Kathleen gathered her bags containing several practical items and stepped off the bus into a muddy puddle by the grass verge. Grey clouds were gathering disgracefully above and she felt the first drops of rain as she hurried across the road and began the short ascent up the tree lined driveway. By the time she looked up and saw the red brick and sandstone mansion ahead in the dip the cold rain was lashing down, whipping her face. As she drew nearer she noticed that there were iron bars on every window and the positive vibes that she had suddenly disappeared into a feeling of unease.

Her feet crunched under gravel and she arrived in the shelter of a porch way. Before she could check her mascara smudged face in the brass knocker the door creaked open and a nun glared out at her.

Every Family Has One

It seemed that the nun was expecting her. She continued to glare at her; then with a sweep of her arm guided her into a small hallway and without saying a word ushered her down a long corridor. The smell of boiled cabbage and floor polish mingled in her nostrils as Kathleen followed the swish of the nun's robe and the sound of her rosary beads click clacking along the corridor to an office at the end.

When they were inside the office with the door shut the nun looked at her again but said nothing for a few moments. The nun went to sit behind a desk, opened a drawer and began to fill in some paperwork. Then she looked up, didn't smile. Kathleen felt the cruel glitter of her eyes drinking her in. When she finally spoke Kathleen was startled and took a step back in surprise.

'The pain on this earth is only the size of a grain of the suffering compared to the vast beach of suffering and torment in hell if we do not do penance for our sin.' The nun waited for the words to sink in. Kathleen didn't know whether she was expected to reply.

'Yes sister.' She said.

'You will address me as Reverend Mother and I will address you as Bridget.'

'I think you have the wrong name... sister... I mean Reverend Mother.'

'I am well aware of who you are. Your mother says you have the devil in you. A troublesome mind. But Bridget is your new name.'

Kathleen's mouth fell open and she didn't know what to say.

'I won't expect any backchat.' It was as if the nun knew Kathleen was working out a reply.

She carried on, holding the stage. 'You have fallen from grace in the eyes of the church and your family. You are here to do your penance and save your soul and of course have the cause of your sin removed from your body.'

Kathleen's heart lurched in her chest and she looked down defensively at her swollen belly and silently spoke to the baby that she had

37

grown to love. *It's ok little Windysella mumma's here for you. I love you even though no one else does and I'm going to protect you from harm.*

She looked at Kathleen's hair.

'We'll have those long curls cut this evening. I'll send someone up to the dorm to cut it after you've washed and put your bedclothes on. 'Tis a sin to be swaying hair around so it is.' She sniffed.

Kathleen felt a sinking feeling and instinctively put her hand up to touch her head. She loved her hair. Had spent many hours in her attic bedroom brushing it, looking at different hairstyles in Jackie Magazine, imagining she was Farah Fawcett Major. It was her best feature and she didn't see what the problem was. It was tied into a bun; neat and out of the way.

'Now. Here's some paperwork for you to sign.' She twizzled the paper round; handed Kathleen a pen and stabbed the place where she wanted Kathleen to sign.

Kathleen wondered what she was signing and hesitated as she quickly glanced at the writing. But it was typed in a tiny font and she could barely read it and didn't know where to begin because there was so much to read. But she wasn't given a chance to peruse what she was signing. The nun hurried her along, stabbing her finger again at the place to sign and Kathleen could sense her impatience as she picked up the pen and fearing harsh words she hastily scribbled her name.

'Good. That's the formalities out the way. Now. Uniform and a linen nighty.' The nun clapped her hands, as if the uniform and nighty were about to spring into the room in a puff of smoke and Kathleen flinched.

The nun got up. Kathleen noticed a large belt around her waist containing a chain of keys and thought how heavy it must be, to wear all day. The nun removed a small key and turned to open a metal cupboard behind her desk pulling out a white nighty with a drawstring and a shapeless brown tunic and handed them to Kathleen without asking her size. The tunic reminded her of being in prison and she tried to remember what the prisoners wore in the series 'Within These Walls;'

a drama portraying life in HMP Stone Park, a fictional women's prison. Whatever those prisoners had worn, she thought to herself, this tunic; coarse to the touch and plain ugly was considerably worse.

'Now... You'll be working in the laundry. The day begins at six.'

Kathleen dared to speak.

'When do we get paid Reverend Mother? At the end of each week? Me daddy got paid at the end of the week. He worked on the docks before he was made redundant.'

The nun stared, speechless for a few moments. And then she began to laugh; a deep throaty laugh. Kathleen wondered what was funny. Maybe the nun found it amusing that her father had worked on the docks; but she had been proud of her father. It had been a hard dirty job, long hours.

'It's reward enough to be here.' She snapped. 'To be looked after, fed and watered, somewhere to sleep. Your reward will come if you're lucky to enter heaven...but after what you've done, getting yourself in the family way you've got a lot of repentance to do. You need to pray very hard.'

Kathleen tried to hold her tongue as she quelled the thoughts rising in her mind. Maybe it was best not to speak.

'The bell will ring at five for you to get up. No lingering in bed. No talking to the other girls. There are twenty on your dorm. You'll find a small cupboard to keep your things in. What have you brought with you? Let me see.' She asked in a clipped voice, snapping her fingers.

The nun beckoned with her hand for Kathleen to pass her bag over and instantly Kathleen was back at school, in her head; reminded of the time that she was suspected of bringing fags to school, summoned to the headmaster's office to have her bag searched. She could still see the contents of her bag strewn across the headmaster's floor, then being ordered to pick up the contents, the headmaster waving the fags in front of her face, crushing them in his hand and then the harsh slipper upon her buttocks. But standing here now she had done nothing wrong - for once in her life – but was being treated in a wretched way as if she had.

One by one the nun removed the contents and created two piles of the items on her desk. In one pile she put her hair brush, hair slides, a book she had been reading on the bus by Judy Blume 'Are you there God, it's me, Margaret' and in another pile she put her nightdress, a few items of clothing, Mr. Daddy, the cloth toy she had made a couple of years ago on her Grandma's Singer sewing machine and a photograph of her dad.

'Now then.' She looked up, her face lined with disapproval. Kathleen waited.

'You won't need this book.' She hissed, picking the book up with two fingers, extended it out, flapping it close to Kathleen's face. 'I've heard about this book. Growing up, fitting in, discovering *who* you really are. Tripe. We know who you are.' She gave a snigger. 'A sinner. Which is why you're here. You can read the Bible instead. It's the only book worth reading.'

Kathleen looked at the ground.

'Who's this man? Your lover? Is it his seed you're carrying inside you?' The nun asked holding the photo of Kathleen's dad with a look of distate.

Kathleen felt her cheeks redden, tears were pricking, as she looked at the black and white photo of her dad in his fishing gear proudly holding a prize trout, leaning against a tree by the riverbank smiling to the camera.

'No. It's my dad. Was my dad.' She muttered.

'Photographs are pure vanity. We don't have cameras here, photographs or mirrors. What we have is love for the dear Lord that we carry in our hearts.' She snapped and with the swift action of her fingers she tore the photo into tiny pieces and Kathleen's heart sank as she watched, the pieces fluttering into a wire mesh bin in the corner, dumbfounded, unable to comprehend why the nun would do this, her only link to her father now gone.

Then she turned to Mr. Daddy, picked him up and held him at a distance as if she might catch something nasty from him.

'What's this filthy thing?' Kathleen's eyes had been fixed on the bin. They darted to the handmade patchwork toy the nun was holding. This time she tried not to show emotion, kept a straight calm face, fearing the nun - maybe enjoying her distress - might toss him into the bin as well. She quickly thought of a reply; didn't want to tell the nun the sentimental value of the toy and how she had made it in memory of her dad.

'It's a charity toy Reverend Mother.' Kathleen wasn't sure what she meant by the statement, hoped the nun wouldn't question further.

The nun thought for a few moments, still holding him at arm's length. Kathleen waited, wondering what Mr. Daddy's fate would be. She glanced at a pair of scissors on the edge of the table and dreaded the thought of him cut to pieces.

'Oh well.' She said. Kathleen could see her suddenly lose interest. 'You can keep it. It's falling apart. Won't last long anyway.' The nun flicked Mr. Daddy's wonky right eye; a black button with hanging threads working lose. Then without warning - giving no time for Kathleen to object - the nun yanked the lose button off, turned and tossed his black eye into the bin.

'Great shot don't you think?' She beamed in satisfaction.

༄

She was guided from the room, clutching her new nighty, uniform and bag, now only containing Mr. Daddy with his one remaining black eye, one pair of knickers and bra and a few toiletries. Out in the empty corridor she could hear the approaching subdued shuffle of soft feet, whispering voices, the creak of doors. The girls were pouring in from the laundry; it was time for dinner. Kathleen breathed in the sulphurous odour of boiled to death cauliflower and broccoli, wanting to gag.

'No talking.' The nun barked. The girls stopped walking, shuffled into line, straightened up and as if to order, dipped their heads to the nun in what Kathleen guessed was a bow. Kathleen estimated there were around thirty girls now in line. Some looked heavily pregnant and about to drop, others looked too slim to be pregnant. Kathleen wondered if there were any from Liverpool or the mainland or whether they all came from Ireland. Suddenly she felt a long way from home and wondered what her friends would be doing. Maybe they would be at the cinema or a disco.

The girls looked up, a synchronized action and suddenly all eyes, inquisitive were upon Kathleen. The nun walked along the line of girls, inspecting each, from feet to head, her keys jangling from the belt; the only noise in the corridor. Now at the front of the line she pushed through a set of double doors and everyone followed into a refectory, lined with long tables and benches. Kathleen, without being told joined the queue, gazing into the hall to the table beyond the benches where hot food steamed from several large metal canisters. The girl in front of her turned around, a reassuring look on her face that said *don't worry you'll be ok. You're not alone. We're in this together* but Kathleen had forgotten the rule of silence and went to speak.

'Hello. I'm Kathleen. What's your name?'

The girl's face melted into alarm.

'Shush.' She said with a frown then turned to face the front.

The nun stopped. Turned around.

'Did I hear someone talk?' She barked.

There was silence. The nun waited, looking from face to face along the line and then turned around and soon she was seated at the helm with the other nuns gathering from an adjacent room and all the girls began to take seats along the benches. Kathleen caught several trying to communicate to each other through facial gestures and hand movements and wondered if they had developed a code.

She waited to be served by an overweight cook with gnarled hands. Beyond the crow's feet and farm tracks of the cook's face Kathleen wondered what card life had dealt the woman and whether she had worked in the laundry for long.

After the unappetizing watery lamb stew that contained very little meat but lots of gristle the girls were led out, along the corridor, again in silence and into a chapel at the back of the house for Mass.

Prayers were opened by a plea for the girls to beg for the mercy of Jesus who had died on the cross for a far greater suffering than they could possibly imagine.

With the sign of the cross the Reverend Mother indicated for the girls to line up in rows, bow their heads and make the sign of the cross and repeat the following words:

He suffered and sacrificed his life so that we may enter heaven. Our penance will allow us to cast off our sins.

'We have a new girl. Her name is Bridget.' Kathleen's cheeks flushed as all eyes turned to stare at her. May I remind you no idle chatter. Silence is golden. It helps you to focus your thoughts on God. You will show Bridget the routines in the laundry and do God's work with diligence. Hard work is rewarded in heaven.'

The evening then passed quickly. The girls were ushered outside and ordered to run around the field several times *to get some fresh air into your gills and to help you work harder and have a clear head to focus on God.*

As she wheezed her way round the field a girl behind her started to talk through puffed breaths.

'You're new. They don't tell you what happens here. When you've had your baby there will be a car waiting on the gravel outside to take it away.'

Kathleen stopped. Too stunned to carry on.

'Don't stop. They'll notice.' The girl said gasping for breath, sweeping Kathleen on with her hand.

Kathleen resumed her run.

'My mam will come and fetch me.' Kathleen felt certain.

'That's what every girl thinks. But I'm telling you - it rarely happens. Best you forget your mum. She's turned her back on you. You're the slut of the family. We all are.'

'Are you pregnant?' Kathleen asked, irritated by what the girl had just said and feeling sweaty and desperately in need of a nice hot bath.

'Was. They took my baby away when she was six months old. I pleaded with the Reverend Mother to say one last goodbye but she wouldn't let me. Told me the baby didn't know who I was, wouldn't remember me and I was nothing to her.'

Kathleen wanted to turn round, sensing the girl's need for a hug but too frightened to stop, knowing the nuns were standing, hawk-like on the veranda watching.

Soon it was time for bed. Kathleen was tired and aware of the early start the following day. They clambered up a spiral staircase to the very top of the house into a long dormitory under the eaves. It was an airless room, with only a tiny barred window at the end. The room was uncarpeted and a bare light bulb dangled precariously from the ceiling. Kathleen put her bag in the metal cupboard next to her bed and looking round to check nobody was watching, feeling behind the cupboard for a suitable place to hide Mr. Daddy until after dark when she would slip him into her bed.

Everybody had washed, cleaned their teeth, changed into white starchy nighties ready for bed. Throughout these tasks there was silence. It was going to be like living with a bunch of mutes Kathleen thought to herself. How was she going to cope? At school she was a chatterbox; nothing could stop her if she had something to say.

Each girl knelt beside their bed to read from the bible, making the sign of the cross, closing their eyes in prayer.

As Kathleen finished her prayers she was startled. A girl was standing behind her, looking down, a sneer on her face. Kathleen got up noticing her piercing raven eyes. She didn't look Gaelic; looked more Southern European.

Every Family Has One

'So who are you then?' The girl asked, looking at Kathleen as if the cat had just dragged her in.

'And don't think you can nick all the best jobs. I've got all the privileged jobs round here.' A shorter, tubby girl with freckles came over to Kathleen, her hands on her hips.

'I thought we weren't supposed to talk.' Kathleen answered, wondering what the privileged jobs were.

Several girls walked over to Kathleen's bed, looking as if they wanted to join the inquisition.

'That's not what I asked.' The girl snapped.

'Kathleen.' She replied. Then she remembered and corrected herself to Bridget. She didn't like this new name, didn't see what was wrong with her own name or why a new identity for her had been created. It seemed odd.

'What do you mean by privileged jobs?' Kathleen asked. 'Do you get paid to do them?'

A titter of laughter broke out. Hands clapped over mouths.

'Joking aren't you?' The tubby girl spluttered. 'Ironing the starched altar robes. That's the best job. But you're not having it. I do them.'

'You've fallen from grace. We all have. Life here is not worth living. You'll soon realise that and want to escape. But don't bother trying. I did and look what happened to me.' The girl with the raven eyes said, pulling her nighty up and Kathleen stared at the healing red gashes on her leg, flinching at the thought of a terrible beating by one of the nuns.

'Who got you up the duff then? Dirty cow.' The girl with the raven eyes asked.

'Leave her alone Martha. It's hard enough here without people picking on each other.' A lanky girl with cropped blonde hair and a friendly face stepped over to defend Kathleen.

'I only wanted to know. Expect you do too Mary.' Martha sneered at Mary.

The other girls sat on their beds watching.

'Did you open your pretty legs and beg him to enter you? Couldn't hold yourself back? Did you enjoy the five minute fumble? Worth it was it?'

Kathleen could feel a stab of anger but with as much determination as she could muster she resisted swiping Martha across the face, knowing it wouldn't be a good start and wouldn't do her any favours.

The girl started laughing, searching Kathleen's face for all the gory details of the conception. Kathleen kept her cool. And in those difficult moments she resolved there and then never to tell a soul about the ordeal with the priest for as long as she lived.

After a breakfast of watery porridge Kathleen joined the throng of girls silently heading out of the back of the house and into the sheds. The stink of chemicals, detergents and sweat hit her as she entered and she instinctively pulled a face and waved the smell away.

'It's like this every day.' The girl in front whispered.

'I don't think I'll be able to stand the heat.' Kathleen whispered back. 'Not in my condition.' And Kathleen had never realized until that moment how much she hated silence. Silence swelled in her head. Made her fear. Made her ponder things.

'We're all in the same boat. You don't have much choice. It's like the heat of hell in here.'

Kathleen peered into huge baskets lining an uneven pathway along the side of the shed, gagging at the sight of the filthy contaminated and blood stained sheets.

'Where are they from?' Kathleen whispered.

'Hospitals, nursing homes, the army.' Kathleen's chest twisted in a knot of sadness when she heard the word *army* thinking now of her father, caught up in the Troubles visiting his sister on the Falls Road. She hadn't seen any TVs and wondered if it would be possible to see

Every Family Has One

the news. Since her father had died she had taken a particular interest in the Troubles, desperate for it all to end.

Soon the machines were brought to life, clanking and churning and wafting clouds of steam into the air. It was a long day in a furnace like atmosphere and by the end Kathleen's legs ached from the standing and her hands burned with the bleach after scrubbing, washing, cleaning and folding all day long. The nuns showed no mercy when they saw her flagging and wiping her brow. She found herself thinking of her mum back at home and wondered if she'd known this fate and whether it would have made any difference and she wondered - not for the first time - how her mother would have reacted to being told that Father Joseph had raped her.

'I can't do this again tomorrow.' Kathleen whispered to the girl next to her while the nun on duty wasn't watching. 'I'll lose the baby. I don't want to lose my baby. I love my baby.'

'You'll lose your baby anyway. We all will.' The words hit.

'I will not.' Kathleen snapped back.

Kathleen's voice, no longer a whisper made the nun turn and glare and march over to where Kathleen was working.

'You will not talk. Do you understand? Otherwise I'll take the leather strap to your hands.'

Kathleen's legs suddenly gave way and she crashed to the hard floor and with the heat, the shock and the humiliating despair of it all with no warning sobs hit and flooded up from her chest.

The nun seemed to enjoy the look of deep distress in her eyes and with a look of contempt she dragged her to her feet and ordered her to follow to an adjoining office. The door slammed behind them and with a snarl of intense hatred the nun ordered her to place her sore and cut hands on a desk, unbuckling her leather belt from her waist she rained down lash after agonizing lash until Kathleen could bear it no more.

Putting her belt back on she gave Kathleen an icy stare.

'We will beat the sin out of you. Now get back to your work.'

Kathleen was struggling in the August heat. It was only a month now until the birth. There were about ten girls who were expecting and it seemed that her pregnancy was the most advanced. With each passing day she found working in the laundry harder and harder. She could no longer put on her shoes for her feet had swollen so much with the constant standing and her back ached with the weight of the baby and having to spend long days standing, bending and twisting. She longed for the baby to be born but a fear gripped her every time she thought about the inevitability of what was to happen after the birth. The thought of being parted from her baby felt like the twisting of a knife in her heart. How could she stop that fate? As she folded and ironed sheets she mulled over ideas. What if she refused to hand over her baby for adoption? They couldn't stop her keeping her own child. What right did they have over her child? If they refused to listen to her pleas she'd ask them to call her mother and she'd speak to her mother and ask her to pick them both up.

This wasn't the 1950s. Times were different. Things were improving for women, she mused. The Equal Pay Act had paved change in the work place and she'd heard somewhere about a Sex Discrimination Act coming in very soon. Maybe that would give women more rights. But she wasn't sure. She hadn't heard the news in a long time. She felt so out of touch with life outside the walls of her apparent captivity. This wasn't fair. She wanted her say. She would have her say when the time came even if they turned round and beat her to death. Either that or she'd escape. That was another possibility. Although they were stuck in the middle of nowhere, with few trees around to hide between, there had to be a way.

Kathleen woke in the night aware that she had been talking in her sleep. *There must be a way. There must be a way.* And then an idea came to her head.

Every Family Has One

Mini vans delivered the laundry each day, returning late to pick up the completed work. It was only about three weeks until her due date although the nuns hadn't been able to give her a certain date. Glancing over her shoulder she escaped the stifling heat and walked into the biting wind to assist the men who drove the vans and unloaded the laundry. So far she had never done this task but there was no reason why she couldn't assist. Each day about three girls helped to unload the vans and there was no rota; it was whoever noticed the vans arrive first, going out to help. She began to lift a basket from one van that had just pulled up and as she lifted it she looked into the face of the driver. His face was kind and warm and momentarily she fixed him with a look of distress and sadness that she hoped might move him to help her. In the seconds that she held his gaze, neither spoke but she could see his eyes transform into a gentle look lit with concern.

'Help me.' She blurted out.

'Bridget get a move on with that basket.' A nun had come out to check on her. Kathleen's heart sank. As she moved to go she noticed the look of concern on the young man's face had turned deeper and she wondered if he would come again and help her next time.

But a next time didn't come for the following day while Kathleen was feeding dirty sheets into the washer she was suddenly gripped with an intense pain, coursing across her stomach and down her legs. She gripped the drum and her whole body felt weak. She thought she would collapse on the floor.

'Don't stop.' The nun barked over at her.

It was only then that she felt a warm trickle, which became a gush and within minutes she was standing in a pool of water imagining that she had wet herself.

49

'I said don't stop Bridget. What *is* the matter?' The nun came dashing over and as wave after wave of pain crashed over her she feared another whipping in the back office but instead the nun stopped, looked down. To her surprise she stopped shouting and a tiny flicker of concern filtered into her face and taking Kathleen's arm she guided her to the office telling her they needed to get over to the mother and baby unit promptly.

Still holding her arm for support the nun passed the Reverend Mother in the corridor and explained that Kathleen was now in labour.

'Stand over there a moment' she said to Kathleen and joined the Reverend Mother a few feet away.

'Will you let Robert know up at the hotel. Tell them to pack and be ready.'

Kathleen wondered what they were talking about. Who was Robert and what hotel? She wondered if Robert was a doctor. She would need a doctor to deliver the baby.

⁓

She was lying on a couch in the mother and baby unit having been in labour for several hours. The pain seemed to go on forever and Kathleen felt as if she were flailing in deep water unable to prevent herself slowly drowning as wave after wave crashed and gripped. She thrashed from side to side, unable to hold back the screams and the tears, despite the nuns demanding silence from her and reminding her that Christ's pain on the cross had been far greater and this was her punishment for opening her legs to a man. If only they knew, she thought to herself. And then one of the nuns leaned in towards her and shouted for her to give one last final push.

'The baby's head is coming. Push hard. It's coming.' She shouted.

Kathleen pushed; her face contorted, her body rigid. She thought she would tear open. And then she made one final attempt before her whole body collapsed in exhaustion and although she couldn't feel

Every Family Has One

anything she knew the baby was out and in the seconds that followed waited for the first cry to fill the air.

But the room was suddenly silent. She looked at the two nuns standing at the bottom of the couch staring at the space between her legs, their faces hard and expressionless, revealing nothing of what was going on.

She couldn't move and couldn't find the words to speak but as the seconds crept into minutes she knew that something was wrong. Hysteria rose as she struggled with one hand on the side of the bed, pain coursing through her as she sat up and looked down to the space where her baby lay, cold, still, drained of life.

A swirling blackness engulfed. She lay back, sobs ripping through her as she watched the nuns swiftly - as if well practiced -without saying a single word wrap the baby into a bundle using a blood stained sheet whipped from under her. Then she heard a thud as the bundle was tossed into a waiting bin.

'My baby, my baby. I want my baby. What's wrong with my baby.' She screamed over and over, somehow mustering the strength from within her lungs while the rest of her body was draining of energy and filling with grief.

But the nun wasn't listening. With her back to Kathleen she stood at the window watching an old Rolls Royce trundling up the avenue popping and spluttering to a halt in the middle of the gravel.

'Reverend Mother, Reverend Mother they're here. What do we do? What do we say?' The nun shouted, rushing for the door in panic, throwing Kathleen a look of hatred and disgust as she grabbed the door handle, her eyes cold as ice, continuing to yell 'they're here, they're here' down the corridor.

Kathleen tilted her head to see a well dressed, confident looking couple through the bars in the window get out of the car, stretch their arms and look around at the scenery, their eyes searching for the entrance to the house. She wondered who they were. Then she looked at the wire mesh bin in the corner of the room and the white bundle,

51

stained with blood, nestled between scrunched waste paper and dirty rubber gloves and bloodied gauze cloth.

Voices echoed in the corridor as several nuns gathered to discuss the visitors in anxious, raised voices. Kathleen strained to listen. What was going on? For a moment they all spoke at once and Kathleen thought how the girls would never be allowed to talk at once. One rule for them, another for us, she thought.

Although Kathleen couldn't see their faces she imagined their satanic expressions and the disappointment and greed lingering in their eyes consuming each of them. Only yesterday she had found out the nuns were not only running a laundry but also running a baby business. One of the only times she could chat to the other girls was in the shower block when they were unlikely to be overheard. She had casually asked if all the babies were adopted and the likelihood of being able to keep her baby. *Your baby will be sold for a lot of money. Probably to an American family.* The girl had told her. Kathleen had been too stunned to say anything but after the conversation she had started to think about it all. Did the girls get a share of the money, she wondered. What was the money used for...to set the girls up after they left the laundry? And how much money changed hands?

'They'll be so upset. They've been waiting for weeks in the hotel for the baby to arrive. They were so looking forward to their new addition, poor lambs. Mrs. Granville was told two years ago that she couldn't have children. This was their only hope. It's so tragic. And it's been a complete waste of time for Mr. Granville. He needs to get back to New York to see clients.'

There were a lot of ums and errs as the voices of three nuns discussed the situation just outside the door where Kathleen was still sobbing, haunted by the image of the bundle in the mesh bin. Kathleen wondered if their conversation had anything to do with her baby.

'Now Sister Bernadette I want you to go back in there, wrap the remains in a plastic bag. There should be some parcel tape in a drawer. I'll have the gardener wait by the tradesman's entrance with his cart. I best go down and offer the Granvilles tea and sympathy. God rest their souls.' She gushed.

'That's fine Reverend Mother. I'll be quick.' And then she was back in the room with Kathleen, her cold presence fluttering around the room, her rosary beads swishing from side to side as she moped the floor and prepared to wrap the bundle with package tape and old supermarket carrier bags.

Kathleen was all too aware that she was a child in the grip of an unending nightmare. She didn't think she could possibly shed another tear but the tears and the sobs kept coming, ebbing away to a splutter when she eventually found the courage to ask for the answers to the pertinent questions she had a right to know.

'What's happened to my baby? I need to know.'

'She was never your baby.' The nun snapped, her face hard and cold.

'She? It was a girl?' Kathleen stopped crying, wiped her face with her sleeve and momentarily smiled to hear the news.

'You don't need to know anything. Just rest a while. You'll be due back on the evening shift in a while.'

Kathleen detected a tiny flicker of compassion in her face as the nun momentarily stopped and looked at her, shivering and shaking, but her concern soon melted away as she prepared a bowl of water and began to scrub Kathleen down, removing the blood and scooping up the spongy dark mass from between her legs that was the placenta.

'Why did she die? Sister I need to know. Please sister.' Kathleen grabbed her wrist. The nun shook her hand away.

The sister hesitated and looked towards the door as if to check whether somebody was about to enter.

'I'm not supposed to say but...'

'Please sister.'

The nun hesitated. Looked at the door again.

'Your baby will be going to hell. She was born out of wedlock and has ruined the lives of a good couple who desperately wanted her.' Her voice was as sharp as sulphuric acid.

'But *I* wanted her.' Kathleen pleaded, her voice rising to fever pitch. 'I'm her mother.' She tried to sit up but sharp pains were stabbing.

A smile of triumph twisted on the nun's lips.

'You weren't fit to bring her up not with her condition.' The nun was quick to scold.

'What condition?' Kathleen frowned, now confused.

'She had a hair lip. We checked inside her mouth. A cleft palate too. Feeding her would have been a challenge. And she was too small to survive. Obviously didn't grow properly. Maybe you're not capable of a producing a proper baby. But I do know that it was God's will. Your punishment for sin. Now I suggest you spend the rest of the day praying while I clear the mess although quite honestly why it should be me and not you - the one who made all this mess in the first place - I do not know. Reverend Mother's orders. We don't question her.'

And with that she scooped up the bundle from the mesh bin and carried it out of the room, the door banging behind her sending a drafty gust into the room.

Kathleen fell into a disturbed sleep soon after she left, the tears lulling her gently into a stupor, but not for long. Voices wafted up from the gravel drive through the open sash window and at first Kathleen felt disorientated and then the trauma of what had happened returned to her like an incendiary device in the head. As she carefully sat up and adjusted her nighty she could see the gardener in his green wellies, pushing a bundle under a large black cross in a handcart, a spade tucked under his arm. Autumn leaves swirled around the cart in the light breeze as he hurried along.

She could hear the gardener asking a nun *which field for this cart?* And knew that they were discussing the burial of her baby. Would there be a headstone she wondered? She didn't remember seeing any headstones in the garden and surrounding land and wondered if any mothers had lost a baby too over the years.

Every Family Has One

Kathleen gasped in horror as she watched the cart pushed along the gravel and climbed down from the bed. Rushing to the window desperate to push the sash open, she found it wouldn't budge. It was stuck and no matter how hard she pushed and tugged she couldn't open it further than about three inches. With blood trickling from between her legs and sweat now turning her body cold she cried out in despair, yelping, calling to her baby. *Windysella, Windysella, Mummy's here.* Slamming her hands hard against the cold window, she descended to the floor, a sobbing crumpled wreck, leaving a trail of bloody, sweaty hand prints on the freshly polished pane.

And then she began to cry *mammy take me home. Mammy, please take me home.* Where was her mother in her hour of need? The wailing went on for some time, until the light started to fade, casting crackling shadows across the drab room. The smell of rotten cabbage indicating it was almost dinnertime seeped up through the floorboards.

The door creaked open and Kathleen - expecting to see a nun - wiped her eyes but a man's hand appeared and emerging into the room she recognised the friendly faced man; the driver of the evening laundry run from Dublin she had met before. Without thinking Kathleen scrambled to her feet and despite the pain she rushed over to him and clutched him as if he were a rock in a turbulent sea. He let her cling for several minutes and neither said a word. Grateful to breathe in the comforting smell of another human being, she enjoyed a momentary warm embrace swaddling her in happiness. She knew it couldn't last, for there were footsteps outside on the squeaky floor heading for the room. He pushed her away but kept her at arms length and they gazed at each other as if in a staring competition.

'I heard your crying so I came up. Here take this. I'll help you escape. I promise.'

She looked into his eyes, could see genuine compassion and concern.

'Why me? There are lots of other girls you could help.' She managed a coy smile, her cheeks flushing.

'But it's *you* I want to help. I can't help all of you. And you're lovely. I love your smile, your pretty face.' He touched her hair and brushed his lips lightly across her cheek.

As the footsteps drew closer he thrust a small folded piece of paper into her hand folding her fingers over it with a look that told her to be very careful.

'Read it later. I'll help you. Promise.'

He stepped away from her, rushing to gather laundry from the basket before the door flung open.

He looked at the nun; a rabbit caught in the headlights. The portcullis was down in an instant as his face switched to a hard, cold indifference for the nun's benefit.

'And what do you think you're doing on this wing? Who gave you permission?' The nun shouted, peering at him from under her glasses.

The man was quick. Had obviously worked out an answer.

'I like to be proactive sister. I knew there was a baby that had been delivered today with more sheets to be collected. Thought I'd save your girls a bit of time. They look rushed off their feet.'

The sister's face reddened.

'Are you offering to do my job? How dare you make those assumptions. Get downstairs now before I report you.' She snapped, turning her attention to Kathleen to search her face for the truth. Kathleen hoped she couldn't read her face and twig what was really going on.

'What are you doing out of bed? She said to Kathleen. 'You should be resting before the next shift.' She poked her finger in the direction of the bed.

Twenty-four years later - 1998
Slough, England

6
Kathleen

March 1998

Drowning out the clatter of hospital trolleys and the squeak of shoes up and down the corridor, Kathleen stared with disinterest at an old battered copy of the Woman's Weekly; a sea of words on her lap as she waited for her scan. She was terrified of what the scan might reveal about the second child growing inside her. Even though it was now twenty-four years since the birth of her first baby - she could remember every detail as if it were yesterday. She would never forget her daughter and had celebrated her birth each year. In her head she carried an image even though she had never seen her tiny face. The nuns would never know the power they had wielded in denying her that one request; a power that still cast its' shadow over her life weaving into every relationship she had.

Someone called her name, smiled, beckoned her into a consulting room. Her heart jumped to her throat. Maybe it was a mistake to come alone. Maybe she should have brought her husband. But she didn't want him to see her like this and have to explain to him how it wasn't the first time she'd given birth.

She stood up. Her legs felt heavy, as if they would give way. It was too late. Like it had been too late before. No going back. She was having a baby. *He only knows half the truth* a voice in her head whispered as she thought of everything that had happened in her past and how she had never shared it with her husband. She had told him about the laundry but said nothing about being pregnant. As far as he was concerned her mother had hated her and that was why she had been sent there. And the more Kathleen repeated the story over the years the more she had begun to believe it. After all this time she was still trying to erase the image of the priest and the pain of what he had done to her. She hadn't wanted him to worry about this birth and what might happen to their baby but she had done a lot of research on the internet about cleft palate and lip and the chances of it happening again were small. According to the Cleft Palate Foundation every parent had a 1:600 chance of parenting a child with a cleft. According to the Foundation there was only a 2-5% chance of a second baby having a cleft and so Kathleen felt reasonably reassured. There were no genetic tests and so she would just have to chance it that all would be well this time around. (See footnote) [1]She had told the midwife her background and had been offered recurrence risk counseling but had turned it down. The midwife had reassured her that feeding wouldn't be a problem if the baby did have a cleft. Sometimes babies with clefts couldn't breast feed but there were specially designed teats to make feeding easier.

The midwife had tried to persuade her to tell her husband. *The truth will set you free – it's like a lion. You don't have to defend it*, she had said at one appointment. But Kathleen didn't agree. Some things were best kept secret in a marriage. And this was one. What would he think of me? And even if he accepted the truth there would be questions. The past raked up, mapped out old soil ploughed over. For his benefit not hers. The past was controlling enough without adding his hands to the steering wheel. She had done her penance.

And yet despite doing her penance she couldn't move on. It was as if she had become the woman she now was on that fateful night

---

[1] See Cleft Palate Foundation at www.cleftline.org

of 12th January 1974. She could remember the precise moment when everything had changed forever. The moment when the light from the moon outside had illuminated the statute of the Virgin Mary near the altar, as Father Joseph was issuing each sharp thrust. The past kept clawing its' way back, parading in front of her, dancing the dance of the devil beside her, next to her, inside her every single day and no matter where she had been to over the years – enjoying a singing career in Dubai, working as a waitress in Wales, then to Rome and Belfast – with many good memories to pile on top of those bad memories - they kept resurfacing, despite the attempts in her head to photo-shop them out.

The sonographer smeared cold gel on her stomach, then moved a hand held device across her abdomen, pressing, pushing, wiggling it around looking for a heart beat. Kathleen was glad she couldn't see the screen, but didn't like the way the nurse frowned, her face set in stone as she peered intently at the screen saying nothing.

'There's a heart beat?'

'Yes don't worry.' The nurse's face relaxed but she kept pressing harder. Then the nurse's face hardened once more and Kathleen could feel her heart banging in her chest as fear mounted. She was glad she was lying down. Didn't want to receive the bad news standing up. Bad news would be the ultimate irony and maybe not such a surprise. It was everything she deserved after all. A punishment from God maybe? *Before you formed in the womb I knew you*, God had said. How could conception be a gift of God, through rape and with foetal abnormalities? It didn't make sense. And if children were a gift of God why had the nuns condemned her pregnancy as a sin?

'Is everything ok? My first baby had a cleft.' She suppressed a tremour in her voice and wondered if the scan would reveal anything. Her first birth seemed so long ago. It was hard to believe she had been a mother before. She had given birth but had played no greater part in the birth and now when she thought of the birth she saw it all in sepia colours, devoid of joy. All she had was the mocking words of the nuns replaying in her head. *You produced a monster.*

The nurse paused and asked if she had spoken about this to her midwife and smiled sympathetically, telling her that sometimes these things happened but it didn't mean it would happen again.

'We can monitor everything closely. You can come back for another scan in a few weeks. Just to confirm everything's developing normally.'

She sat up, anxiety rising as she stared at the posters on the wall; but their words couldn't reassure her. More than anything she worried about explaining to her husband why she needed a further scan. She also worried about him being able to attend the appointment – for he often worked abroad - and the nurse blurting out her background without thinking.

The nun's words still echoed in her head. *You've produced a monster.* Would she produce another monster? Were scans reliable? She couldn't relax until the birth when all would be revealed. Was she carrying a defective gene? Where had that gene come from? Were abnormalities punishment for sins? The way she'd treated her mother? For allowing herself to be alone with Father Joseph? For placing the temptation in front of him? *No. That's ridiculous* an inner voice interjected. Or was it? Part of her still tossed those questions around. And if God were a loving and merciful God why would he have created a baby with defects? *Every child created in His image.* What did that mean? And why should a child suffer because of its' mother's sins? Were the circumstances of life the direct result of sin?

She remembered a passage from John chapter 9, verse 1-3 in which Jesus was asked *who sinned this man or his parents that he was born blind?*

Neither this man nor his parents sinned, Jesus had replied. *This happened so that the work of God might be displayed in his life.* Jesus went on to heal the man. He created a blind man to show how he could heal, how His power worked, how only He could relieve suffering. But even with faith suffering could not always be removed, healed. The only thing

Kathleen knew was that despite those abnormalities she would have loved her baby, turned that suffering around into love. She would have accepted her baby no matter what the deformities.

Competing theories tossed and turned in the washing machine of her mind. She was tired. Wished she could press the stop button.

༄

Her baby son was now several weeks old. The birth had been swift and with the aid of pethidine - in the main pain free. When she had looked down at her son for the first time she felt a rush of love and a deep need to protect him forever. She lay in bed cradling him, watching him sleep. The rose-leaf softness of his gentle, fragile skin invited the touch of her finger and the warmth of her smile. But these feelings would crash, without warning, swinging like a pendulum, minute to minute, hour to hour. She couldn't understand what was going on. Maybe she had the baby blues. It was a widely discussed problem but she tried to dismiss it. At her six-week health check she had the opportunity to discuss her mood when the midwife asked a series of routine questions but she was so terrified of the social services taking the baby away that she gave false answers, revealing nothing of the extent of her emotions. But as the days and weeks went by it had become a pattern to feel happy to burst one moment, then crash the next, like a wave with deep sadness as she recalled the traumatic birth in the laundry. Having the next baby seemed to heighten this sadness because she found herself contrasting and comparing the two experiences.

Sometimes it was easier not to answer the phone than make more excuses. Why couldn't they leave her alone? Invites for tea, Costa coffee mornings, meet ups in the park, lunches, post-natal exercise classes. Her head swam in a cloudy soup with the thought of conversations about sleep routines, feeding, nappy rash, cradle cap, mastitis, dummies. It was tedious. She didn't want to be a part of it all. She didn't feel a part of it all. The only person that mattered now in the whole world was her baby. And no one was going to take him away. She looked down at him cradled in her arms and planted a kiss on his downy forehead.

☙

It was a week after the baby's four month check and he was filling out; plump legs, cute dimples on his cheeks, chubby arms. The doctor had carried out routine checks and weighed him. Everything was fine. He was a healthy baby. There was nothing for Kathleen to worry about and yet she found one thing after the other to fret about. If he slept for long she would rush to check he was still alive. If he felt hot she was convinced he might have meningitis. And when it came to his jabs she read all the alarmist articles online, unable to decide whether to have him vaccinated.

It was three in the afternoon. She had got up to make a cup of tea and sandwich returning to her bed. She hadn't stopped breastfeeding. What would the gaggle of women think to that she wondered? But she didn't care. It felt right. Secure. A necessary luxury. All the time she cradled him he was safe. Safety was everything. She remembered a quote from Shakespeare. *Out of this nettle, danger, we pluck safety.* But she had no idea what it meant.

All the time she fed him no one else could touch him. It was the perfect excuse. What gave them the right to hold her baby? He was a fragile being, like a precious piece of fine bone china. She intended to breast feed for as long as she possibly could. She couldn't take her eyes off him; felt entranced, hypnotised by his beauty, his powdery smell, his warmth, his soft skin. He was perfection and the more she stared at him, tracing her finger around his little face, planting delicate kisses on his cheeks the more she wondered what her first baby had looked like. *You've produced a monster.* The nuns' harsh words came back to her and the way they had tried to reward her and dismiss her feelings with a new set of rosary beads and a bottle of holy water.

She could still hear the triumph behind the nun's southern Irish accent, the deep and throaty voice, the words veiled in cruelty. Words were a powerful drug; a drug that seeped into the subconscious and became a part of you forever. Words were like scars etched across the body. Once they had escaped from the mouth they couldn't be retrieved, taken back. All she'd wanted was to see her baby. Why hadn't they let her? Why had they been so cruel? None of it had made any sense. Just a glimpse would have helped to lay her to rest.

The net curtains danced gently in the breeze. She could hear owners whistling to their dogs, children playing on the Common. She couldn't muster the energy to sit up. A tsunami of exhaustion swept her body.

The landline was ringing. She looked at it; didn't answer. Then her mobile started ringing. She sighed. This was his tenth call since breakfast time. Didn't he have work to do? Reluctantly she pressed the green button.

'I've arranged for mum to help you tomorrow.' Her husband casually said.

Kathleen took a deep breath. Closed her eyes. Why did her husband always refer to his mother as *mum* rather than *my mum*. This grated in Kathleen's head. Her own mum had gone; had long forgotten her. It was as if his mum had become her mum too. She tried to remain calm. Didn't want her voice to climb in hysteria and receive a repeat of his layman's diagnosis of post natal bloody depression; with it the big dirty label *mad new mother*. But her head screamed *Please no*. Her heart started to thump. She felt clammy. Her nighty was wet with milk. She didn't want that woman near her baby. Didn't want her to pick him up, cuddle him, change him. *This cannot happen. Why are they doing this to me?*

'No. I really don't want any help. You're only away till Friday. I can cope.' She snapped, immediately regretting her ungrateful tone.

'She'd like to see him.' He said in rising cadence. He never gave up. It was her baby. No one else's.

'She's not coming to help me. End of.' Kathleen snapped aware that her attitude was starting to put a strain on their marriage.

'She just wants to see the baby. It is her first grandchild darling. You've got to let other people hold him at some point. You can't keep him all to yourself forever.' He reasoned.

'Can't?' Kathleen bristled. A rope of anger tightened across her stomach. 'And *you* can't tell me what I can and cannot do. I'm his mother.'

'She's not taking him away. No one is.' How dare he tell her what she could and couldn't do.

'Darling no one said they're going to take him away. I wish you'd talk to the health visitor about this. It smacks of paranoia. I hate seeing you like this.'

'Look I know what's best for him. I'm his mother.' Kathleen reminded him.

'No one's disputing that. But what if you get ill? Someone else will have to look after him.'

'I'm not ill. Tell your mum not to come. Please. I'll be out. At a coffee morning.'

'That sounds nice. You need to get out. It's not doing you any good sitting in bed all day.'

'I'm not sitting in bed.' She lied. How the hell did he know what she was doing? She was fed up with him telling her that what she was doing was the wrong thing, the right thing. Why couldn't he just back off and let her get on with it? She hated his opinions, the way he was judging her and judging what was best for her and for the baby.

'Really?' He didn't sound convinced.

'Did you sleep well last night without me?' He asked. *Better*, she thought to herself. She could sleep well with the baby when he was away but when he returned she knew she would resent having to share the bed with her husband.

'Apart from the sound of foxes mating.' She always woke to the blood curling sound of foxes mating; sounds which mingled in her dreams as a recurring nightmare, taking her back to the cries of the other mothers in the laundry as their babies were taken from them, whisked away for adoption.

'You're a funny thing darling but I do love you.'

In a huff Kathleen didn't feel like saying *love you too*, but as she put the phone down she knew the rebuff would hurt him. She got up to close the curtains and the world outside, crawling back to bed; her baby nestled in her arms. The bed was her pond, small and safe and she didn't want to venture away from it into the big ocean. She pulled the duvet over her head, pulled her legs tight to her stomach.

When was this going to end? She asked herself.

7
Kathleen

July 2003

Kathleen had heard that West Wittering was a magnificent beach; the best along the south coat. It wasn't far from Slough; a two hour run, mainly motorway.

But as soon as she pulled off the A27 and saw the lengthy queues on the approach road to the beach she knew it had been a mistake to come. The vision of her garden and paddling pool sprung to her mind; less stressful, now more inviting. Her son was shrieking in the back *are we nearly there yet?* He was tapping his yellow plastic bucket with the spade as if it were a drum; a noise that grew louder in her head with each inch travelled and as the car slowly nudged forward she was beginning to feel as if she was trapped inside a metal baked bean can, clawing her way out, unable to breath, slowly deprived of air.

She was surprised to find that her hands were shaking as she passed the money to the waiting car park attendant sitting in his wooden booth. And then she looked around; taking in the sea of cars filling every space into the far distance. This was like arriving at the long stay car park at Heathrow. How would she find a space? Find the car on her return? She couldn't process logic, think of a landmark then chart the route to the car. The familiar tightening of her chest had returned, her mouth felt dry and she wondered if she would faint again, like she had several times before when she felt this way.

In the back of the car her small son was chattering. *Can we swim? When can I build a sandcastle? Can I have an ice cream?*

Getting out of the stuffy car the cooler air made her feel better. She leant against the burning metal taking deep gulps of air. She was doing this for her son, she reminded herself. *You can't keep him at home every day*, she chastised, *not on a beautiful summer day.*

She was glad that her friends hadn't come too. She didn't want them to see her like this. When she was like this all she could do was to shut the world out, ignore the phone, not return the calls, cross over the road if she saw a friend; pretend she hadn't seen them. To everyone around her she was the fun loving, flamboyant, gregarious woman who joked and made them laugh. But she couldn't keep it up all the time and that's what they wanted. They didn't know the real her: the woman who was drowning in her nightmares; the daily struggle to get up, the struggle to function as a parent. It was all a front. And sometimes she couldn't keep up that front. It all became too much.

∽

It happened shortly after lunch. They had paddled in the sea, watching the graceful flight of the silvery grey terns and cormorants hovering over the shallow water then plunging down to catch small fish. They had built a sandcastle, filled a moat, eaten their sandwiches.

She felt drowsy, laid back on her towel, her head on her handbag, her hand linked to her sons as he twizzled his plastic ball with his other hand. She drifted off, not intending to, then woke disorientated, the bright sun scorching her face, unsure how long she'd slept.

Where was he? He couldn't be far.

She grabbed her bag, stood up, looked around, feeling groggy. The beach was packed. She spun round, scanning in each direction, looking for a small boy with blonde hair. Soon she was shouting, people were staring, the scene froze like a video on freeze frame. Seconds seemed like minutes. Time was dragging. She was shaking again; the pain in her chest and the dizziness back. And before she could see the nice lady, her face full of concern, holding his hand guiding him back to her, her son clutching his plastic ball Kathleen's head was spinning, her blood pressure dipping as she collapsed into the sand with one thought buzzing through her head.

I can't do this. I can't carry on.

8
Kathleen

September 2012

Kathleen had been sick several times but didn't tell her husband or son. It felt as if her inners had been nuked. A cold fear slithered through her body as she walked along the school corridor and into the meeting, her head bowed low, sunglasses hiding her red eyes. Why was she putting herself through this? Why did she put herself through any of it?

Allowing him to go to friends' houses for example where she knew there would be danger: head and back injuries from trampolines. Or he could get killed on the way to their house from a car accident. But he didn't have to go to friends' houses for tea with all the hazards that entailed: food that he might choke on or get food poisoning from, hazards like windows, viscous dogs, cats that carried germs. And the pressure to prevent him walking to school on his own, or with neighbour's kids was tearing her apart. She had to continue driving him in to school, as long as she could. A stranger might pull him off the pavement. He might faint on the way to school and how would she know? He might get bullied along an alley way, he might not look properly crossing the road... The worries never ceased. And worrying was draining.

She couldn't let her son see her like this. It wasn't fair. The school trip meant everything to him. It was his coming of age. His initiation. He'd been talking about it throughout primary school and into middle school and now it was upon them. But it had come round too quickly. She couldn't believe he was now thirteen. He was nearly as tall as she was.

She'd painted a smile on her face over breakfast, feigning her excitement, asking questions but inside dreading every answer. He was filled with a manic happiness: planning midnight feasts, showing her photos of Kingswood and the activities that awaited them. *It's only a week* she kept telling herself. One week of his life. Monday through to Friday. Four nights. Five days. October 2012..it would go down in her mind as one of the biggest tests of her parenting. She wasn't sure if she would survive the week. But he'd be back, if all went well and there were no accidents, under her watchful eye. But was his first taste in independence really worth this amount of stress? This was her battered attempt to confront the darkest parts of herself; the demons she had wrestled with since his birth. She knew that there would never be a right time to cut the apron strings. It would always be a double-edged sword. The truth was she would never let go. And all the time she felt this way she couldn't move forward. But letting go surely would mean she no longer cared. And there was no one in the whole world that she cared for more.

There were aspects of his life that she could not control. He had to go to school – but she could control the rest of his life and was determined not to loosen her grip.

She slipped into the school hall hoping no one had seen her, taking a seat at the back. The head of year began to explain the format for the week; the departure time, what to pack and not pack, the programme of activities: climbing, abseiling, go karting, fossil hunting, swimming and an end of week barbecue.

Her breaths were now coming in short rasps, her chest felt tight. Visions of her son falling while abseiling, drowning while swimming, blurred the view in front of her, as a spell of intense visceral fear engulfed. It was as if she had entered a lion's enclosure. The room was starting to spin. She gripped the side of the plastic chair steadying herself until the waves passed and then raised her hand mustering courage to ask a question.

'You said that they can't take a mobile with them. But can we phone them? In the morning and evening?' She asked.

Suddenly all eyes had turned to look at her. Although several of them were her friends and knew her well and the extent of her day to day parental anxieties and gave sympathetic knowing smiles in her direction she felt like the freak in the room; the protective mother who wrapped her son in cotton wool. It was an expression threaded across every face in the room, even those of her friends. She could feel the blood of embarrassment pulsing in her head.

'That's not the general idea. We'll phone you if there's a problem. We need them to experience what it's like to be away from home for the first time.' Ants started to march across the base of her spine as the words *away from home* slowly sank in.

The parents were muttering, whispering to each other. Paranoia engulfed as she sensed they were all talking about her and her extreme parenting. Then the teacher smiled.

'Think of it as a nice break. Maybe you'll get together for an evening out. Enjoy the break, glass of chilled wine, feet up. That's what I say.' The noise in the room rose as laughter and chatter broke out. Kathleen felt like the condemned woman at the top of the scaffolding about to feel the noose around her neck, reminded that at least she'd been offered a nice glass of chilled wine.

After the meeting the parents disbursed and she hung around to ask again about phoning each day.

'I see you're very nervous about sending him on the trip.' The teacher rubbed her arm in sympathy.

'It's his first time away from home. He wants to go but I don't want him to go if I'm honest.' She took her sunglasses off, her face more wrinkled than her years, the strain of worry showing in the bags under her eyes.

The teacher frowned, reflecting back her pain.

'Have you met Joey?'

'Joey?' Kathleen thought this was another child in her son's class.

'Come this way.' She took her arm as if guiding a cripple and led her along the corridor to one of the classrooms. As she walked in she could hear a cage rattle and a soft grinding noise and two eyes watched her from behind a cage.

'Our African grey.' The teacher announced.

Kathleen was confused. The bird started to ruffle its feathers.

'Birds aren't meant to be caged. It's for our pleasure. Their feathers are too bright, their songs too sweet. They don't want to be kept in captivity. He's like your son. There comes a time when we need to let them go, let them live their lives, discover themselves. When we open the cage to feed Joey he flies out because he wants to go. Your son wants to go. He wants to use his wings. And the part of you that knows it was wrong to imprison him in the first place rejoices, enough though his cage is drab and empty because he has gone. It's nature I'm afraid.'

Why did I always think I was a strong person who could cope with anything that life threw? She asked herself as she fled the corridor. *I'm crumbling and I can't pull myself back.*

Part 2
Set in a town near Slough, England

8
Jacko

October 2012

Jacko woke dazed. Gradually the realization that he had killed someone the night before seeped into his consciousness, like tiny droplets of ink spreading through water, then hit him; a hammer to the head. His heart coiled in terror. He struggled to sit up, pushing the plump white pillows beneath the small of his back as his body carried the weight of fear. His head screamed in pain. The haunting laughter of the children came flooding back - happy from their week away, parent free, yet tired and looking forward to seeing their parents again – turning in an instant to deathly screams.

His eyes adjusted to the dazzling lighting and stark surroundings wondering what day of the week it was. Nurses were rushing around, trolleys, visitors, bleepers, chatter. How had he ended up in hospital? Somewhere between losing control on the dark bend and the present there sat a void. His brain couldn't piece it all together.

Shards of memory fluttered into his waking brain. Why the fuck had she been standing there, dressed in black, waiting on the grass verge on that dark and lonely road? Why couldn't she have waited at the school like all the other parents? Part of him thought about how reckless she had been. Maybe she had been drunk; not in control of what she was doing. Part of him felt a sense of desperation. How could he not have seen her? Surely the light from the cottage close by had illuminated her figure. And underneath all of these thoughts wormed the truth: he wasn't good at night driving and should have told his manager before agreeing to drive a busload of school kids after dark. But the ferry from the Isle of Wight had been delayed. They should have arrived back at the school in daylight hours and he should have joined his mates in the Dog and Bucket – the usual Friday gathering to watch the footie on the big screen, washed down with a few beers.

This was the first year the coach had been delayed. In a flash he recalled the grand reception of previous years; of waiting emotional parents gathering along the railings of the Underwood Middle School, chattering in their cliques, sharing stories of how they'd enjoyed their week of freedom while the kids were away or how they had really missed them; couldn't wait for their return. Some years their brothers and sisters would make elaborate welcome home banners and tie them to the railings. In his mind's eye he could see parents scooping their kids into warm embraces, plastering them with kisses, smothering them with cuddles and delight. He could see kids thrusting pocket money gifts wrapped in candy striped paper into their parents hands; dinosaur fossils, postcards or key rings picked up in the Bembridge tourist shop. But not this year. A flash of blue lights had surrounded the coach. Shocked children had been carefully escorted to the roadside. A roadblock put up. And then he'd fainted.

He closed his eyes to filter the scene from the night before but the haunting look in her eyes filled his mind as guilt coursed through every vein in his body. He couldn't erase the image of her dark silhouette underneath the horse chestnut tree. She reminded him so much of the Scottish Widow advert; a beautiful woman in a black cloak and hood; a spectre of death. Jacko recalled the catchphrase to the advert: 'life feels better when you have a plan.' In the few seconds it had taken to lose control on that bend his own life plan had imploded. The image now planted in his mind's eye would be etched across his guilty mind forever. In those seconds before impact he could have swerved, he could have braked, he could have thought faster. And if only his driving skills had been better she would be alive today and his conscience salvaged. But this had happened and he knew that the course of his life was now changed forever.

The thought of stepping into a driver's seat again filled him with terror. He lay back on the pillow, his stomach churning, bile rising in his throat. He reached out and pulled a brown cardboard bowl towards his mouth and spewed the remains of the carrot and meat dinner; the last meal he'd shared with those happy kids on the Isle of Wight.

Had this really happened? He was struggling to believe.

༄

'Are you a close relative because you *are* aware that visiting time isn't until two?'

Jacko was lying with his back to the corridor staring out of the window towards the Chilterns. It was still early but had felt as if he had been awake for hours. Cleaners had been busy around him emptying rubbish, changing the water jug beside his bed and generally clattering about. His head throbbed with each beat of his heart. His mouth felt parched. His lips cracked. Who was the woman in the corridor asking the nurse to see him, he wondered. Trish, his wife wouldn't be along until much later. He was expecting the old bill to be the first to pay him a visit. He imagined they had cordoned the road off, measuring the skid marks, assessing the road and conditions, setting up signs to appeal to the public for information. Although he had answered a ton of questions, taken a drink driving test and given his version of the accident he knew they would be back to check more detail and establish facts. He had killed. His coach had killed. And inevitably a formal investigation would now take place. But he knew and they knew it had been an accident. He was driving well within the speed limit. It had happened suddenly, giving him no chance to swerve and she hadn't seen the coach coming.

'Yes, yes, of course I'm a close relative.' The visitor was insistent. Jacko didn't recognise her voice. She didn't sound like anyone he knew. Why was she visiting so early in the morning? He didn't have long to ponder. Her shoes screeched to a halt behind him, she coughed loudly and prodded him in the back.

'Oi.' She poked again. He flinched, arched his neck to see who it was.

'You took the life of my best friend... My only real friend. You bastard.' She spat.

Jacko turned, his body tangled in swathes of linen and looked up at the flushed face of a woman he reckoned to be in her late forties. Wrestling with the sheets he pulled himself up, unnerved by the simmering fury and accusation in her eyes.

'Steady on lady. Who are you?'

'Never mind who I am. I'm a mum at the school. My son was on the coach too. So was hers. Those kids will be traumatised for the rest of their lives after what you did. Death by reckless driving. Were you drunk? I hope they lock you up, throw away the key.' She spat, leaning towards his ear as he lay motionless.

'Of course not.'

'Well I hope they do you for dangerous driving.'

'You don't come in here making accusations. You don't know what happened. You weren't there.'

She began to cry. Jacko looked away, didn't want to look at her pained face. He felt bad enough.

'You better go. The nurses are lovely. Why don't you have a chat with them. They've got tissues.' He gently told her.

'I came to see you. What happened last night?'

'I'm sure it will be splashed all over the local papers at the weekend, with a biased version of the events. Why don't you wait and read the Slough Express?'

'Lives will be changed forever after what you did. A boy no longer has his mother. How will he cope? You've no idea how hard it's going to be for his father as well. What's he supposed to say to his son? He won't be able to cope without her. She did everything for her son. They were so close. He'll never get over this. And his father will probably take him abroad now to be close to his parents and work. God knows how my son will cope without his best friend. Of course none of this concerns you. You don't see the impact of what you've done, how it cuts across so many lives.'

The woman looked exasperated. Her arms were flinging all over the place, her eyes shooting in all directions. He didn't know what to do, what to say. He'd never lost anyone. Didn't know how it felt. He couldn't empathise, yet guilt washed over him even though it had been an accident.

'And to think she very nearly didn't send him on the trip. That was her greatest fear. An accident. In fact she feared lots of things. If you hadn't killed her it would have been someone else because you're obviously a bad driver and only a matter of time. You shouldn't be driving.'

'And you think it will be easy for me to get behind the wheel after what happened. I don't think so. That's if I haven't lost my job. You think I'm going to sleep easy? Not have nightmares?'

She looked away, didn't say anything for a few moments, seemed surprised by what he was saying. And then she leaned in closer, fresh tears forming. He could feel her warm breath upon him as she whispered.

'You're evil. Truly evil.'

And with those last words she turned to go, leaving him wracked with a litany of emotions tossing and turning in his head.

9
Faye

August 2014

Faye had been waiting for over an hour. The doctor's surgery was particularly busy. She had flicked through several Home and Garden magazines, swiped a couple of recipes from Woman's Weekly, checked her iphone. With her eyes now closed she was back to thinking of Katie, her image filling her mind. Beautiful Katie. Her lovely smile. Her radiance.

For most people in her situation nighttime was the worst. Not for Faye. Katie was in her head in the middle of the day when she walked down the high street in Trentum, where they both lived; a small market town close to Slough. Like Elvis Katie's lookalike was everywhere. Darting across the road in a long black coat, her face hidden behind large sunglasses, whatever the weather or time of year. Faye could see the back of Katie's head; tumbling dark curls in the distance, weaving around crowds of shoppers. Yet when she went to tap on her shoulder it wasn't Katie. It was someone else: someone older, or someone younger, someone with heavy make up or someone with a tired looking face. Never Katie.

She often heard Katie's voice or thought it was her; usually in the charity shops in nearby Marlow or Windsor. Katie loved the charity shops in the better off towns. For her it was worth going further afield. And Faye had to agree. *We'll pick up designer dresses, Armani handbags, Karen Millen t shirts for less than a tenner* Katie would whoop. Katie had always known what suited Faye, the colours that worked with her skin.

Faye looked down where Home and Garden sat on her knee. These days Faye wore torn jeans and a scruffy t shirt. Back then, in the Katie days she had looked glamorous, just like Katie. But the Katie glamour look had gone. In its' place was the dowdy look. The look that said *well it will have to do.* When Faye went into charity shops these days she couldn't focus. It wasn't the same. Her eyes flitted over every rack and then she would leave the shop, feeling lost, adrift at sea, not knowing where to go, what to do.

In charity shops Faye imagined Katie undressing in the cubicle, shouting from behind the faded curtains. *Oh my God my bum looks big in this* or *wow it contours my figure perfectly.* Faye could see Katie swooning in front of a long mirror, hugging a silk dress to her trim body. *What do you think darling?* Katie would ask. Faye had always felt special when Katie asked her opinion. It was nice to be valued. And proud that it was Katie asking her and not some other friend. And nobody had ever called Faye darling or sweetie before. They were words that made her feel truly loved and when Katie said them she said them with conviction with a smile that reached her eyes.

And by the way shall I pick Tim up from school, give him tea, give you a break? Katie had asked so many times.

Katie had been a godsend after Trevor's death; having the kids to tea, keeping them overnight so that she could work at a nearby factory or supermarket – anything to make ends meet. Sometimes she had brought round home made pies and other delicacies, packed under foil in a wicker basket.

Tea shops, coffee shops and in particular Ringo's were the hardest places to go in nowadays. It seemed that Katie's voice echoed around the walls of Ringo's cramped tearoom and her laughter in the cups that tinkled, the cutlery that clattered. She could see, in her mind's eyes the way Katie used to smooth down the chintz tablecloths before placing her cup and Victoria sandwich on the table. It was hard now to go in there and Faye had gone right off Victoria sandwich. Just looking at them made her stomach sink. The waitresses all remembered of course. Well it had been the talk of the town after all. They gave Faye their looks of sympathy, asking how Faye was in that sickly tone strangers have in situations like this.

How's Ed? They'd ask. *Poor lad. It must be so hard and for his poor dad. How's he coping?* Too many questions thrown at her like missiles, yet no answers. She didn't know. When they asked Faye she would look into her teacup for the answers as if the leaves contained an update. Katie had been one of life's givers. Never a taker. Always a listener. Always there when you needed her. Faye wondered who had been there for Katie. Some aspects of Katie's life had been a mystery. The way she had flipped from being gregarious to being sullen and withdrawn, shutting herself away for weeks yet not explaining what was wrong. She had been hard to tap into. Hard to get to the bottom of. Yet Faye hadn't missed a deep sadness at times behind Katie's pale eyes. Katie hadn't revealed much about her past, her family and who she was before she married. Life had been consumed with children, Faye now mused. Perhaps this was the way it was for all women; abandoning their old lives at the garden gate when they married and had children. And now, when it was Faye's turn to do the giving she wasn't able to. Ed and his dad had gone. They hadn't given her a chance to help. *We'll be moving to Dubai where my parents live. Ed needs family around him. They can do the childcare. That's where I met Katie. She was working in a bar in the Burj Khalifa as a singer. You must come out sometime, visit.*

A flight to Dubai would cost a fortune and on the pittance I earn, no chance, Faye wanted to scream at him. But it would be nice, Faye often thought, to take Tim to see Ed. Not that Tim ever mentioned Ed. Come to think of it, Faye thought to herself Tim didn't mention any of his friends.

Every Family Has One

Maybe that was why she was now sitting waiting for the doctor to see her. There were things that needing addressing, issues needed solving.

⁂

'It's about everything and nothing.' Faye adjusted her bottom in the cold plastic chair, flapping the clammy August heat from her face, eyes glancing round the doctor's consulting room as if the answer to something and nothing was contained within those four white walls.

'I just wanted your opinion...' Her voice trailed off.

In embarrassment her head darted to the sink in the corner of the sterile room and the boxes, vials and packets of syringes stacked on a shelf and books containing all the answers to questions not contained in the doctor's head. Then her eyes returned to his sympathetic face and gentle eyes; a face she had come to know and trust over a long period of time covering a catalogue of problems.

'If something doesn't feel normal very often it isn't. How can I help?'

It didn't matter that his nasal hair was a dense forest and a distraction as he spoke, or that his thick wild eyebrows moved up and down like window wipers at 90 degrees. For he had a warm Welsh lilt to his voice that could easily lull her to sleep or calm her fears.

Her eyes were now fixed on the white lino.

'You'll probably think I'm just a neurotic mother. Rather like Katie. The type who rings with a raised temperature, panics at the first sign of a rash.' Her voice was cracking.

'I've never thought that. You've done an amazing job bringing three children up on your own and coping after Trevor's suicide. What's troubling you?'

'I don't know where to begin. It's Tim... he's slowly dying. Little by little. The light inside him is growing dimmer with each passing day and one day that tiny flicker won't be able to survive any longer and will be finally extinguished. I'm sorry to be vague. I haven't come here with tangible symptoms that you can look up in one of your books and tell me what the matter is.'

She sighed. Without Trevor, without Katie it seemed the whole world was resting on her shoulders.

'And how are *you*?' His voice was soft, almost a whisper and Faye felt like a baby being rocked softly to sleep by a lullaby. Their eyes held. With those four words he had opened her soul and the tears came tumbling and the sobs came crashing. These four walls were the place she came to cry and purge her soul in the presence of Dr. Owen. Where did she begin when the clock was ticking and the waiting room was filling and the phone in the reception never stopped ringing and ringing; desperate patients with more pressing matters than hers – all pleading to be seen.

'My son exists as a ghost floating between his room and the kitchen. I'm living with a ghost and I don't quite know when that happened or why that happened or what I've done or haven't done.'

Faye closed her eyes. It would have been easier if her son had been born evil, a sociopath, cold and adversarial from a young age; rather like Kevin in Lionel Shriver's 2003 novel 'Let's Talk About Kevin.' At least she might have understood him better.

'The girls are so different. Chrissie is alive: chatty, sporty, energetic. She's at that lovely age. Nine. She does ballet, football, tap and drama. Shayne, Chrissie's dad sees her regularly and is supportive.

And Meg is alive too; feisty, opinionated, confident. The girls enjoy my company. They like coming out with me. Meg comes late at night, sits on my bed for a chat. We go out for lunch, for breakfast. We talk about all sorts of things. She's like a best friend. But how could twins be so different in character? Meg outgoing, Tim silent. I don't know who Tim is anymore. One day I woke and Tim had gone. A new Tim had arrived.' Just saying his name seemed to sap her energy.

'It might be delayed grief.'

'But he never knew his dad. He was too young.' Faye whined.

The doctor said nothing for a minute, allowing her time to collect her thoughts. She looked at him. His lips were cracked. Beads of sweat on his brow glistened in the light streaming through the window. She wondered how many hours he worked a week. Suspected it was a great many.

'He's the silent shadow in the corner: the one that mutters but doesn't speak; the one that whispers but doesn't shout. The one that used to cry all the time when he was little but now he's a cardboard cut out and cardboard cut outs don't cry do they? Sometimes it is as if he is an imposter. When I look at him I can't connect with the fact that I gave birth to him. It's as if he isn't mine. I find myself trying to remember his birth so that I can reconnect with him but all I have are shards of memory. I see his baby cheeks pitted with dimples and I remember him; the boy he was; Timmy Tankers. But it was all a long time ago. Sixteen years ago. There's a disconnection between him as a young boy and now.

He creeps up behind me and he towers over me but says nothing. It's like walking along the beach, buried in your thoughts accompanied only by your shadow. He asks if we have any more biscuits or he asks for money. He's a vessel to be filled. I'm just the ATM. The taxi driver. The cook. I exist as wallpaper in his environment. It's like having an adult in the house except that he isn't an adult and he doesn't connect like an adult. But neither is he a child anymore. I'm waiting for something to change. For him to emerge into a new being but I can't see what that being will be.'

Faye sighed, her eyes rested on the windowsill and a Blue Tit pecking at a feeder and she paused before making the big statement.

'I don't think he likes me. I'm pretty sure of that. And...'

The doctor didn't answer.

She dabbed her eyes, feeling the heat burn her cheeks.

'And I'm not sure *I* like him.'

Then she looked at the doctor, shook her head. Felt a surge of guilt. Tim was a likeable boy; placid, gentle with a wry humour. There were the odd funny things he would say at the dinner table.

This meal has a high potato sausage ratio. He had said the previous evening. The way he lined his chips under his burger bun *like Yogi Mitzel in the yog pod.* Whatever that meant. *And I'm going over to a friends for a hearty chat.*

The doctor made no move to interrupt.

When she had emptied her thoughts from the vessel, nothing more to say and repeated her worries several times over he turned to his computer and she wondered what prescription he would prescribe for this nameless complaint of hers with its' invisible symptoms. The screen sprung to life.

'I know the teenage years can be a challenge. It's really not easy. Especially when you're trying to do everything on your own. Does your brother... Steve still have the kids to stay? He seemed to step up to the plate of fatherhood after Trevor's death?'

'My brother was great. I was very lucky to have him. I had no other family. Katie was there though. I couldn't have coped without her.'

Faye looked away, finding it hard to continue and the doctor reached out his hand and gently rubbed her arm with that same look of sympathy plastered across everyone else's face when Katie was mentioned.

'But unfortunately,' she carried on, her mind snapping back to Steve, 'Steve's now living in Spain: new job, new wife. So everything's down to me.'

'You're doing a great job you know. You should be proud of all three of those children. But I have to say he's a teenager and staying in their room *is* what they do. Rest assured that *is* normal. But at the time you feel you've lost your son. Well you have. Temporarily I suppose. But he'll come back. You see.'

He smiled warmly. He'd unlocked the padlock to her soul, taken her hand softly in his and led her through a gate into a big empty field. But she was now standing in that field completely lost. Where did she go from here?

What would you do Katie? What do you think is wrong? She silently asked.

'My own son was exactly the same. He's now 30 and he's come out the other end.'

This was his way of admitting her to the club of disaffected teens. They were both members. Except this was different. His kid was normal. His kid still had both his parents. Tim's dad had jumped in front of a train when Tim and Meg were only five years old. Not that Tim knew the full facts. *Daddy was ill* was all she had ever told the twins. *Cancer.*

'When he starts back at school you could suggest he joins a school club. What does he enjoy doing?' The doctor suggested. Why did doctors always state the obvious, Faye wondered. As if she hadn't already thought about this.

He wasn't getting it, but he'd listened and that was maybe all Faye needed at this stage.

'Nothing. That's the problem. He's given up any interests he had – Judo, Scouts, the Duke of Edinburgh. His only interest is the computer. He sits in front of it all day. But what can I do? I can't take it away now. It's too late. It would be like slamming the door after the horse has bolted. I should have set the rules years ago, but I thought it wouldn't matter.'

Faye stared at the doctor as if he had all the answers. But deep down she knew he didn't. This was surface chat. In the five minutes they had available he could only tap the surface. This was the top soil of the problem, not the inner foundations.

'He'll soon be busy studying for his exams. And then in the next year his life will change again.' The doctor reassured.

'Take a look at this website.' He turned to look at his computer again. 'You can always give them a ring, have a chat.'

She leaned towards his desk, took out her iphone and noted down 'Connexions.'

It was a service she already knew about. Inwardly she chastised herself for not looking it up myself.

And as she left, the same question burned inside. What was wrong with her 16 year old son? And what did his future hold?

10
Faye

August 2014

It was the day after the visit to the doctor and concerns about Tim were still bubbling below the surface of Faye's mind. At some point she knew she would have to confront him and try to get him talking. She had asked him a couple of times why he never said much and his answer had always been the same: *I've got nothing to say.* She would ask him questions about his day at school and all he would say was: *I went to the toilet. I ate my lunch.*

She had allowed this to go on for too long; living in hope that change would happen naturally, in an evolutionary organic way.

As she washed up the evening dishes Faye looked out at the overgrown lawn and wondered if things would have been different if Trevor had been still alive. If only Trevor had opened up to her; told her about the financial mess he had been in rather than turn aggressive and abusive. *I blamed myself for so long. I didn't know why he was so aggressive towards me,* she had told Katie so many times. Yet all along Trevor had been deeply depressed, then turned to the doctor for anti depressants. *How could I not have seen it coming?* She'd asked herself many times.

These and so many questions Faye asked herself daily and all the time aware that her consumption of the past and the unresolved issues stopped her focusing on the present. But it was hard not to dwell on the past, to fester, because the past usually impacted on the present. *Some people are dwellers* she had told Katie. *I try to forget the past* Katie had replied.

As Faye washed up she visualized Trevor at the table helping Tim with Maths just like her own dad used to help her at his age. She visualized them going out for an evening walk or to hit a few balls at the golf range; all the normal things dads and sons did. But Tim was in his room as usual; coming down to eat, then back to his room, returning later to ferret the biscuit tin. Faye wondered how this pattern of life had changed from only several years ago when he would watch Coronation Street, Doctor Who or Eastenders with her and Meg. But now the lounge had become the girl's room; Faye, Meg and Chrissie snuggling up together to watch a girly film or just have a girly natter and giggle - all the time Tim in his room, doing his own thing.

Suddenly the silence was broken. Faye put down the cloth, dried her hands.

'You creepy, creepy little weirdo.' Meg was screaming outside Tim's room. Chrissie - also upstairs - was crying.

'For God's sake. What's the matter? The sooner you lot go back to school the better. This Summer's dragging by.' Faye shouted from the bottom of the stairs and with leaden feet began to climb.

Meg was hammering on her twin brother's door with both fists, her face burning in fury.

Chrissie was hunkered against the wicker laundry bin in the corner of the landing clutching her ballerina jewellery box, knees bent up and sobbing.

'I hate having a twin brother. Why did you have to give birth to him. Why did I have to share your womb with him? Why can't he just go and live in Spain with Steve and leave us girls to it? He's a creepy retard. Have a look at his Facebook.' Meg screamed.

'Don't be so bloody nasty. Snap out of it.' Faye screeched, opening the door. Meg, pressed against his door now stumbled into the room, falling onto Tim's bed. Faye followed. A blast of air as the door opened whipped a flurry of photographs into a frenzy, fluttering to the floor. She cast her eyes around taking in the scene and froze. What the hell was going on she wondered.

Rooted to the spot, Faye's breath caught in her throat. Everywhere she looked there were photographs. She clapped her hand to her mouth and gasped.

Tim had been in the loft, ferreting through photographs. A trail of pictures - like a forest carpet of leaves - scattered from the ladder, across the landing to his room. But the photos he had selected - to decorate the walls - had one thing in common: Darius. Faye stared at the face of the man she had very nearly married. But thank God she hadn't. A chill passed through her body as she remembered his abusive words towards her children and to her.

Tim pulled his earplugs out and grunted and they repeated their questions demanding to know what the obsession was with Darius.

He gave them a hard, cold stare and shrugged. They persisted. Meg went over to him and digged him in the ribs.

Faye stared at the montage Tim had created: Darius standing by the Baltic Fleet pub in Liverpool close to his birth home. Darius by the mural on the Fall's Road in Belfast where they had discovered a clue related to his missing younger sister Kathleen. And one of Darius by a lake in Wales; where they had searched for Kathleen one weekend. Darius in dark glasses sitting in the desert in Dubai; another location where they had hunted for Kathleen having been told she had been a waitress in the Burj Khalifa. Every picture told the story of her two-year relationship with the man she had met over the internet in 2009. Their relationship had ended in 2011.

Faye stared as she wheeled back in time with mixed emotion. In many ways it had been - for her - a wonderful time. Darius had been led to believe, by their mother Maria that Kathleen had run away from home. In 2008 however their mother had confessed that Kathleen hadn't run away from home at all. She had sent her daughter to a

93

Catholic Magdalene Laundry in the 1970s to atone for her sins because she was pregnant, just 14 years old. Kathleen had never returned. As his mother had approached her final years - sick with a heart problem - she had started to dream of seeing Kathleen again to ask her forgiveness for having sent her away. (See footnote) [2]It had been her dying wish to find her, to find out what had happened and so Darius and Faye had travelled the world on and off, when Steve, her brother or Shayne, Chrissie's dad were happy to have the kids, looking for Kathleen during their two years together. Faye looked at the pictures on Tim's wall remembering the search that had stretched over several continents.

Despite social media and a range of internet tools they hadn't found Kathleen. They had picked up a few clues along the way. The most haunting clue had been a hand made cloth toy, in the shape of a gingerbread man found at the burned out laundry in Southern Ireland where Kathleen had toiled; an unpaid slave for the Catholic Church of Ireland.

Darius had been convinced that Kathleen had made the soft toy; a conviction confirmed when they had visited Belfast and seen it painted on the side of his auntie's house with a caption next to it related to their father's death, in the Troubles in 1971. But what had been very strange about this toy was the fact that Faye had recognized it. She thought she had seen a similar toy, given to Tim when he was born. Despite searching the house she had not been able to find the toy to compare it to the one they had found in Ireland. Was it a coincidence or had the same person made both toys? At the back of Faye's mind was a disturbing question: did she know Kathleen? Had she met her before? But when she thought about this idea - despite the world being at times a small place - it seemed ridiculous, far fetched.

Faye was aware that Kathleen had been found – a week before Maria's death. Kathleen had written to Darius and Maria but hadn't

---

[2] Footnote: Please see 'A Catholic Woman's Dying Wish' available on Amazon.

wanted to see them; telling Darius and Maria that her life had moved on and she wanted the past forgotten. Faye knew that a black cloud would always hang over Darius for he would never know the truth about what had happened to Kathleen, but at least he knew she was alive and well and that was - after all - what mattered.

Faye could have understood if Tim had made a montage of photos of his father. There were no photos of their dad anywhere on display in the house; because a very painful door had closed the day Trevor had jumped from the platform in front of the 7.52 to Paddington.

Over the years they had asked questions about their dad but Faye had always been evasive; wanting to protect them from the truth.

But pictures of Darius -this *was* curious. The kids should have long forgotten him.

'Why?' She screamed at Tim, trying to process the scene around her.

Tim had been busy: cutting pictures, pinning them to the wall and making what looked like a scrapbook with a title 'my hero.' The bed, the carpet, his desk; littered, the floor; a graveyard of memories. Faye felt exposed. Violated. Memories destroyed. Her past invaded. All respect trampled upon. An era gone.

Is Tim having a breakdown? What the hell is happening? She asked inside. *Katie what is going on? I need you to help me work this out,* her head screamed. But Katie hadn't been around much during the time she had dated Darius. She had only met him once, briefly. The period between 2009 and early 2011 had been a void in their friendship although Katie had still had Tim to stay and still picked him up from school to help out.

'But why is all this bothering *you* Meg?' Faye suddenly wondered, looking at Meg who was red faced and teary. The photos he was chopping up weren't Megs. They had nothing to do with her.

'He's been posting pictures of Darius on all my friends' Facebook walls. He's photo-shopped some of them. They're pissed off with him.

95

Why the hell would he do something like that? Darius was just a jerk. And Tim's a prat.'

'Why?' Faye looked at Tim who was sitting at his desk playing League of Legends and listening to Pink Floyd, 'We don't need no education,' his back to them.

Faye faced Tim. Looked him in the eyes she saw mischief – the type of look he used to give as a toddler when he'd hidden Meg's dolls. He turned back to his computer screen.

'Go away.' His voice was cold.

'Why are you so obsessed with Darius?' Meg asked again.

'He was a cool guy.' And then he let out a light laugh, enjoying the mystery he was creating.

'Oh for God's sake. You're a complete weirdo.' Meg yelped, her hands flying up, her eyes wide and saucer like.

'Welcome to the city kids. Where there's hope on every corner and gold on every pavement.' He suddenly said in an animated way. Faye's heart jolted. He had remembered one of Darius' key sayings. For several moments she said nothing, wheeling back in time, capturing that wonderful humour Darius had; the way he could trip out a one liner for every occasion and every emotion. In her heart she knew she missed him, bitterly but looking back upon the past with rose tinted glasses was for foolish romantics. The truth was those glasses had fractured in several places.

The silence was broken by his next quote, delivered in a lilt. 'Fits like a glove kids.'

Meg started laughing. 'I remember Darius saying that. When he used to park the car.' And soon all three of them were laughing at all the funny things Darius used to say, trying to recapture the exact way he said it, the tone, the rise in cadence, the accents he could put on yet all tinged with Scouse.

And when the laughing had ebbed Faye snapped back to mummy mode.

'Now...get dressed. It's two in the afternoon for goodness sake.'

She pulled back the curtains, opened the window to say farewell to the smell of sweat, Lynx, computer heat and empty crisps packets. The room smelt like a busy London underground train in rush hour.

'Can you go now?' He asked, suddenly returning to his former self as the laughter faded away.

'Are you not going to do anything Mother?' It was a command from Meg, not a question.

'The photos are gone. I can't bring them back and I don't know what to do.'

'Oh my God. What about my friends? They'll hate me now.'

'Can you all go now?' Tim repeated in a flat tone like an old tin pan. Faye struggled to recall a time that he'd ever got worked up about anything. She'd never seen him angry. When he was small he was always crying. She couldn't remember what he'd cried about, just that he'd cried frequently. And everybody telling him not to cry; *shut up you baby*. Yet with Meg it was different. She was always angry, loud and expressive; making her point, her presence filling the room.

Faye walked out onto the landing still puzzled but decided to leave it for now. Chrissie was still clutching her jewellery box.

'And what's the matter with you? We need to get out and do something. This has been another wasted day. Six weeks of school holiday entirely wasted.' Faye said looking down at Chrissie.

'Blame that on Tim too. He never wants to leave his stupid room. Retard.' Meg shouted at the door. 'I'm going to do something to your computer later so watch out.'

'If that stupid idiot doesn't want to come out with us that's his problem. He can waste his life sitting in his smelly bedroom in darkness. I don't care.' Meg gave the door a kick.

Chrissie went over to Tim's door and kicked as well.

'Not you as well. Stop it. Let's go to the park.' Faye urged.

'Parks are for babies.' Chrissie said.

'Shopping? Both of you?' Faye asked.

'I'm working soon.' Meg said.

97

Chrissie gave Tim's door a kick.

'Stop kicking. That's enough.' Faye yanked Chrissie away.

'He's stolen all my money from my ballerina box.' Chrissie whined.

'Money?' Faye had been wondering why she was clutching the ballerina box and crying but hadn't thought to ask why.

'All the tooth fairy money I've collected and money from under my daddy's settee cushions. I had £32. It's all gone.'

'That doesn't automatically make Tim responsible.' Faye pointed out.

'Well it won't be Meg. He's stolen it. I know he has.' Chrissie was crying again, her face turning red.

'We can't prove it.' Faye opened Tim's door. This time he turned round to look at them.

'Did you?' Faye hated accusing. There was no proof.

'Chrissie.' Faye called back to her. 'Maybe you put it somewhere else. Maybe you lost it.'

'I didn't. I didn't.' She wailed.

'She's so careless with money.' Tim gave a muffled laugh with his sleeve over his mouth. Then he pulled his sleeve between his teeth.

'Look in his room. I bet you find loads of Pringle tubs under the bed. That's what he's spent it all on.'

Faye went back downstairs, her mind more confused than ever.

She half wondered if she should meet with Darius. Tim was posting pictures of him all over Facebook and it was better he knew about that than find out from some other source then contact a lawyer. She never knew what Darius might do. Making an enemy with him was not a prospect she relished.

When it was quiet, a few hours later she decided she had to ask Tim what was going on in his life but knew it would be a hard conversation.

She peered round his door, gagging at the cloying smell of body odour and crisps. He turned round startled, took his ear plugs out and instinctively scowled and asked her to go away.

Undeterred she sat on his bed wondering what her opening sentence would be and out of the blue it came to her.

'Have you heard from Ed lately? Does he like living in Dubai?'

'Nope. Should I have?' He turned back to his screen.

'Well we used to spend practically 24/7 with Ed and Katie. Just wondered if you were missing him. Who do you hang around with these days?'

'Just because I don't bring people home doesn't mean I don't have friends. Most people are on Facebook.'

'Doesn't sound very personal.'

'Ed was too much of a mummy's boy. It was getting embarrassing hanging out with him at school anyway.'

'I expect he'd appreciate an email though, a call maybe? He must miss it here...'

'Why are you thinking of him?' Tim suddenly snarled, turning to her and she caught a fresh whiff of Lynx. Faye recoiled in shock, didn't know how to respond.

'Because he probably needs your support.'

'And what about me? After dad's death?'

'You were too young. It was hard for you to understand.' Faye suddenly felt her face drain of colour at the mention of Trevor.

'Why do you never talk about dad? Why aren't there any photos around?'

'Because it's hard Tim. It's really hard.' Faye stifled the tears, couldn't continue the conversation. She got up. Left the room.

11
Faye

September 2014

Faye waited until the twins 16th birthday was over, the long Summer holidays ended and the return to school for the Autumn term before searching their rooms for the missing money from Chrissie's ballerina box. In Tim's room she wanted to take a closer look at the shrine he had created to Darius and to gain clues as to what was going on in his life.

Under Chrissie's bed she found the Ballerina jewelry box where she kept her money: tooth fairy money and coins found littered across her daddy's house. Her dad – Shayne – had an incredibly untidy house. His hallway and stairs looked as if somebody had taken a black bin bag and thrown the contents. The hallway was littered with stacks of unopened junk mail, estate agent and Chinese takeaway flyers, dirty yogurt pots, nails, cutlery and a whole manner of other things including a dollop of ketchup on a credit card that had been there for as long as Faye could remember.

Shayne was a classic hoarder; keeping everything from a whole flotilla of gravy boats to a collection of 50 or more sherry glasses to the complete set of Ordnance Survey maps of the UK. But the one usual find across his house was money and Chrissie had quickly turned this into a small enterprise: going round the house collecting the change and returning from her fortnightly visit with a sack of loot. Shayne, to his ignorance knew nothing of this for he had no control over his house and rarely tidied up.

The jewelry box, normally locked had been broken into. On top of the box the dainty ballerina was broken too. And a large tin with a picture of a rabbit on the side - designed to be filled then opened with a can opener - had already been prised open. Faye knew it wasn't Chrissie who had opened it. What the hell was Tim doing stealing a small child's money? Didn't she feed him enough? Why did he need to buy his own junk food; crisps, cakes, cola?

She found so many different things in Chrissie's room that she almost forgot about searching Tim's room. But what she found in Chrissie's room was all very normal for a nine year old girl:

1. A huge stash of sample toothpastes swiped from the basket in the dentist's waiting room.
2. Enough hair bands to set up a rival to Accessorize.
3. About 50 lip glosses contained in such vessels as a miniature handbag and a very tiny knickerbroker glory glass.
4. Fairy dust. (But no miniature Dyson)
5. A dolls' house toilet with a massive poo that was way out of proportion to the size of the toilet. It was strategically placed under her bed; but like a cocktail parasol in a rainstorm it would be of no use if she got caught short in the middle of the night.
6. One sticky lolly with a centipede in the middle, stuck to the carpet.
7. A pair of socks with the feet cut out and rolled up into two doughnuts with felt tip dots across them to make a smiley face.
8. A collection of teddies that seemed to multiply by the week. *Would she notice if I chucked a few in a charity bag,* Faye wondered. Katie would not have hesitated she thought to herself.

Faye had long treated Tim's room with extreme caution, picking up his pajama bottoms with a pair of tweezers, transporting them at arms length to the washing machine. Faye picked her way around the garland of used toilet roll, dotted with blood and green snot. She knew that in the secret undergrowth; the hidden, dark murky world beneath his bed lurked a whole manner of things that either smelled rotten or threatened to return to life. She dreaded getting down on hands and knees to discover something new. She knew that she would find an exploding lunch box containing green, pongy ham sandwiches, a brown squelchy apple core and a crisp packet folded over, tied into a fancy ribbon. Every September she found an exploding lunch box; languishing there, pushed to the back, dated circa July 20th, the last day of the Summer term.

The Wagon Wheel emporium had been an on going situation in his room for as long as she could remember. The addiction, the obsession, the longing for those round chocolate biscuits was a theme in his bedroom. She was used to retrieving empty wrappers from around his room as well as crisp packets and sweet wrappers and crème brulee glass pots, complete with spoon still standing in the pot. About three years ago with a couple of friends he had created the Wagon Wheel Appreciation Society of Rydon High and posted a few home made songs and adverts on You Tube which had generated several hundred hits. His appetite for Wicked Wonderful Wagon Wheels had developed into an interest in the Wild West. He had developed a dress code of roper-style cowboy boots with spurs, a trophy buckle round his signature western jeans – usually Wrangler. He still ate copious numbers of Wagon Wheels but the attire now sat in his wardrobe gathering dust, having grown out of the novelty; and back to wearing trainers and sweatshirts.

Faye couldn't see under the bed for there was so much rubbish as well as a heap of towels and underpants. She cleared as much as she could, delving through the undergrowth like a potholer. Snaking her way on her tummy it was as challenging as a Kenyan safari on foot. She didn't have the skills or expertise of Indiana Jones in the Temple of Doom and succeeded in knocking over a full opened can of pink fizzy drink which bleed through the carpet creating a massive cloudlike stain.

'For fuck's sake Tim.' She cursed getting up.

As she swept a damp cloth around his room she found several interesting items:

1. An application to change his name by deed poll to Ahmed Abdullah.
2. A homemade 'Merry Capitalist's' Day card with a message inside saying 'I hope you continue to fund capitalist conglomerates by purchasing meaningless cards and gifts for your friends and family.' Love from a wayward vagabond.
3. A pair of John Lennon style sunglasses which he didn't need on account of a Summer spent hidden away in his room with the curtains pulled firmly across.
4. A pink stocking cap.
5. A Sherlock Holmes style monocle with a chain.
6. A collection of vintage old lady plastic spotted rain bonnets in their cellophane wrappers.
7. A piece of black fabric tied into a knot.

How was she going to break the news to Chrissie that if he had stolen her money it was being spent on stocking caps and old lady rain bonnets? It was farcical.

But it was the wall that disturbed her the most; the pictures of Darius pinned with Bluetak and in the middle the slogan 'My Hero.'

There were some things about his room that had remained unchanged for months, even years. A broken two year old calendar hanging on the wall, set to February; A collection of books gathering dust on the shelving: from Enid Blyton's Famous Five series, the

Harry Potter series, Killer Underpants, Captain Underpants and other books centering around the theme of farts and bottoms – eventually developing into a taste for Anthony Horowitz, The Game of Thrones and The Hunger Games. He'd learned to read young. As a little boy Faye always made a habit of sitting him on her knee every evening to read a few books – the mark of a good parent who wanted to see their child do well. She could still - if she tried - recite the words of his favourite book from nursery school about a dog in a pet shop, which he'd adored and wanted read over and over. At 9 he had a reading age of 14 but sadly computer games were then discovered and The Call of Duty and Minecraft consumed many hours.

Faye closed the door holding a bundle of his dirty washing. She had decided that she was going to contact Darius for a chat. But she knew that wasn't going to be easy for she hadn't seen him in a few years.

But if Faye hadn't knocked over the fizzy drink can she might have gone further under his bed and discovered something hidden in the undergrowth; something much more alarming than a few crisp packets and a few photos around the wall.

12
Tim

September 2014

Dear Katie,

    My English teacher told me once to write a letter to offload, even though you might never send it to the person. She said it would make me feel better.

    When I was a kid the same teacher used to send me to a room to sit on my own to draw pictures of dad. I thought it was a weird thing to do. Sometimes the lady from learning support would ask me questions about dad then smile at me. She'd write them down, put them in a folder, hide the folder in a metal filing cabinet. I didn't understand why. I do now. But why didn't they present me with the folder of my memories when I left? The memories were fresh back then, although jumbled. Dad on the beach with an ice cream splatted on his head. Dad on the golf course in checked shorts. Dad and me lying on the carpet in the lounge watching Shrek together; him tickling me to death. But now all I see are cloudy memories. It's hard to remember what he looked like. There are no photos of Dad around the house to jog my memory. Where are they? Did mother destroy them and if so why would she do that?

Nighttime is the worst time. I hate being alone: the cold bed, the silence, the glow of my iphone for company until sleep takes over. I miss your hugs, your motherly perfume, your lips brushing my cheeks, the tickle of your curls, your whispered *love you* in the darkness and the gentle squeeze on my shoulder to reassure me you were still there, would always be there, as you tucked me in next to Ed.

Mother has long given up on bedtime kisses; silently retreating to her room, not even calling *night everyone, sweet dreams, love you*. I'm glad she doesn't kiss me though. I'd hate that. If I slip out into the night air now would she even know I'd gone? Would she care? I went out at three last night. I can do whatever I like really. She can't stop me. But I can't go tonight. There'd be trouble in the wood. He's got a knife. I'm scared Katie. I've got no money again.

It's ten. The night is always long. I pull my duvet cover over, my hand groping between the bed and the wall. That's where I hide him. If mother found him she'd say I'm too old. She'd give him to a charity shop – or worse – chuck him in the bin. His face is battered, grimy. One eye is missing. Some threads are loose. I can feel tears prickle as I sing the song you taught me a long time ago. *He sings and sways and sways and sings...*

I miss your songs, especially when Babouska and Ivan, the Steiff Bears joined in. They were always farting and burbing, pooing and weeing. Ed and I laughed until our bellies ached. Then you made us creamy hot chocolate with piles of sugar. I can see your pretty face. I met a girl, Bella. She's a younger version of you. I thought I was in with a chance. She came round every Saturday. Mother didn't even notice I had company. We played League of Legends together for hours. Then when I tried to kiss her she said she didn't fancy me. *You're too spotty* she said. I hate my face. And I hate my t shirts. They all come from BHS. I want cool t shirts and a hat. I want a red suit for prom. But mother says my school trousers will be fine and she'll buy a tie from a charity shop. Mother's always saying she's got no money but when the BHS t shirts no longer fit she'll buy more. I don't want to wear gay, retarded clothes. She bought me a new duvet the other week with a map of London Underground on it. It was well retarded. The type of thing autistic kids would like.

Bella doesn't come round anymore. She's going out with Alex. He's a rugby player. He's over six foot and looks well fit. I've got a girlfriend now though. A proper one. She told her mates we're going out. She's called Lisa and lives in Holland. I'll go to see her soon. She's got to clear it with her dad first. She says she'll buy me a ticket. I can't wait to kiss her. We chat for hours, sometimes all night over Facebook. But I'm really worried about her. She's always slashing her wrists with her dad's razor. She showed me the blood. It was gross. She was in hospital last year. I think she took an overdose of paracetomol or something.

Oh God I can hear Chrissie crying again, in bed, still upset because of the money. Should I crawl into bed with her, give her a little hug? No. She'd only push me away.

I feel guilty. But where else am I going to get the money? Chrissie only pilfers it from her dad's house. It was never really her money. She's got nothing to spend it on except buy a few crappy plastic toys from one of those pound shops. My need is greater than hers. I'm now running up a tab; a tab that will soon turn into a debt. I'm so scared Katie. I can't stop myself. Maybe I should never have started but I miss you, I miss Ed and it was the only way to fit in to this new gang. It helps me though; it's the only thing that drowns nightmares, helps me to forget, makes me feel happier again. People use it to relieve the pain of cancer so why can't I use it too, for my pain? The pain you caused?

Why did you warn me? You shouldn't have hinted what you were going to do. It was a heavy burden on my shoulders. I can never tell anyone what you said that night. Mother would be devastated to know the truth. It would destroy her.

Sometimes when I take it, it fucks me up. Stops me concentrating in class. Stops my brain working properly. It gives me ridiculous random thoughts. Makes me sleep in too long when I need to finish an essay. But I'm waiting now for the big one. The big one will solve all my problems. Will reunite me with you. It won't be easy. But I'm sure Darren's dad will help. It's his department after all. I don't need to tell Darren's dad everything; the real reason why I need to make it.

Maybe Chrissie will have some more money after her next weekend with Shayne. I hate stealing but Mother will replace the money. Like the tooth fairy she'll come in the night, fill the ballerina box back up.

Mother doesn't give pocket money. It was nice when you gave me money, treating me as your other son, making me feel special. *If you want money you need to do a few jobs* Mother says. So I washed the car, hoping for a few quid but then she changed the goal post. Washing the car is apparently a 'family chore' and doesn't warrant pocket money. *You live here; we all have to muck in.* So I cleaned my room, hoping for money but she said the floor was still messy. Whatever I do it's never right. When I was younger; when household chores seemed exciting I'd enjoy washing up and drying the dishes but after several attempts Mother lost her patience with me; told me *just leave it, you don't do it properly, the plates are still dirty and you're sloshing water all over the floor.* Nothing is worth the effort any more. She doesn't appreciate anything I do.

Tim x

13
Faye

September 2014

'What's this parcel? Tim's been getting a lot of parcels lately.' Meg said picking up a jiffy bag on the doormat and giving it a squeeze and a shake. It was a school inset day and she had been upstairs studying and Tim was out.

It was a small package addressed to Tim. Taking it through to the kitchen she carried on squeezing it, trying to guess its' contents before tossing it onto the kitchen table.

'Probably just another part for his computer.' Faye said dismissively. Tim had spent months building a computer. She knew his late father, who had been a computer engineer for Microsoft would have been very proud of his son and suddenly felt a stab of sadness as she visualized father and son building the computer together.

'He should have just got a laptop. He's pathetic. That computer takes up his whole room and its' bound to break down. He's not thought what he'll do when that happens has he Motheroon?' Meg moaned.

Faye filled the kettle, reached for tea bags.

She passed Meg a steaming mug. But as she turned she could see that something was troubling Meg.

'I think we should open it. See what's inside.' Meg said with a concerned look.

'Leave it. He'll want to open it.'

'But where is he getting the money to order things on Amazon?' Meg persisted.

'Maybe left over birthday money.' Faye casually said.

'His birthday was months ago. Motheroon he spent it all on computer games. He's bought all the computer parts he needs. You should know that.'

In that moment Faye was hit by the brutal truth of Meg's words. The fact was she didn't know very much about her son's computer project and chastised herself for not having taken more interest.

'If you open it you're invading his privacy.' Faye warned as she watched Meg's finger teasing the corners of the parcel.

'Well I'm going to open it.' Meg had decided. And Faye, powerless next to her daughter, felt her victory.

Meg tore open the jiffy bag and pulled out a plastic package and Faye turned to see Meg looking at a bag of brown woody shards.

Both looked at each other puzzled. Then Meg turned on her six-inch heels and headed for the stairs.

'I'm going to see what else is in his room.' She called back. She was doing what she had always done as his twin sister; still violating his private space but this time she was the adult taking the appropriate action. Faye was the child flailing in deep water.

Faye tore open the plastic and took a shard to her mouth to taste and smell it but it was odourless and tasted of wood.

'It's just wood chippings Meg. Probably for a school project. It doesn't taste of anything.' She called up from the bottom of the stairs.

'Christ mother don't eat it.' Meg rushed to the top of the stairs, her eyes full of alarm. Faye raised her hands in mock defeat.

'Well I don't know. See what else you can find up there while I search for the company name on the side of the parcel. It says Opux Health, Birmingham.' Faye was secretly pleased that Meg was taking control. Her hands were shaking as she fired up the laptop. It was a warm day but she played cat's cradle with her hands to warm them, blowing hot air between her fists then rubbing her face as she shivered in fear. Her stomach tightened as she typed the company name into Google, relieved that Meg had initiative and was searching through his room, unlocking Pandora's box. It reminded her of the time that she had frozen to the spot - hysterical, unable to do a thing when Chrissie had cut her head open on a metal bench in the play park with blood pouring and the open wound gaping like a huge pair of Afro Caribbean lips while all the other mothers rushed to her help and somebody called an ambulance and somebody else gathered the children up.

Faye couldn't find any trace of the company and within a couple of minutes Meg appeared at the doorway, visibly stunned, clutching a plastic bag of zip lighters, a set of small weighing scales and two large tubs with the names of chemicals on the side. Faye froze, A stunned silence thickened the air between them. The reality of what was going on in Timmy's life started to hit her.

Meg was hopping from one foot to the other in the doorway screeching a mantra of *oh my god oh my god* over and over and all Faye could think to say was *shit* and then the spell was broken and it was time for action as Faye dashed to the kitchen drawer, pulling out a crumpled Sainsbury's carrier, thrusting everything into it. Picking up her keys she headed for the front door trying to decide whether she was heading for the doctor, the school or the police station, leaving Meg shivering in the hallway. Only when she had flicked on the ignition and began to reverse the car up the driveway she decided to take it to the school and ask for their help.

Faye had just picked up Tim from the station after his day out with a friend; he rarely went out with friends. The items were now safely with the school; the head of year 11 promising to chat with Tim the following day, when school resumed, then report back to her.

I must talk, I must ask, I must confront, I must magic my mothering skills. She chanted in her head as they drove home from the station.

'You've caused me a lot of trouble today.' Faye began at random; breaking the silence as she drove. She was aware of how ridiculous she sounded, as words mashed in her brain. A confrontation with Tim was the last thing she wanted.

'Huh. Sorry,' Timmy muttered in his usual robotic tone and Faye wondered why he wasn't curious about why he had caused her trouble.

'Don't you want to know why?' Her pitch was now sharper.

She sensed his shoulders rising in the seat next to her, his hands firmly in pockets. Her eyes remained fixed on the road ahead and children, dressed in green uniform darted across the road at every opportunity.

'You had a package arrive today. Want to tell me what it is?' She asked.

His shoulders rose again. Her words ebbed into silence.

'Some brown woody stuff. What is it?' She persisted when he didn't reply.

'It's nothing.' He quickly dismissed.

The silence became suffocating. It was as if they were stuck in a lift together. They passed through two sets of traffic lights and the throng of school children slowly trickled away.

'It's to do with legal highs isn't it?' The words had escaped her mouth.

'It's not legal highs.' His reply was quick.

'Then what is it?'

'It's for a project. It's nothing.' He replied and she was glad they were in the car. There was no escaping her question.

'Well I'm worried.'

'It's not legal highs.' He drummed again.

'Mr. Richards will decide about that. I've handed it into the school.'

'I'll tell him it's for a project.' His flat tone disturbed her. Why wasn't he defending himself more strongly? Why wasn't he cross that she had handed it in to school?

'What project?'

'Just a project.'

Faye couldn't think of anything more to say. She knew he was skirting the truth. The gulf between them grew wider with every inch of the journey until the car was on the driveway and he was out and back into the sanctuary of his room.

Faye heard Meg go into his room, despite his protests for her to leave. Faye went up and stood behind Tim's door listening to their conversation.

'Timmy just tell me. What is it?' Meg was asking him.

'It's for a project. Go away Meg.'

'What project?'

'Get out.'

'Pleeeeeeease tell me.'

'I'm going to sleep now. Go away.'

'But it's only 6 o' clock. Why do you need to sleep at this time?' Meg shrieked down at him.

Faye imagined Meg standing in front of Tim, arms folded like a schoolmistress, while waiting for him to spill the truth.

Meg tried another tack. 'Mr. Richard is going to call you to his office tomorrow. He'll get it out of you. They might even call in that Police Officer that works there.'

'They don't scare me. That Police Officer is only about twenty.'

'Richards will.'

'I'll tell him it's for a project.'

'You're a pathetic loser. And look at your bedroom. You can't keep expecting mother to tidy it. There's toilet paper everywhere, your duvet looks grim, crisp packets, towels, yogurt pots everywhere. Ugh get a grip will you, you're in year 11 now.'

Faye went to bed wondering what the next day would bring.

14
Faye

September 2014

Dear Katie,

I'll come and visit you tomorrow as soon as the meeting with Mr. Richards is over. I'm terrified about what I'm going to find out. It's been a dreadful day. It feels like the turning point in our lives and everything is about to come crashing down. I'm suspecting the worst, but it could of course be nothing.

You're the only one that can help me; help us. You understand my past. You were so much a part of their childhood. Everything's that's happened, all the decisions I've made. You were there, picking up the pieces, offering your wise words.

I can see your concerned face and your watery eyes. You'll clasp my hand and say to me *darling, sit down I'll make you a nice cup of tea* and it will no longer be my problem it will become our problem. You'll go into your kitchen; always clean and tidy while I tuck my legs up on your fine Cavendish upholstered sofa from John Lewis with its Bancroft stripes and its Serpentine springs until I hear your stovetop kettle whistle and the gentle padding of your stockinged feet behind me on your plush springy carpet as you hand me a steaming cup of finest Fortnum and Mason Earl Grey tea in a dainty Wedgwood butterfly tea cup! And it will be all cosy as it always is in your lovely home; with the table lamps on, whatever the time of day and the radiators gurgling, the boys playing upstairs and our tea cups balanced on our knees, our bodies in symmetry as I tumble out my troubles and you focus your eyes on the magnificent horse chestnut tree outside; the heavy branches which seem to caress, the shade hugging our hearts.

I need you now Katie more than ever. *You are my rock. Faithful one, so unchanging, ageless, I depend on you, I call out to you, again and again.* Do you remember that hymn?

Yours ever,
Faye

15
Faye

September 2014

Mr. Richards called at 10am, asking Faye to *get here immediately, this is very serious.*

She pushed through the double doors. The receptionist - seeing her sobbing - unlocked and pulled the glass door across the counter pushing a box of tissues in her direction. She signed her name in the green visitor's book and took a seat in the waiting area. While she waited a mother of one of Chrissie's friends and also the Methodist minister's wife, working as school nurse, dressed in a navy uniform passed by on the other side of the glass doors, separating the reception from the corridor. She stopped, beamed through the glass, a look of curiosity on her face as to why Faye was visiting the school. Faye's heart sank as she opened the door, dreading her cheeriness and upbeat outlook on life. She asked why she was there and Faye was candid, spilling her fears. Faye expected a stunned silence when she had finished explaining, but the woman's face remained unchanged. *This is so typical of bloody Christian do-gooders* she thought to herself. It was as if Faye had merely popped by to pick her child up for a routine dentist appointment; a minor inconvenience to the daily routine. The woman had nothing to say, no advice to give.

Every Family Has One

'So what did he tell you?' Faye asked eagerly as soon as Mr. Richards' door was closed on the quiet corridor outside.

'Thanks for getting here so quickly.'

The morning sun streamed through a side window striking the gold and silver sports trophies on display like a match, adding warmth and energy to the room and a feeling of success she struggled to share.

Faye stood waiting in front of his desk. In that moment she knew that Tim had spilled everything to Mr. Richards. This was a man in a professional role with years of experience of coaxing information from students but a part of her felt a deep inadequacy that she hadn't been able to coax the information from him herself.

He gave his canary yellow tie a hard yank as if this was a cue to begin any meeting, then pulled out a chair for her, walked around the desk, wafting Armani and exuding an air of slickness as he sat down. It was his job to protect the school, its' reputation, its' pupils. But beyond the school community did he really care what happened to his pupils Faye wondered.

'It's not good news I'm afraid. It's more serious than I imagined.' He shook his head.

Tim's life flashed before her eyes in the punishing seconds as she waited for him to continue - a random series of photographic memories that welled with intense emotion. She saw Tim the toddler with dark glossy curls, beautiful olive skin and dimpled chin, speeding round the lounge on his yellow plastic car, shrieking and happy. Then he was four in a swing laughing, wearing a Buzz Lightyear outfit. Giggling in a fairy dress; the mischievous boy who liked to be different. Playing pass the parcel on his fifth birthday with real packing boxes for it was the day they'd moved into the flat. How could she have orchestrated such an enormous event to take place on the poor kid's fifth birthday? But as ever traumatic events were turned around by Tim's adorable humour. Faye hadn't planned party food, party music but Tim suggested using

119

the noisy neighbour's music and the leftover scraps from their school lunch boxes.

'I was right?' Faye asked.

She knew she wasn't the first parent to face this nightmare. But this was *her* son and he was *only* 16, *very* bright and in a matter of months would be sitting his GCSEs.

'At first he thought he could pull the wool over my eyes. I've been in this game long enough. I told him so. He said it was for a creative project. Oh God what do you call it?' Mr. Richards clicked his fingers and they were caught for a moment trying to think of the creative project Tim had been referring to.

The pleasant lilt of his Glaswegian accent offered a small blanket of comfort but didn't stop the butterflies in her stomach.

She glanced beyond him at the evidence of the game he'd long played: various framed teaching awards and certificates adorned the wall of his office, spanning a successful 30 year career at Rydon High culminating in the final accolade of Deputy Head. And the Colgate smiles of his four daughters beamed down from a shelf; all having attended Rydon, despite being out of catchment and all having achieved straight A's in every damn subject.

Mr. Richards:

The successful teacher.

The successful parent.

The model citizen.

And in all probability the perfect adoring husband.

'I have to say I'm gob smacked Faye. Until today your son wasn't even on our radar. A four year unblemished record and glowing reports. Not a single detention or unauthorized absence. He was heading for A's in his GCSES. Maybe he still is. But this isn't going to help.'

The next few moments disappeared in a blur as the facts were presented to Faye and a long list containing names of things she had never heard of before on mustard yellow school headed paper, passed across the table for her to examine.

She studied the yellow paper and asked him to repeat the names of all the items Meg had found in his room. Suddenly she remembered all the ridiculous things she had found in Tim's room only a week before: the vintage old lady bonnets and the monocle with the chain. Whatever next, she thought to herself but this was something more enormous than old lady bonnets.

'Ok. He has tubs of calcium hydroxide, some white vinegar and zipper fluid to make a psychedelic compound called...' And then he pointed to the word written down... Dimethyltrptamine. 'He was planning to make it, take it. He says a friend bought all the items and the friend wants to sell it on the internet.'

'He knew how that was spelt?' Was Faye's first thought as she struggled to digest what was going on.

'I had to look it up. Never heard of it. It's a highly dangerous hallucinogenic drug; possibly the most dangerous drug there is. The trip is about as intense as you can get. One trip can mess someone up for life. People have described seeing deserts of rats; they've killed themselves because the trip is so real and so frightening. People have regressed back in time, been confronted by emotions and events in the past. The Amazonian people make it from plants, drink it to connect with the spiritual world. It's a class A drug, carrying a prison sentence of 7 years maximum but to manufacture and sell it; well the sentence would be higher obviously.'

Faye was struggling to take it all in. It felt as if she was floating on the ceiling observing another woman's life.

'Give him his due he was very honest with me.' Mr. Richards let out a light laugh and suddenly humour had found its' way into the dark cloud that hung in the room.

How had these plans been happening under her roof without her having any inkling? It didn't seem possible and then it dawned on her. He was living a secret life within his computer taking him anywhere in the world, across so many dimensions of life, good and bad. His room was a shell. She couldn't see what was really going on.

'But wait a minute. How would he have made it? In reality? He doesn't know anything about Chemistry. He's got no equipment, no knowledge.'

'I really don't know. But I tell you it's raised a chuckle in the Chemistry department. They're quite impressed, in a dark sort of way.' Again he laughed. Faye could see them sitting in the staffroom, amused at her expense.

'He did tell me he can access the dark web. You need to get parental controls.' He warned her. But Faye wondered how she was going to be able to do that with her basic knowledge of computers and from what she'd heard controls slowed up computers and made it difficult to search on Google because so many key words were blocked.

As she considered all of these issues she noticed a shadow move across Mr. Richard's face when the amusement had died down.

'But that's not all...' He began and once more the sky in her world came crashing down as he prepared to drop his next revelation.

'There's something far more serious. He says he needs to take cannabis to cope with life. He doesn't want to go on...Has been planning to end his life.'

'Wha'?' Faye couldn't digest this new gristle.

'Why would he go into drug production if he's planning to top himself?' Faye laughed at the irony.

This was every parent's worst nightmare.

'With the drugs my main concern, from my point of view is his use in school.' He paused, drew breath through his teeth, his eyes lit with a new concern.

His point of view. Great. Faye thought. He's only bothered about him taking it on school grounds. But where did he become introduced to drugs? She wanted to ask. On school grounds of course. *So you should be concerned Mr. Bloody Richards.*

'He told me cannabis makes him feel better. He says he feels worthless.'

Every Family Has One

The word *worthless* hit like a spark of electricity, snagging in the air. Faye was a condemned woman in the dock guilty of the worst parental crime: making your child feel worthless. She had given him everything, been there for him, so why did he feel worthless? What had she done to make him feel this way?

Into the hollow pain she filled the next moments with Tim's early childhood; a nervous energy, spluttering memories to Mr. Richards of his angelic face; the adorable little boy with dark curls and a cheeky smile, so happy and fun to be with. The memories flitted before her eyes: his first steps across Katie's lounge, the enormous sandcastle he built on the beach with Katie and Ed, his dancing in front of the TV as the news broke about the Twin Towers and zooming round pretending to be an areoplane. And then the memories started to flutter away, like ashes in the gentle breeze, sinking back into the murky waters of the present and the future that lay ahead.

Blaming herself was all she could do. He belonged to her. She was his mother. Had housed his body. His soul was her responsibility. Yet along the way they had become separated; like a tank jettisoned back to earth from its' space rocket.

Time. She had not given enough of her time. She had allowed him to do too much alone, separated, experiencing life on his terms. He'd been given too much independence. And too much independence was just as damaging as too much protection, too much smothering. Suddenly she thought of Katie and how different their parenting styles were.

Maybe if I'd held onto him tight and secure like Katie did to Ed.

'He says he's not being bullied. We can rule that one out.' Mr Richards added. Bullying hadn't occurred to Faye.

16 wasted years. Years of watering the plant, feeding it Baby Bio, positioning it to the sunlight, watching it grow, admiring it. Seconds to hack the flowers. *Who now felt worthless?* Her inner voice asked.

123

'He changed after the death of his dad. He was only five. At seven and eight he started getting stomach cramps, scared to go to school. Was he being bullied? I don't know. I was called back to school several times to pick him up. And that was when I started worked nights at the factory. Katie stepped in and Tim to stayed over at hers and Meg went to another friend.. She was amazing. There are few friends like her. But gradually he started wanting to spend more time at Katie's. At one point it was as if he lived there. Katie...' Her name slowly dissolved into the air as the image of Katie appeared in front of her eyes.

Faye was aware she'd been rabbiting. He was now checking his watch, but she'd barely begun, needed help.

'Take him straight to the doctor. Get an emergency appointment. In the meantime I'm going to refer him to the child mental health team for an urgent appointment.' Mr. Richards was now in practical mode, following protocol.

'Then go home. Talk.' Mr. Richards said.

Talk. The word bounced mockingly in her head. *How?*

Mr. Richards scraped back his chair. The bell started to ring. Doors were banging, the corridor filling. Laughter. Shouting. The pounding of feet in the corridor became the heavy boots of the challenge ahead.

He looked down at her, put a reassuring hand on her shoulder. She remained rooted to the chair clutching the yellow slip of paper containing the list of unpronounceable words, her head filled with everything she didn't understand and couldn't grasp. Into the bustle of the corridor she would go, a boat cast adrift at sea with a storm kicking up.

'Just tell him you love him.'

The words were bird song in the air between them but a pummeling fist in her chest. He smiled, grabbed the door handle and the smell of school lunch came flooding through.

I love you.

She couldn't tell him that; he was too old for such platitudes.

And then she saw him, his dark curls hanging limply around his face, sitting in the reception area waiting to be taken home. He stood up, face expressionless, his usual self. Who would know? Who would guess? He didn't look suicidal. Had she really just had that conversation? But Trevor hadn't looked or acted suicidal the day before he'd jumped in front of the train. To onlookers Tim was probably waiting to be taken to a dental appointment, not contemplating the end of his life.

They looked at each other and it was as if she was seeing her son for the first time except that she wasn't and she didn't know what to do. It was as if he had just stepped off a plane and she was supposed to meet and greet and welcome. But they both stood wooden, not knowing whether to smile, cry, embrace. A tapping voice in her head told her to hug, but with the security of the spot she was standing on her body refused to respond. Weakly she raised an eyebrow and one side of her face hoping this would be acknowledgement enough of his pain, distress. It was all she could manage.

In the car a commentator was talking about the Scottish referendum on the World At One. She turned the radio off, fishing for words that wouldn't come. When they came there was no warning, like vomit.

'It's my fault. This is my fault. Not yours. Do you understand? You have to know that little Tanky. There's a lot you don't know about the past. Your daddy... We messed up not you. Then your daddy died. That wasn't your fault. He was ill. Cancer. It was out of our control, my control. But it's all in the past now, best forgotten, put away in a box. We can move on.' She was spilling clumsy sentences and as soon as they were out she was regretting them and regretting the lie that came with ease. Fuck. Cancer. What was she saying?

'I...' The words were stuck, square in her round mouth they refused to come.

She tried to form them, practice them in her head. *I love you Tim.* He knew she loved him. It was something every child took for granted, wasn't it? She asked herself. He didn't need the sickly reminder.

'Oh I don't know Tanky.' She finished the sentence with a sigh.

'It's not your fault.' His voice was quiet.

'Yes it is.'

'No it isn't.'

They were in pantomime territory and she couldn't find the cord to pull the curtain.

'You need counseling.'

'I don't want counseling.' His voice was firm.

'You're too young to know what you want.'

A mist of silence crept into the car and Faye made every effort to disperse it.

'Tell me what's going on. Talk.' Faye pleaded.

'I don't know what you want me to say.' Tim mumbled his words, as if swallowing them back.

His flat response halted the conversation. She didn't know where to go from here and so they continued the short journey to the doctor's surgery under a cloud that lingered but wouldn't burst. The intricate algorithm of what to say to him had already defeated her.

༺ ༻

Faye was an amateur at getting an urgent doctor's appointment passively accepting the excuse always used. *There are no appointments for the next week.* The receptionist looked on the screen and told her to return at four. This was the start of a journey and piece -by -piece she was about to learn how to toughen up, use and abuse the system to her advantage and use the words *my son is suicidal* in order to fix an instant appointment which she was to learn were called *red flag appointments*. Learning to manipulate the system was essential in a medical world that groaned under the strain of Coalition cutbacks.

Every Family Has One

They got back in the car. Without an appointment the urgency to the problem had suddenly gone, rather like a flooded house after a storm - you learned to eat your tea in a boat.

Get an urgent doctor's appointment.
Go home and talk.
Tell him you love him.

None of the above was going to happen. Not in a hurry. Faye turned the engine on, didn't know what to do. She felt like a fraudulent mum playing the role as if in an advert, condemned to watching him slowly drift away.

He sensed her hesitation but sat wooden in the passenger seat clutching his bag, his muddy black loafers resting in the footwell, obliging to go wherever she took him. *I must talk*, an inner voice chanted.

But as she reversed she knew she couldn't. This was a hill she couldn't climb, yet had to climb. And when she looked up it was steeper than Helvellyn.

'I want to go back to school.' He said.

She was relieved, though hated herself for feeling that way. For a few hours she could breath again, until he returned. She could put the problem on hold. Go home, have a cup of tea and a comforting Hob Nob.

So she took him back to school, a leaden blanket of silence shrouding the car.

༺༻

It was 6pm. Meg was in Tim's room crying, hugging her brother, in shock after hearing about the meeting with Mr. Richards.

Faye stood at the bedroom door watching Meg plead with Tim to open up and tell her what was going on. She walked away and as Meg closed the door on them, feeling the weight of the problem lifted onto Meg; Faye heard Meg say those three words to Tim. *I love you Tim.*

Faye's body felt as if it would sink. Meg had the courage to say the words but to Faye they were American and sickly. She looked back at the door, hand hovering over the handle, willing herself to go in, but it was easier to leave them be.

Faye then began to get ready for a date with a man she had met on line, unsure why she hadn't cancelled with everything going on. But as she got ready she looked in the mirror and told her reflection:

I don't want to see him, he's not my type at all but it's been arranged for days and I don't want to let him down. His company might take my mind off the events of the day; an escape, for a while. She instantly started to perk up and thought of a busy pub, a glass of wine and maybe a good snog in the car park afterwards.

As she applied fresh make up and chose a low cut dress flaunting her cleavage, a splash of zesty perfume wafting around the bathroom Meg came in - a look of disbelief on her face - her blue eyes wide and accusatory.

'Where the hell are you going Motheroon?' Her body was bent forward.

'On a date.' Faye leaned to the mirror applying pink lipstick.

'Oh my God. Your son is in there, really sad and you're going on a date.' She screamed at Faye.

'I need a drink.' Faye turned back to the mirror applying eye liner.

'But your son needs you.' She leapt forward clawing Faye's arm, a moggy cat about to attack, the copper strands of her thin hair swaying.

'I won't be long then.' Faye said wearily.

'Curfew is 10pm Motheroon. Not a moment longer. I bet...' And Meg stepped back, examining Faye's face, looking her in the eyes. 'You're only going for a snog. Yes I knew it.' And soon they were laughing.

But when the laughter had died Faye came to a decision.

'Alright. Alright. I'll stay in. Like I've stayed in for the past 16 years bringing you lot up.' Faye trilled, arms flying to mock defeat. 'Is Tim going to come down, sit with us? Or is it to be another evening with everyone sitting in their rooms because if it's the latter I might as well go out on the date.'

'We could go to the cinema, have a meal, get Tim talking over fajitas and cola.' Meg suggested.

Faye agreed, internally grumbling about the cost of feeding three in a restaurant, followed by three cinema tickets and the futility of it all. Would Tim talk over dinner she wondered? Probably not, came her answer.

And so she took the twins into Slough for a Mexican and then to watch the thriller just out, 'When I Go To Sleep.' Chrissie thankfully was with Shayne for the weekend.

⁓

Over a seven layer burrito and heart warming Enid Blyton ginger beer -that promised so much but delivered none of the love found in an Enid Blyton children's novel - Meg filled the silent cloud that hovered over them with nervous banter and giggles - mostly apologies for how she'd treated Tim since the year dot - interspersed with chatter about school work, teachers, music, friends. Faye listened; waiting for her opening, which - when it came - made her look silly and out of date in the world they lived in.

'Don't you know how that works on your iphone mother?' Meg was saying, as if the world would end if phones weren't used to their full potential. Faye felt inches tall, began to think about the evening she could have had. She wasn't sure how the conversation about phones had begun, but knew that with teenagers all conversations began and ended with iphones.

'Honestly Motheroon. It was a waste of money you buying an iphone. You don't use everything on it. Oh my God. And why are you on that contract? You can't be paying that much. Nobody pays that much.' Meg carried on the mantra.

They were briefly silent as the twins got out their phones to check messages. Faye thought about telling them to put them away but decided that tonight she would give them a wide berth.

'What are you chuckling about?' She asked Meg.

'You need to get with it Mother. Look at this.' Meg was laughing and turned the screen for Faye to see.

Faye peered at the screen as Meg explained what she was looking at: a small black creature with a fiery tail called a Charmander; a made up figure that somebody had had tattooed onto their body while drunk and it had caught on.

'It's gone viral Mother. Viral. Do you know what *viral* means? Facebook is old now. You need to get onto Snapchat and Imgur and Reddit. Oh maybe not. You're a bit old for all of those.' Meg was whittling on and laughing, leaving Faye on a different planet. And all the time Tim sat saying very little.

Feeling small Faye started to skillfully swing the conversation; the need to gain one-upmanship with her daughter. She knew that Meg was partly to blame for the way things had turned out. The names she'd called Tim over the years, the selfish things she had done; taking toys, destroying his belongings, making sure she got the best of everything, slamming his opinions down, talking over him. Meg had been first in the queue for everything and he had taken the back seat, seemingly happy for *ladies to be first*.

'I'm so sorry Timmy for calling you weird and a retard.' Meg said looking up, doe eyed. It was as if she had read Faye's thoughts.

'Yes. You made his life difficult sometimes. Like I made my brother's life hell calling him a spas.' Faye said.

'Wha?' The twins looked at each other, confused.

'It's short for spastic. Not a word people use these days.' Faye told them.

Tim grunted, pulled a face.

'You should stop internet dating mother. And stop going on Facebook. It's not doing Tim any good. Oh my God adults really should NOT go on Facebook.'

Meg strung out each word, her mouth a coy carp, her eyes as wide as a Philippine Tarsier - the mammal with the largest eyes on the planet.

'Any more orders?' The waiter came to ask. Faye smiled at the irony of the question.

'And you shouldn't sit at your computer so much. You need to talk to your kids more. Play board games with us. Do something.' Meg ranted with a leer.

'Oh shut up. Just shut up.' Faye looked away wounded, the strain killing her as she tried to fight tears and the desperate helpless feeling inside. How she longed, in that moment for Trevor to be back with them, helping her through this mess.

'And another thing...' Meg began. Faye's heart sank again.

'You need to buy Chrissie a bra. She's got bath plugs. Surely you've noticed? That fried egg stage is sooooo embarrassing. You don't understand Motheroon. She needs a bra to cover the pathetic, cringey lumps. Ugh. I remember that awkward stage.' Meg's copper hair swayed as she ranted on.

Meg rested her head on Tim's shoulder again, her hair gleaming under the spotlights, her sapphire eyes teary. He flinched, not particularly comfortable with her concern for him and the amends she was trying to impose on their relationship, set into stone over the years. It was, by now a relationship that was familiar to him, Faye suspected.

'Are you struggling with any courses? Maths? Science? Mother will pay for tuition if you are. Won't you Motheroon?' Faye's heart sank as Meg fired the suggestions. Where was she going to get the money for private tuition if he was struggling at school?

'Yeah.' Faye said quietly, in a non- committal way. All enthusiasm to try to make amends now gone.

Faye looked out of the window as Meg and Tim discussed exam boards, reading lists, different teachers and all the topics of conversation she couldn't join in.

Opposite the restaurant a couple of homeless people were hunkering down for the night in a shop doorway. She conjured up an image of Tim in a doorway, skeletal, grey faced, a sleeping bag keeping him warm. Visions of the film Trainspotting drifted into her head. She turned to look at him. He was letting Meg do all the talking like he had done for the past 16 years. His caramel eyes were pools of sadness; a murky emptiness she wanted so desperately to understand.

The end of the film resonated a special sadness for Faye. She wiped a tear from her eye, hoping Tim wouldn't see her as the mum and the son in the film embraced each other; a tender reunion she didn't in a million years imagine would happen in her own home. It was as if Tim - the old Tim - had been abducted by aliens, spirited away to a different world, replaced by this stranger, bearing the same name, with traces of familiar features returning graciously from time to time.

It had been a long day. When they returned home Faye said goodnight and it was as if a new and scary dawn in their lives had broken. She stood on the landing looking at Tim's door, listening to the silence. The door was the barrier; a Belfast wall separating two opposing communities. A fortress. Inside was a forbidden den; the internet gateway to a world she didn't understand, feared, hated; a world that had transformed her innocent son into a malleable zombie.

She hovered on the landing, thinking all sorts of thoughts.

I should have insisted the computers be used in a family area. Why the fuck was I so casual about it all? Why wasn't I a tougher parent? Ground rules. I didn't have any. This is my own fault she chastised.

But deep down she knew that it wouldn't have made a scrap of difference because hand held devices had arrived and all the advice then quickly became dated and irrelevant.

She shivered. Looked at the door again before turning to go back to her room.

I'm more scared than I've ever been in my entire life she thought to herself. She crept up to Meg's room to see what she knew. Most of the time the twins coexisted under the same roof surrounded by the shrapnel of their arguments but she knew there were times when they came together, felt a connection, a united front. Deep down they did love each other, they did care, but didn't always show it.

When the twins were born Faye's mother, who also had a twin had said that twins were two souls split in two and would be there for each other no matter what. *They're twins. They'll always have each other. They'll feel each other's emotions.* And maybe they did. But it had never felt like that. They had fought like cat and dog over the years, pulled each other's hair, called each other names. They were a comedy of constant comparisons; anything but two peas in the same pods. She worked hard. He didn't. She was organized; tidy room, neat piles of study books lined across the floor. His floor was a forest of crisp packets and dirty underpants. She drank ginseng and ate fresh berries to stimulate the brain when revising for exams and counted her 5 a day. He sneaked in fizzy high energy drinks and wonderful wicked wagon wheels and went for days without cleaning his teeth. Mealtimes were a nightmare. He wouldn't eat anything unless it had a face. She wouldn't eat anything unless it came from the earth. She loved couscous. He called it a plate of sandy beach and refused to eat it. She loved spinach. He said it was pond algae. Or maybe these were just normal boy -girl differences, Faye wondered.

Like two trees growing too close in the forest he had failed to thrive, didn't bloom into the full and green tree that he should have grown into. She had stolen the light. Everything had been centred around her and what she wanted; from clothes to trips to presents. *He who shouts the loudest gets* Faye had always believed. That statement was so true now.

They were non identical twins. Didn't resemble each other in any way. He had beautiful dark curls and striking brown fudge eyes and looked like a younger and more unkempt version of the actor Rufus Sewell. Meg's hair was like fine lengths of copper wire. She had striking blue eyes like topaz gemstones and resembled the actress Nicole Kidman. From day to day the twins operated like a clunky army vehicle driving through the deserts of Iraq on square wheels. She wondered if they would cut ties when they each left home or whether they would persevere in the familiar war zone they had created.

Meg pulled Faye into her room and asked what was going to happen.

'Have you got a plan mother?' Meg ordered like an army corporal and Faye bristled once again with the official title of Mother.

' You should turn the internet off. Don't let him use the internet after nine. He's on it all night.' She carried on.

'That's an idea. We'll wait and see what the professionals say on Monday.' Faye said, her usual evasive self.

'Oh my God you've no idea what he's up to on the internet have you mother?' Meg stared hard at Faye for the answer and Faye felt like a naughty school child summoned to the head's office for a stern ticking off.

'He's not well for Christ's sake.' Faye insisted.

'He's perfectly well Motheroon. He knows how to get into the dark web.'

'The onion router? He's downloaded it?' Faye asked.

Every Family Has One

Meg started to laugh hysterically, her mouth wide, flashing her metal tracks.

'Mother don't pretend to know all about the dark web when you don't. Oh you're so funny at times.'

'I looked it up on the internet.' Faye said, feeling as if she were a teenager herself caught in the middle of a group of chiding bullies as Meg mocked her words, laughing more, snorting like a horse let loose in a paddock.

'You don't *download* anything.' Meg stretched out the words as if talking to a slow learner. Faye shriveled in size.

'Is it a separate processor? The dark web? He's built that computer himself. He knows everything there is to know.' Faye chanced the question expecting further mockery.

'I don't know but he says it's dead easy to get into it and from there you can go anywhere. He's tapping into a dangerous world. You need to do something.' Again Faye was asked to solve the issues but at the same time mocked for her ignorance about the modern technological world.

'It's beyond me. Beyond any parent. I could put child protection safety on the Wifi. I could turn the Wifi off at nine each evening. I could insist he uses it downstairs...' Faye was running through all the ideas as if standing before her employer outlining how she was going to move the company forward. But Meg wasn't interested. She had moved to the next rung of the ladder and was looking down again.

'I think you should start by *talking* to him. It's that basic.' She said and Faye, reeling inside, knowing she was so right just wanted to slap her.

'He won't talk.' She was exasperated.

'Take him out. To London. Insist on going out with him for the day. Tomorrow. Do it.' Her words were lemon sharp. She stabbed the air with a painted finger.

She couldn't contemplate that idea. What would a day alone with her son be like?

135

But that was what Faye decided to do. She would take Meg's suggestion and tell him in the morning that they were going out. As Meg said *don't give him any ifs or buts, do it*. They were going out. He was going to get out of bed in the morning. Have breakfast. Get dressed.

She went to bed already dreading the idea of being alone with her son. What would they say to each other? Would she have the courage to say all the things she needed to say?

16
Faye

September 2014

Dear Katie,

...and at the end of the meeting Mr. Richards said *go home and talk*. My heart sank. How do I start a conversation with a brick wall? You would never have let your relationship with Ed slide down to this level. Am I the only crap mother out there?

This morning I looked in the mirror and wondered what I was supposed to see. I don't know what I'm feeling. I was in a state of shock yesterday. My first reaction was *what a crap parent you are* that your son feels so worthless. Why is it in life that the real troubles are the things that never cross our minds? Or do we just bury our heads in the sand? Or is it that as parents there are just so many things to think about, consider, take into account that we cannot do it. Parenting has become a paralysis, a thorny bush and we are all struggling.

When I went to bed I looked at his bedroom door. He's a stranger. He's no longer that gorgeous little boy with the dimpled chin; the one we both remember so well. He's the enemy within. It's like the Muslim women you read about in the papers whose husbands turn into Jihadis. In the space of 48 hours he has become the black sheep of the family. They say that every family has one. Someone who trips up and needs a hand to get back up. Will I be able to pull him back? Will anyone? I don't know where to go from here but the professionals will all be descending on Monday, like ambulances at the scene of a road accident.

But there comes a time in a child's life when they need to take responsibility for their own destiny. That's what I believe. We stifle, we protect, we guide but our children must walk the path of life alone – ultimately. I wish you could have seen that but you had to protect Ed didn't you? You wouldn't let him make mistakes. You were a suffocating mum. Maybe things would have been different if you hadn't been like that. I don't know why you were. I'll never understand. You thought you could control Ed. You couldn't. We don't have that power to control our kids. It's beyond us ultimately. We can't rub their wounds away or dab that pain with herbal oil 31, made in Switzerland the cure for all pains imaginary and real. We can't keep dosing them in Calpol. They grow up. That's the sad fact Katie. They grow up. They fly the nest. They aren't ours to keep.

I want to come over to yours tomorrow. You can cut a slice of your finest chocolate cake; silky smooth chocolate parceled as love and concern and present it to Tim and maybe he'll explain it all to *you*. You always said you had a special bond with Tim; that you could see inside his soul. I don't know what you meant by that.

There are no salty tears to dab. No flushed chubby cheeks to kiss. This Timmy doesn't cry. I'm his mother but I can't dab the tears anymore. He's a teenager. It's the way things are. Do you remember reaching for the box of Bloomsbury and Tate luxury tissues that were always on your coffee table?

How am I supposed to react? There are no tantrums. No shouting. No throwing things around the room. No

Every Family Has One

anger. No challenges. No reason for me to shout back. He's too old for me to slap his hand, take a toy away, send him to bed early. You can't do that when your son is thinking of selling drugs. You have to tread carefully. You don't want to do anything that would risk his life. If I take pocket money away he'll owe it to his dealer; *drugs on tick mate until you get a job* but they'll be conditions attached Katie. A fist through the face...nice.

Timmy is too big to sit on my lap. Too big to tickle. Too big to blow raspberries on his belly. Too big to distract with CBeebies or offer a warm bottle of Ribena or a treat. I don't have the ability to turn his unhappiness around with the treats and the quick fixes of the past. This is new territory and I must delve into the past for the answers but there's so much more to this – aspects to the problem I cannot possibly understand unless he talks. But he's not going to. Is he? You took all that away from me. You made him want to be with you, not me.

I could gather up and buy all the Wickedly Wonderful Wagon Wheels in the world and let him pig out but what good would that do? This problem won't disappear in a gloop of biscuit nougat and melt in the mouth chocolate.

So how does a parent react to silence?

Go home and talk. Tell him you love him. Mr. Richards thinks that's job done. Parent dismissed. Problem removed.

I've spent all day trying. Doing what Mr. Richards said. I took him to London today. I didn't want to go. I didn't know how it would be. It was Meg's suggestion.

I went in his room this morning and announced that we were going to London; just the two of us. He told me to go away. Parent in room - it triggers an alarm. *Go away* on repeat until feet are removed from room.

Come on we're going to have a mother son day out in London.

Surprisingly he didn't object. He made it easy for me. Strange. He refused to go anywhere with us as a family all Summer holiday. But now he obligingly went.

On the train I asked if he minded going to London with his old mother and he just shrugged and said 'nar' in a faint voice I could barely hear. He stared at the floor of the train the entire journey. I asked where in London he would like to go. He stared out of the window, shrugged.

When we got to Blackfriars we followed the literary bench trail in the City. But it was about me looking at the map, working out where we were going. There are three tours. You have to find the benches. They are painted in bright colours and depict a different famous bench. I wanted him to pose for a picture at each bench but he waved my camera away and slumped onto the bench with his hands in his face. Not even Anthony Horowitz's book 'Alex Rider' raised an eyebrow or Stephen Hawkin's 'Brief History of Time.' Probably not the best of ideas for a 16 year old but I couldn't think of where else to take him. I don't know what he's interested in. He doesn't say. I suggested the Tate. He shrugged. I suggested London Dungeons. Again a shrug. He doesn't reveal his opinions. Not to me. I'm his mum. I guess he's not supposed to. His answers are yes or no. Nothing more. Maybe they are always other peoples' thoughts. At least I cannot decide who he is because without his opinions I cannot judge him and I don't want to have to judge him. Not really. But all the time he holds it all in I'm left with questions unanswered in my head, but sometimes questions inside the head are easier to live with. It's that truth dilemma again. Do we really want to see inside someone else's head? If we could see inside our children's heads how would we cope? What did you Katie put in his head?

I wish you'd been able to come with us. You and Ed. Do you remember the day in London we had? I can see the boys walking along the wall next to the Thames, at the South Bank and us holding their hands tightly. And watching jugglers and clowns and other street performers and the boys running round in circles. They always had to take their plastic swords wherever we went.

Do you remember the man with a pole who asked the audience for a kid to come up and feel his pole? You practically wet yourself laughing.

We saw a flame thrower, a man dressed as a bronze statue, a stall selling sweet hot nuts. No comments from him. Then we stood on the Millennium Bridge and looked at the views all around. My mind floated to different eras across a wide span of history. I imagined plumes of smoke, the river crowded with boats. I imagined men in bowlers carrying umbrellas dashing across London Bridge. I thought about the docks and the warehouses and barrels of rum and whisky being loaded and I closed my eyes and wished I could be transported to a different time when we didn't have to worry about the internet.

I said to Timmy *Imagine living here by the Thames. Wouldn't it be wonderful? All the lights at night and the amazing views. Where would you live if you could live anywhere?* It was an easy enough question. I waited several minutes and had to prompt him for an answer. He didn't answer me. His face looked haunted, drained of colour. He needs fresh air. Exercise. We walked on and we came to the Tate. I stopped. He stopped. We both looked up. I said *What an incredible building.* He said nothing. We went in and looked at all the strange paintings. Smudges of paint on canvas. I said, *Strange paintings aren't they? I wonder what was going through this artist's head when they painted it.* He didn't reply. He stood next to me, a shadow that never left my side all day; a lingering cloud of part Lynx, part body odour.

And then I saw a poem under glass. I read it. I think he did too. I saw a hollow faraway look in his eyes staring back in the reflection of the glass; a look that haunted me as much as the poem did.

The poem read:

"Once there was a mother of a son. She loved him with complete devotion.

And she protected him because she knew how sad and wicked the world is.

He was of a quiet nature and rather intelligent but he was not interested in being loved or protected because he was interested in something else. Consequently at an early age he slammed the door and never came back. Later on she died but he did not know it."

With you around Katie there was never silence. You didn't allow it.

Love Faye.

17
Faye

September 2014

It was Sunday and Tim was back in his room. Faye knocked. Went in; hit by the thick fug of body odour, dead crisp packets and computer heat. She tried not to recoil. His room was a petri dish of furry toast and grey- flecked cheese waiting for lab testing. Empty glasses, straws still inserted, balanced precariously on each newel post of the bed threatening to fall at any moment into the sea of clothes like an item of rubbish discarded from a cruise ship. His face was a picture of thunder of the high seas for having been disturbed. He lay on his bed, headphones inserted while she surveyed the scene of teenage devastation. He inched further up the bed, like a spider scuttling to a hole.

'Your room always smells of computer heat. Have you cleaned the fans lately? What about the air flow around all this equipment?' It was as if her voice had engaged before her brain. The question was idiotic. *I'm nagging again* she chastised herself.

'Go away.'

'We might need to put an internet screening, child lock system on your computer. What have you been looking at the dark web?'

'Go away.'

143

She stood awkwardly in the doorway, an unwelcome visitor peering into an animal enclosure.

༼ྀི༽

Faye came out of his room feeling tortuously lonely, the weight of the problem heavy upon her shoulders and standing on the landing suddenly missed Trevor bitterly.

She picked up the phone. Who was out there she could speak to? She thought of her brother but knew that he'd just tell her *to go easy on the lad; don't make him talk; it's hard living with a bunch of women.* And she knew he was right, in part.

She scrolled down. This was a Chris Tarrant phone a friend card. The buzzer was lit up; everyone waiting anxiously. She hovered for a few moments over Katie's number, tears pricking the back of her eyes. It was still programmed in; a painful reminder.

Tim's problems weren't easy problems to share with just anyone, especially not local parents. *My son takes cannabis.* Word would spread like wildfire. He'd lose friends. People would judge. Label. Demonise him. Turn him into a drug dealer. They'd want to keep their kids well away. But who could blame them? She'd be the same. She could understand this attitude but desperately wanted to share the problem with someone.

She wished she could phone, hear Katie's voice again. Soak up her wisdom, her empathy, her understanding... of Tim as he then was.

But she dialed her cousin in Scotland whom she saw a couple of times a year, thought the world of and who would have some understanding of the situation, maybe able to help; at best listen.

'Oh Faye I am not surprised. It was obvious to me from a very long time ago that Tim was a withdrawn child.'

Really? Was he that withdrawn? He wasn't when he was young. He laughed. He screamed. He joked. Katie remembers. She's the only one that does. Katie I need you... Faye's head screamed.

'He's always kept his emotions tightly locked up inside. I have observed him as a worrier, an incredibly sensitive child, a child who didn't know where he was supposed to be, a child who was an observer rather than a doer... Some of that is his personality and *some* external factors. He's a beautiful child darling. He still is. He's meddling in a nasty world but he's still your boy.'

Faye pulled her legs to her body, dabbed the tears from her eyes as she basked in her cousin's soothing and wise words.

'I blame divorce and Trevor's death. The only person that can really help me understand is Katie.'

'Katie...oh darling. It's hard, I know. You miss her. And maybe Tim misses her too. Have you considered that? They were very close. She was a second mum to him after all.'

This was a thought Faye hadn't considered but a very plausible one. They were silent for a moment while Faye digested what her cousin had said.

'You need people around you to help at a time like this. To be brutally honest Faye - yes, I have always said that the Trevor's death must have had a huge impact on him - I have never hidden that from you. Yes it's really sad. But it's something that has happened and cannot be undone but you are now at a crucial time to do something now.' Her words were bullets of truth, jarring, hard hitting and designed to shake Faye up like a tin of jelly beans.

'Stop the grieving and self -criticism - we all hold guilt - honestly I do it all the time. Now is the time for positive action.' She could see her cousin drumming the air.

'It's hard Faye but believe me I have had to really pull it out of the bag and dig deep for my kids.'

'I can't help it.' Faye whimpered.

'It's not easy being a parent of any age. And even harder I imagine being a single parent. There comes a time when every parent thinks they've failed. This is your moment and like any moment in life don't let the moment pass. Some advice will be good; some not so good.

That's the pick n mix of parenting. It's all a maze with no clear route out. But get some help for you.... Ask the doctor. He will be able to refer you. Go private. Dig deep.'

Dig deep? Into the pot of imaginery gold?

'It will mean that you will be able to be seen almost immediately. You haven't got the time to wait to be seen.'

And who did she imagine was going to pay? She had no money left over after paying the bills. All on the measly £6.79 an hour she earned at the local recycling factory. Counselling wasn't cheap. That would be the food budget gone.

'Family counseling. That's what you need.' She was off on one, stating the obvious but it wasn't going to happen. Tim was unwilling and unlikely to open up and until that portcullis had risen communication was going to be impossible.

'It's going to be hard.' It was as if she was reading her thoughts.

The conversation had now become tedious, like journeying a steep mountain. Her head ached. Tiredness washed over her, thoughts spinning in a vortex, draining her energy. She knew what needed to be done. Any outsider would see that. But no one could see what she could see from the inside, because her role was unique. She was his mother.

Her cousin rattled on, heart in the right place.

'A counselor can throw up all sorts of stuff. He may have unresolved anger. Kids blame. Too many people have left his life. You're not thinking about it all. Inward anger is more frightening – you don't know what's going on inside someone. Self harm is a consequence.' Her cousin warned.

The word grief suddenly loomed large in her mind tapping at every corner.

'It's as if Tim has died. It's death without the burial. This is pent up grief for the loss of family. The loss of his dad. Katie told me to protect them. Oh God she was the world's number one in protective mothers.' Faye said, chastised herself now for not having revealed the truth to the twins but she was painfully reminded of why she had done that and the influence, at the time of Katie.

'I must have been so wrapped up in my feelings, what I was going through that I stopped communicating with the kids.'

'Well Meg isn't going through the same as Tim. This is to do with Tim not Meg and I'm telling you he's a very withdrawn child. There's an inner anxiety, inner conflict that's not been dealt with. That's why he had tummy aches and wouldn't go to school. Remember? When he was at primary school.'

Faye knew she had made a very valid point.

'This must be a terrible time for you sweet heart - it must have rocked your foundations to feel that all this has gone on under your nose for years.'

What has gone on under my nose for years? Faye's inner voice questioned.

And then as if to answer that inner voice 'I'm not really talking about the drugs, the wanting to die and the possible drug selling as this is just a by product of how he is feeling. His actions now are just an expression of his confusion and his distress. But it's now your job to take the reins and guide him in the right direction as best you can.'

Ugh. So the ball is in my court. And how am I supposed to turn things around? Faye wanted to scream. He won't bloody communicate!

'You'll have to pay darling.' Faye felt a lump of irritation descend. Her husband was the director of a multinational company. People like that could throw money at any problem. They didn't have to worry about the NHS in crisis following Cameron's austerity programme. They could afford to go private. But they failed to understand the plight of single motherhood and what it was like to struggle on the minimum wage. She longed for Labour's return to power and its' promise of an increase in the minimum wage.

'You need help now not in four, six weeks time darling. And you can get help.'

But Faye felt as if she was drowning.

18
Faye

September 2014

It was the start of the following week and time for action. Faye had always had a good relationship with her local GP. She wanted to know what Tim had said to him at the appointment on Friday.

She sat down in the plastic chair beside his desk recalling her previous visit to see him, only a few weeks before.

In his late fifties Dr. Owen had a big belly; an indication maybe that he didn't take life and health too seriously. She found this strangely comforting.

'I'm worried about his long term. I see him on the margins of society, not adjusting to different situations very well. Another child in his year took his life, over the Summer holiday. Jumped in front of a train. I'm wondering if that might have influenced Tim's suicidal thoughts.'

'That boy was my sister's son.' He said, nursing his ginger beard.

'Oh God. Shit I'm sorry. I had no idea.'

'They're still going through an inquest.' He pursed his lips, retaining a professional demeanour despite the fact that he was closely connected to this tragedy.

'How serious are Tim's suicidal thoughts?'

'I didn't see him. It was a locum...'

'And I can't tell you I'm afraid. Patient confidentiality.' He taped his nose.

Faye raised her hands in defeat and felt tears begin to prick.

'How am I, as his mother supposed to help him if everything is shrouded in this top secrecy?' This was like climbing a mountain without the right equipment.

He studied her face for a few seconds. Their eyes locked. Then he turned to the computer, which sprung to life at the touch. She noticed the damp patches under his white shirt. A light breeze drifted through the open window dispersing the smell of his body odour.

'I'm not supposed to share this with you...'

'He's only 16. He's still a kid really.' Faye was pushing her luck, she knew but was feeling desperate now.

'Ill read out the notes.' His eyes were serious. 'But if you say that I told you I will deny it. Do you understand?'

'Yes. Of course. Thank you so much.' She groveled. Although he said nothing she knew he felt the same disdain as her about confidentiality.

He scanned through the notes, looking for relevant bits to read out.

'He said he feels worthless and has been feeling like this for a couple of years but recently the low moods have got a lot worse. He came out 6 out of 10 on the suicide at risk scale. Says he smokes cannabis every week. Pays about £10 a time.'

'You know he's been into the dark web? Ordered products to make a class A drug.' She said checking he knew the situation.

'Have you ever been into the dark web?'

His question startled her. He might as well have asked her if she'd ever used a vibrator. Of course she hadn't. Why would she want to? At the back of her mind she imagined the police were monitoring everyone who tapped into the dark web - but they didn't live in a police state. This was England.

'I wouldn't want to.' She quickly said, thinking his question irrelevant.

'It's easier than you think.' A shadow moved across his face. She wondered if he had been into the dark web and for what purpose.

'And how easy would it have been for him to make DMT?'

'Easier than you think. With a bit of research, a bit of know how.' The doctor's eyes glowed with a deeper knowledge than she was giving him credit for.

'Not from a bedroom.' Faye laughed.

The doctor shrugged. His eyes darted from side to side as if to say *think outside the box a minute.*

'He couldn't have sold drugs over the internet. Not at his age.' Faye said.

'I think he might have needed bitcoins.'

'Do you know of a private psychiatrist that's good?' Faye asked. Not that she had much intention of throwing shed loads of money at the problem.

'The problem is if you go private the child mental health team might not take him on. You *should* get an appointment to see someone in the team in the next few days. They'll be contacting you very soon.' He reassured her.

'And are they good?'

'Sometimes. Not always.' This didn't bode well. She was pinning all her hopes on the child mental health team.

⁓୦

The following day the professionals began to swoop, a flock of seagulls each with their own expertise or lack of it and each raising more questions, the answers of which Faye didn't have.

First on the phone was Sarah, a family support worker at Rydon High, a quick chat to arrange an appointment.

Next up was Dave, the school's police liaison officer who explained his role: teaching some PSE classes, taking some assemblies and generally being on hand for issues as they arose. He wanted to meet Tim with Faye to explain some of the implications to him of his actions that he might not be aware of. He explained that it wouldn't be on record but that he did need to be scared a little so that he was made aware of the seriousness of what he was doing and the implications of cannabis use.

'Have you found anything else in his room?' He asked Faye.

'No.' Wasn't it all serious enough? Faye thought to herself.

'Can you bring it in if you find anything?'

⁓

Next up was Sally, the substance misuse officer and the conversation led on to Tim's use of the computer in his room.

'I shouldn't have let him use the computer in his room.' Faye said.

'You decide the rules. It's your house. You pay the bills and if you decide to cut off the internet you do that. There is a group you can join as a parent. It might give you the confidence to know you aren't alone in all this.' Sally said.

She was right Faye thought but she wasn't relishing the thought of taking the dummy away from the baby.

'And what about DMT?' Faye wanted to probe her about the making of drugs.

'I need to do some research. I don't know much about DMT I'm afraid. I don't know how easy it is to make.'

Jesus. She's an expert and she doesn't know.

A wave of exasperation washed over Faye.

'Do you think this is all related to that series, Breaking Bad?'

'Does he watch it then?' He asked.

Dumb question. Obviously... otherwise why would I be asking? Faye asked inside.

It was getting late. As she went upstairs to bed she saw the light glow from the bottom of Tim's door and wondered what measures she should put into place. Maybe she should insist on the door being open. Maybe she should restrict his internet use, maybe turn the Wi fi off at 8 each evening.

She hovered outside his room; fist ready to knock feeling uneasy. A bridge had been crossed in their lives and nothing would be the same again. She dropped her fist. It was useless. Why was she bothering? But an inner voice interjected and the words of Churchill were suddenly in her head. It was a bizarre moment.

If you're going through hell keep going.

She raised her fist. Knocked. Went in.

'Get out.' He fired his opening shot. She was becoming used to this hostility, almost condoning it - for she had never tried to change it - but now when she needed to she had no idea how she could break it. Her eyes flickered round the room, taking it all in quickly before he tried to push her out. There were three screens set up on his crowded desk. She could see the blue screen of Facebook, then Reddit and Minecraft.

'I just wanted to talk to you.' She hovered in the doorway, wondering whether to risk perching on his bed.

'Go away.' His responses had become robotic, predictable.

Do you want to know what the worst thing I've ever done before is?' She was now starting to feel awkward as she began to talk.

'No go away.'

'I'll tell you anyway.' She took a deep breath. Swallowed her rising nerves.

'Go away.'

'I threw a brick through the neighbour's window once. When I was ten.'

'Well that was stupid.' Suddenly he reminded her of his father. The morose shake of his head. The flash in his eyes; arrogant, dismissive, condescending. Her mouth gaped in silent frustration as she tried to quell the rising emotions and destroy the image of Trevor before her eyes. When had he morphed into his father she wondered? And why, like Trevor couldn't he discuss his problems? What if he ended up like Trevor...on the train tracks because he couldn't express his emotions?

'Yes I know. But sometimes in life, particularly when we're young we don't think of the consequences. I could have killed someone. Scared an old lady to death. But at the time it was a dare. I thought it was funny. But it was any thing but funny. We're carefree when we're young. We think nothing can touch us. I don't know why you were planning to do what you were going to do and I'm not here to judge but you could have hurt someone. You could have made lots of people very ill.'

'Go away.'

'And that's not all...'

'Go away.' The go aways were raining down now like a series of bombs over Helmand Province.

'I did shoplifting.'

'I would never do that.' His eyes had turned frosty. When he looked this way she found it harder to believe she was his mother.

'Actually a lot of young people do it. Of course it's wrong. Any theft is wrong. Sometimes when people get into drugs they have to steal to support the habit – so they become embroiled in two crimes and it has a huge impact on others too and then they get into trouble with the police. Thankfully I saw it was wrong but that was after I got my friend into it too – at that point it wasn't just making me bad it was making someone else bad too. It was so easy. That was the worst of it. Like taking drugs it's so easy but all these things have implications and we don't always think of the implications when we do them.'

'Go away.'

'Who's your dealer?' Faye chanced the question.

'Go away.'

'Not until you tell me.'

'There are lots of people.'

'What do they look like?'

'They've all got horns and wear red capes.'

At least he was talking. This was a start, despite his surly attitude, Faye thought.

'Don't be sarcastic.'

'Well you think all drug dealers must be evil. They're just honest people trying to earn a living like the next man. They're entrepreneurs, businessmen.'

She thought how grown up he suddenly sounded, although incredibly niave.

'A dishonest income.'

'Depends how you look at it. In some countries it's legal. It's pretty harmless. The Green Party want to legalise it.'

'Well it isn't legal. For good reason. Do you get talking to them? Do they offer you stronger stuff?'

'What would they talk about? Nice weather for three in the morning in a bush.'

Faye looked away, disgusted by his surliness.

'I just want to know who is ruining my son's life.'

'There is one main guy. He only sells trusted stuff.'

'Does he smoke it too?'

'Of course. They all do. He needs it to get through the day. Something happened to him that messed him up. Poor bloke. He was offered counseling. That was crap. Then he discovered the wonders of cannabis to drown the pain, never looked back. And the best of all is that he can afford anything he wants. Nice car, nice holidays, big TV.'

'Yeah but companies start to ask questions when you hand over shed loads of money.'

'There are ways of covering the tracks.'
'And what pain are you drowning Tim?'
He shrugged. Faye waited but no answer came and then he looked at her as if to ask *why are you still in my room?*
In the background the phone was ringing. Tim looked towards the door his eyes nudging her to answer it.

～

It was now Friday and as Scotland woke to a no vote in the referendum for independence Faye woke with the worry of the meeting that lay ahead with the police officer at the school.

'It's been an amazing campaign. The Scots have become politicized. The whole country has been galvanized behind the campaign.' A commentator was saying above the cheering crowd. She turned the radio off, day- dreaming above the news about how wonderful it would be if Tim got involved in a political cause. But other than the referendum - which was now over and was in Scotland; so remote from the south of England - what was there to be involved in? This wasn't the 60s when there were big causes to follow. And he wasn't a Muslim learning to be a jihadi; not that she wanted that for him.

～

Faye arrived at the school where she met Tim in the reception area and together they were ushered along the corridor – which smelt of old PE kit and dust- into a small office where the police officer offered them both a chair and explained his role at Rydon High.

'I deal with legal issues as they arise related to individuals. I have files of several pupils. I'm sure the names of the pupils won't surprise you Tim.'

Faye wondered how often *issues* arose. It was sobering to think that secondary schools now had resident police officers. Things were

155

certainly very different, she thought to herself thirty years on from when she was at school. As the officer spoke she asked herself some pertinent questions: when had this change happened and what had precipitated the change?

'You're not in any trouble Tim. That's the first thing I want to say. We aren't going to prosecute you. This is not a formal interview. I will be taking notes and will write a report but you are not under arrest.' He spoke slowly, softly and Faye thought that he looked too young to be a police officer. *I must be getting old,* she told herself.

Tim sat with his hands in his pockets, the expression on his face set and unchanged; more relaxed than she'd have wanted him to look. She had expected wet eyes and a look of fear but neither came and Faye concluded that either the gravity of the situation hadn't sunk in yet or the man was an everyday sight around the school and not somebody to fear even though he was a police officer with police powers.

'I'd like us to be honest with each other. Tell me what has happened.' He said calmly with a reassuring yet professional look.

Tim shrugged. Looked at the floor. Then in a quiet voice, the breath of a dying engine he mumbled an answer.

'So you were planning to manufacture a class A drug?' He let the words linger in the air. 'And sell a class A drug on the internet?'

Tim was quiet.

'What do you understand by Class A?"

He shrugged, said nothing so the officer gave an answer.

'Do you know what the consequences of supplying a class A drug are?'

Again a shrug. He folded his arms.

'You could be facing a ten year prison sentence.' The words filled the room like a thick mist.

A lump rose in Faye's throat. Tim sat wooden. They both looked at him, as if waiting for the big crack that never came.

'And how would you cope with prison?' He added when the mist of the words had settled.

'Alright. I guess.' Another shrug.

'Really? You sure about that?' He persisted.

He's still a little boy, Faye's head screamed. *He knows nothing. Like a small child running into the road to fetch a ball – how could he know? How could he see?*

'So why is an intelligent boy like you doing this? It doesn't make sense. Is this a risk you're prepared to make?'

'I wouldn't have got caught.' The words splatted across the room like blood in a slaughter house. Faye was incredulous.

'Well... you say that, but how do you think we would have come into contact with you?'

Tim shrugged. Eyes to the floor.

'We might have found items on you. We can intercept the post. Items that arrive at the post office without an address on the back maybe. We work with the post office Tim. In fact we work across every agency. We build up intelligence on people. It's all about intelligence policing. Do you know what that means?'

'Yes.' His answer was firm this time.

'And you were already on our radar. We knew about you. I could probably tell you a lot about you. Even in sleepy Trentum we have intelligence.' His lips twisted as he waited for Tim to soak up the answer.

Faye's cheeks started to burn. She couldn't look at Tim. Felt she was betraying him. He wasn't stupid. He would see how the officer was cleverly bending the truth; a white lie to jar him because he hadn't managed to crack Tim yet. To Faye it felt like a desperate attempt. But then she looked across at him, examining him for traces of unease, the hit by a truck look but the only unease seemed to be her own, welling inside and for a different reason. She knew this tactic wouldn't wash. He would see through the glaze. Of all the useful things the officer had said this clumsy, well - intentioned white lie would be the one take away from the meeting.

'Have you looked at the PH levels of DMT? And you were still prepared to give it a go despite the difficulties involved.' He asked.

There was a pause.

'I guess.' Another shrug came.

'We have a huge drugs department at New Scotland Yard. We do internet research. We have spyware that flags up a person's IP address. Which site did you buy the items on?'

There was silence. But no cracks. No tears. No reddening of cheeks. He was holding his strength, maintaining his composure well.

'A trigger would have occurred. After all it's in the public's interest to prosecute. It would only be a matter of time. You were lucky. You came this close.' He made an action with his thumb and forefinger, 'to messing up your future.'

There was another silence as the officer let his words sink in. Faye glanced out of the window and over at the head of year sitting observing from the corner of the room.

'You can change your future. You can do it now. If your computer knowledge was channeled in the right direction you could be going places, doing great things. You have a bright future if you take the right path Tim.' The officer smiled warmly, despite Tim's wall of silence he was doing his best to win Tim over.

'You're lucky to have a mum that cares. Most parents when phoned to collect their child from the police station will say *keep him*. They don't want to know if it's anything to do with drugs. Your mum's amazing. She's one in a million.' The officer glanced across at Faye who blushed under the much needed compliment.

'She acted swiftly, got all the professional support she could and I've never seen the authorities respond so fast. A week later and there's been real progress to get you help.'

But Faye wondered how true that really was and whether it would have any effect.

Where are you Katie? She asked herself as she listened to the police officers closing words. *Where are you?* Tears were threatening to well as she struggled to focus on the haunting image of Katie that was welded to her mind.

Every Family Has One

Meg was laughing, hovering at Tim's bedroom door determined to ignore his protests for her to go. Faye was tidying her room, half listening; a prick of inadequacy stabbing every now and again as she caught the odd word, wishing she had Meg's persistence; determination to break Tim's wall of silence. There was something radiant and confident about Meg. She didn't feel awkward around Tim's silence; attacking the silence from every angle, keeping the communication channels open; even though sometimes she was harsh and aggressive. But Faye was different. Self-conscious, timid, questioning of her own abilities as a parent, essentially gauche about being demonstrative she lacked confidence with her own kids, as teenagers. It was as if they had morphed into different people; people she no longer knew. Despite Trevor's tragic death in hindsight she had found their early childhood much easier. As small children they were more predictable, more open, more loving.

She walked over to her bedroom window looked out over the warehouses of the nearby industrial park in Slough and the thick bank of cloud crawling across the sky. She longed to be transported back to those early years when they came to her freely, sitting on her lap for a cuddle. She closed her eyes breathing in the memories of kissing their soft downy heads, their cheeky laughter and all the excitement that simple things in life brought, conjuring all the smells and the sounds of those years.

The fact that they were twins didn't help. Even though their characters were very different, even though they'd fought and argued bitterly over the years and didn't always understand each other there was a special bond between them she knew could never be broken. Sometimes they shared each other's pain and triumphs but these were never shared with Faye, their mother. She simply oversaw the day to day of their lives, facilitated things, fed them, clothed them, put a roof over their heads but when the chips were down and they needed emotional support they had each other because that was what being a twin was all about. It was a lifelong relationship.

Something caught her ear. She went to her door. Listened.

'The police were talking rubbish. They said they had sophisticated spyware and that I was already on their radar. It's crap. Course they don't.' Faye heard Tim say.

'Really?' Meg laughed casually, made no comment; maybe not wanting to slam him down, take the police heavy line

'Don't tell mother.' Tim lowered his tone. Faye strained behind the door listening.

She remembered a saying she'd heard a long time ago.

When you go to war take all your weapons with you. Slowly the *weapons* were gathering but she hadn't yet worked out how to use them to good effect. She was at war with her son; a cold war, which was intensifying but deep down she knew that really she was at war with his problems, his issues, not him, her son.

༄

Several days later Faye woke, swimming in a soup of anxiety. She had to do it. She'd been told by all the professionals she had to do it and yet it seemed the hardest thing she had ever had to do. When the twins were young she'd taken toys away, no problem; even when Meg had kicked off in Sainsbury's, lying on the floor screaming, legs kicking, thrashing. Despite the full - blown tantrum she'd stuck her ground determined to win the battle, ignoring the gazing eyes and shaking heads of onlookers. But toddler tantrums were different; not easier just different. There was the assurance that as the parent you were stronger, older, bigger, in control and you were going to win the battle. You were calling the shots and you had all the power. But with a teenager there was no such assurance and the stakes were so much higher, the issues kicking off much greater. She'd been told long ago that you had to win the small battles when they were young to win the big battles when they were older; advice that now rang true.

I've pussyfooted around for days. *I need to get on and do it* she told herself as she dressed. *Before he gets back from school.* There was nothing like the present.

And so while he was at school she carefully began to dismantle his computer, coiling the cables, lifting the unit. Thick layers of dust wafted from the desk and the top of the unit. With the hatch to the loft down she climbed the ladder wedging it into a free space. Then she hunted through his room guiltily gathering any gadget she could find; an old Nintendo DS, an ancient Nokia phone, his Kindle Fire and gadgets she didn't understand: something called a Xda Exec and a Psion 5 series.

As she poured coffee she kept reminding herself of the reasons she was taking the gadgets away. He needed to reintegrate back into family life. He'd become a lodger. She wanted to 'starve' him so that he'd have no option but to join her in the lounge to watch TV and maybe even play a board game, she hoped. The professionals had advised her to build his computer use back up gradually, setting rules, time limits, building the trust again. If she didn't do this nothing would change. She'd always known that too many hours on the computer was bad for his well being but she'd allowed unfettered access, no questions asked; a let him get on with it attitude, knowing this laissez faire attitude to parenting was wrong.

She had called Young Minds and they had been very helpful; pressing the point that counseling, if he agreed would be the best course of action but they also suggested the removal of the gadgets in the short term. *It's like removing toys from a toddler. As he starts to talk and boundaries are reestablished you can begin to reintroduce them little by little.* Faye knew that if she didn't remove the gadgets the fundamental issues – his low mood - would be kicked into the long grass and remain there.

And after that she sat down to work out what she was going to say to him when he got home. In her head she formed a speech and in the hours that followed learned the speech word for word, knowing that when the words tumbled out they would be wooden, disjointed and unnatural.

Why was it so hard to relate to a teenager? Why was she scared of taking the computer away? These were questions that kept reverberating around her head.

∽

It was after five in the evening when Tim returned. He came into the kitchen to ferret in the fridge.

Faye took a deep breath and began to explain to Tim why she was taking his computer and gadgets away.

'Why?' Tim asked with a Kevin and Perry look on his face.

Every carefully crafted sentence Faye had prepared was slayed in an instant. She felt as defeated as a crushed ball of paper. Tears started to prickle at the back of her eyes but she quickly pulled them back, trying to remain calm, composed.

Having spent all day preparing what she was going to say she now threw her hands into the air, in mock defeat and called for Meg to come down to reinforce what she'd told Tim.

'Change the passwords Meg on my security preferences. Tim is going to have some time without his computer. So he can reintegrate into the family. Get him off the dark web and doing other things.'

'Other things?' Tim asked, his nose turning up. 'I don't like sport. And I don't like Pathfinders since Ed left.'

'So you are missing Ed?'

Tim shrugged, looked embarrassed.

'And I'm not sitting down here with you. Why would I want to watch the Jeremy Kyle show or some stupid romantic film with Meg, Chrissie and you.'

Faye gave a heavy sigh. Leaned on the worktop.

'I wish your dad was here. He'd know what to do. He'd get you interested in golf or cricket or take you to a car show.' Tears were forming in Faye's eyes and Meg and Tim looked at her awkwardly.

'Would he? Would he have done anymore than you do?' Tim asked.

'You can't even be bothered to come to my parent meetings.'

'Oh don't you throw that at me.' Faye shouted. 'It's not that I can't be bothered. I find it just a little too hard walking into a big hall filled with happy couples sharing in their kids' achievements. It's a reminder of what I don't have.' As soon as Faye had said her piece she felt selfish. She had lost a husband but they had lost their dad.

'Oh God I'm sorry.' Faye simpered.

Meg's eyes were filled with tears but she couldn't read what Tim was thinking. He looked as if he was working out his next missive.

'How exactly did dad die? Cancer?' Well how come there's a newspaper in the loft with him on the front page? Devoted dad takes his life.'

Faye's world came crashing down. She felt her blood sugar suddenly dip, her face turn an alabaster white. She grabbed a chair before she felt herself go.

Nobody spoke.

'I found it a few months back.'

'Tim I'm sorry. I didn't want either of you to blame yourselves. Your dad had depression. That's why I'm so worried about you. The drugs. The suicidal thoughts. When someone takes their life it's a very big step. The idea of death becomes more attractive than life. Not many end up feeling like that. She wanted to say more but suicide was not a subject to dwell on, particularly with kids.

'When am I getting my computer back?' She was surprised by this sudden switch in conversation.

'Let's see what the professional say. See how things go. Maybe a week? Don't you want me to tell you what happened to dad?' She asked.

'Not really. I read it all.' His voice was cold. 'And fine. I'll just have to go round friends' houses instead. They won't mind.'

19
Faye

September 2014

Dear Katie,

    The big ship sails on the alley alley o, the alley alley o on the last day of September! Do you remember singing that song every year?

    There's a stillness to the air on the beach at Eastbourne this evening, that only late September brings. Do you remember when we used to drive all the way down to Eastbourne for our little jaunts out?

    The sky is a pale enamel blue, reminds me of the crockery on your Welsh dresser. The sea is still, like a millpond - as if it's given up the fight. Rather like me. It's scattered with tiny diamonds; all the people I miss shining down from heaven.

    Chrissie's collecting shells and doing handstands near the water's edge. Now she's stumbling over rocks in her new white socks. She's choosing pebbles to put on our fireplace. A couple of people are swimming; maybe their last day before the weather turns. A new season. Life goes on. A child in pink gives her doll a swim. I don't know what's brought me here Katie. Maybe to be closer to you. Maybe to enjoy Chrissie as

I used to enjoy Meg and Tim. *Used to*... what happened Katie? Did they just grow up or stop wanting to come here?

Seagulls sit on guard on the breakers; bouncers at a nightclub. One of them turns to look at me, his eyes piercing as ice. He knows I'm a crap mother.

I'm feeling disappointed. I was putting all my hope in yesterday's child mental health meeting at Trentum hospital. I've heard it called the 'crash team' - a term that conjures up all sorts of images: a medical team with equipment to treat a cardiac arrest hovering over a dying person in a hospital theatre, or a day out at Brands Hatch.

But Jesus Katie. You would have laughed. The guy we saw was old and crusty, ready for retirement. He wore a tatty tweed jacket, a mantle of dandruff; snow around his shoulders and he kept adjusting his hearing aids. He's probably on a six figure salary because he's got a degree in psychology and years in the job but the advice he gave was so basic, so obvious. It's actually quite patronizing for a parent to be told stuff they already know. What a waste of NHS resources he is! Number one, he said go to bed early. Number two: turn all gadgets off at 9pm. Number three: eat well and get some exercise. Number four: think about a new interest you can take up. Durrr! As if I hadn't thought about all these things. Oh and his parting words were *Tim you're a bright lad, you will do well in your exams*. How the fuck does he know? Not if he doesn't do any work he won't. Not if cannabis fucks his short-term memory. Katie.... Tim has given up working. I never see him do any work! How is he going to pass his exams? I'm so worried. Long term will he end up unemployed, a couch potato for life? It would be such a waste.

I hoped the mental health team would have the answers, (see footnote below [3]) would turn things around in the same

---

[3] For information about Camhs go to www.youngminds.org.uk

way that attaching defibrillator paddles to a patient in cardiac arrest would. But all the crusty geezer did was prescribe medication. Fluoxetine. It's Prozac. And we all know about Prozac...

I couldn't have got through those early days after Trevor's death without you. I think Tim is carrying the pain. Crusty geezer didn't accept this reasoning. Told me not to blame myself. But of course I do. If I'd taken an interest in the finances; seen the bank statements; seen that we were so much in debt and that the mortgage wasn't being paid I wouldn't be in the mess I'm in now, renting for life. And he wouldn't be dead. He robbed me of the chance to help him. I feel so angry with him. How can I feel angry with a dead man?

Tim needs counseling and crusty geezer didn't offer counseling.

But maybe crusty geezer did offer Tim counseling except that everything's so bloody hush hush, top secret confidential that mum is the last person to know! Ugh. How I hate this PC shite world of ours! Who at the end of the day is best placed to help him? His mum. But they make it difficult for us to help our kids. The world's gone mad.

When I close my eyes and I think of you, you're right here with me, living it all with me, holding my hand over the hot coals of parenting a teenager; your spirit in the rolling of the waves, your soul alive in the breeze, warming in the sun. I'm smelling the air. Mixed with salt, tar and Mr. Whippy. Your fragrance wafts by in my head. I'm trying to capture it and bottle it. In the sound of the sea I hear your voice whispering. You're trying to help me, you're trying to reply back through the waves. I can hear you. I'm smiling.

And in my head I can see Ed, Meg and Tim as toddlers chasing the waves, screeching. I can see us nattering, you pouring tea from the Thermos.

The clouds today are a city of high-rise tower blocks. Last week they were aeroplanes. I'm looking for the window you're peering out of. But all things pass, for nothing remains the same and tomorrow will be a new day with different shaped clouds.

The dappled sun is dipping as I write. Red spears the sky. A wasp buzzes near my feet. Is it you prompting me for dinner? It's getting late; the air is chill. The hairs on my arms stand like iron filings. Time for toasties in Notarriani's or the other cafe where the waitress always asks *will you be wanting the side salad; it's just that customers never eat it and I don't want to put it on your plate if you don't want it.* Christ Katie. When we asked for kids did we ask for the side salad that became all the extra problems? The lettuce leaves of life.

There's an ice now to the breeze as if someone's opened the fridge door.

Seagulls are circling, like planes queuing to land.

Dogs scamper over the shingle, their collars singing a melody.

And now Chrissie wants to set up a business; making necklaces from shells. A speed-boat drones across the metallic surface of the sea, drowning her out. Maybe she'll make a necklace for you.

A tanned man in his 80s is getting dressed.

You'd love it here.

We're turning to stumble up the mountain of shingle and the Dotto train trundles by. On the side of the train is an advert for TJ Hughes, advertising massive old lady knickers. You'd laugh. We'd both laugh. Now there's an advert for Oakleaves: unique retirement living for the over 55's. Jesus. That's me in a few years time. By then Chrissie will be a teenager. I can't do it all a third time. I'm dreading her transformation into those teen years. I don't want to do it all alone Katie.

Not without you. But I signed up for motherhood didn't I? We all did. We have no choice. We have to paddle on, doing all we can do, hoping for the best.

I know you've only slipped away into the next room Katie love. That's what the poem says, although you never heard it being read. I know you're waiting, for me, for us all I suppose, though some more than others. And I know that Tim will be a happier boy when he sees you again, but I don't want him to choice the route his dad took. Oh Katie how can I stop that happening?

Whatever we were to each other Katie we still are. Life means all that it ever meant... but why doesn't it feel this way? Why is life so cruel? Why am I so alone?

Love Faye

20
Tim

September 2014

Dear Katie,

I'll never forget that last night when I stayed over at yours. Meg and Chrissie were farmed out somewhere else, as usual but I always went to yours. *Company for Ed* you always said. I think you would have liked two kids. I don't know why Ed was an only child. Being an only child sucks. Poor Ed. Although sometimes I wish it was just me. Or me and an older brother. That way Mother would be the only girl in the house and it would be men versus women. He'd protect me at school, he'd show me how to pull a girl. But he probably would have been just like Meg and called me a jerk.

That last night at yours I came down stairs for a glass of water. I sat on your cold granite counter, swaying my legs. I couldn't sleep. You brought me a blanket, wrapped it round me, told me I looked like a woodland creature, all snug, then gave me a kiss on the head.

Your eyes looked sad, as they often did. Ed's dad was away. I never knew what he did for work but he always seemed to be working abroad. I remember thinking *when I'm older I* want a job abroad. *I want to fly on planes to distant places and eat at posh restaurants with people called clients.*

I want to be like Ed's dad and earn plenty of Benjamin Franklins and buy a fuck off house that everyone will envy so that I don't have to live here with three stupid girls.

If I ever have to go away, you said *remember I'll always love you. Remember how special you are, aim for the top; you're bright, your teachers say you can go places, do well in life.*

Mother doesn't have a clue what my predicted grades are. She always says that she finds the national curriculum way too confusing. Levels and assessments, attainment targets, end of year targets and grades. She hasn't a clue what they all mean. She doesn't bother to read school emails. Says the newsletters ramble on about sport and other stuff she's not interested in. But you were up to speed Katie. You made sure I never missed things going on. You reminded her. Without you everything has crumbled. There's no one to go to parent meetings. Steve's in Spain. Mother should go; she is the responsible parent after all, but she says she can't go because they are all happy couples holding hands and it only reminds her of what she doesn't have. Last year when I was ill she couldn't be arsed to pick me up from school so she told the school nurse that she wasn't at home; was at work but they were ringing the landline so they knew she was lying. So instead I just lay there on the couch in the medical room with the disgusting smell of school dinner wafting under the door making me feel even worse, wishing I could go home and snuggle up in my own bed.

When you said you had to go away my first thought was *oh no I'll be going back to mother's horrible marmite sandwiches.* Mother doesn't buy ham or turkey like you do. She says meat is too expensive. She doesn't buy yogurt tubes or Baby Bels either. We have marmite sandwiches on white bread, an apple and a value biscuit from Sainsbury's. I preferred your packed lunches. They were really yummy. I looked forward to them.

But now when I think about what you said... I know. I know Katie what you meant. I didn't know then, but I know now. Mother must never find out. She would be devastated.

Love Tim

21
Faye

October 2014

Over the coming weeks Faye muddled along researching depression, local services run by the council and she rang Frank, the drug support website and Mind hoping for answers. She found the support fragmented. She had to do all the investigating herself. No one professional seemed to be coordinating everything and unless she had looked for help it didn't fall into her lap. She wondered how some parents coped in this quagmire of disjointed information.

After a week she conceded that removing the computer and gadgets hadn't worked, for Tim had just come home later from school each evening; often as late as 9.30, having been to a friend's house, probably playing on their gadgets. She hated losing battles but this was one battle she had always known she couldn't win for the age of technology was firmly here and fight all she liked it wasn't going to go away.

Far from taking on board the mental health unit's advice Tim went to bed later and later each night. At first Faye tried to set the rules: insisting he turn the computer off at 8.30, then lights at 10pm to get a good night's sleep but little by little this regime broke down as it slipped her mind to remind him. Very often she heard him padding up and down the stairs until the early hours, telling her he was thirsty or hungry. She couldn't keep up; had to re-stock the fridge with snack pork pies, sausage rolls every couple of days and she found more and more elaborate places to hide biscuits and cakes. She joked to friends that she needed a priest hole or one of those secret rooms beyond a bookcase; the type you often see in National Trust properties.

And then there were the occasions that he'd sneak out of the house very late coming into her room with odd reasons to go out. He was gasping for air, needed a walk. Even the torrential rain outside didn't put him off. He said he was nipping out to buy a packet of Hobnobs. 'Heavenly Hobhobs' as he called them. Or 'Wicked Wagon Wheels' or some other snack. On one such occasion the rain was battering the windows, the latches tapping in the gusty wind and Tim still insisted he needed to buy Swiss Rolls.

'I've got Swiss Rolls. And the shops are closed. It's 10 o bloody clock.' Faye said from her bed. She was getting tired and ratty with this daily evening occurrence.

'Yuk.' He shuddered. 'They're value ones. I want proper ones. And there's always a shop open somewhere. Just because you've never seen one open doesn't mean there isn't one open.'

Faye tried to stop him; rushing downstairs after him, watching him disappear into the rainy darkness. When he'd left she returned upstairs watching him from an upstairs window with Meg. When she heard the key in the door an hour later she was ready waiting, Meg stood behind her swearing and as thunderous as the weather outside.

'Ok. Let's check your pockets.' Faye calmly said, patting each pocket, finding nothing, wondering where it was hidden. The porch, where he was now standing smelt woody like a camp fire.

'I know you've been smoking. Getting stuff from dealers. Just admit it.' Faye shouted.

'You're clothes stink.' Meg joined in the shouting match, swooping in like a hawk, poking, jeering; Faye not pulling her back.

'Where the hell is your life going Tim? You're going to end up dirty and smelly and no girl will want to kiss you. You're an idiot. You're just like all the other losers I come across at school.' Meg started banding names around.

'You're going to fail your exams. Oh my God. Is that what you want? Is it? To end up in the Poundstretcher doorway, a total waster? You think you're so clever taking weed don't you? It's not clever. It's pathetic. It's what losers do and you're now one of life's losers. Look at all the ones that took it in last year's year 11. They flunked their exams because they were out of it.' Meg went on, poking him in the chest, provoking and glaring right into his face.

Her voice had spun out of control, filling the hallway rising to a high decibel that couldn't be calmed. Meg was on a roll, a steam engine at full speed, while all the time Faye stood above them, half way up the stairs, her hand over her face in despair, half thinking that possibly this was what he needed: a jolly good shaking up to come to his senses. It wasn't an approach she advocated but couldn't see how it would do any harm. And perhaps the onslaught was better delivered by Meg, his twin sister.

'Memes Meg. Memes.' Tim muttered back. Faye hadn't the foggiest what he was saying. He was living on a different planet.

'What the fuck.' Meg suddenly didn't care about her language, oblivious to Faye behind her, the barriers were down; the gloves were off.

'Meta humour Meg.' Tim continued to mystify them both with his puzzling words.

'What are you on about?' Meg snapped, an irritation in her voice.

Faye was glad that Meg had no idea what these words meant either. Whatever the words meant he was doing his best to deflect and Faye felt a tug of her heart looking down at him, vulnerable, struggling.

'My future's in Syria. Fighting for the Jihad.' He attempted a weak laugh, easing himself into a corner, his dark curls falling around his face and his caramel eyes shining up at her under the hall spotlights.

'Don't talk like that Tim. That's serious stuff. It's not funny.' Faye snapped from the stairs.

'Well I might go and fight for Isis. I've had a holy calling from above. My Jihadi friends need me.'

'You're not a Muslim. Grow up.' Meg snapped.

'I could pass as one with my dark hair and olive skin. Anything has to be better than living under this roof.' He muttered.

'He's just talking crap mother. Ignore him.' And with that Meg turned to go back upstairs to her course work and pot of green tea. And Faye followed on, leaving Tim wafting a smoky aroma around the hallway.

༺༻

The following day Faye made a discovery.

When she returned from shopping Tim was at home with a friend she had never met before. An unknown pair of huge trainers sat in the hallway. She ascended the stairs. A blast of smoke escaped his room as she entered. Tim and another boy were perched on Tim's messy bed, amid towels and dirty underpants.

Fury started to rise within. *How fucking dare they smoke in my house, risking my house insurance, was the first thought that sprung to her mind.*

'Sorry... who are you?' She stared down at the boy she didn't know, whose dark, wavy hair was even longer and thicker than Tim's. He looked quite intelligent in black glasses.

'Declan.' He replied with a shifty look on his face.

'Well what the hell are you smoking in my house for?' She started to scream in his face.

'I wouldn't smoke in someone else's house.' He defended himself.

'Don't lie to me. I suggest you go home. The room stinks. Have you any idea, either of you what you're doing to your bodies? No...

because at your age you don't bloody care. Old age seems a long way off, but then you'll discover lung cancer and emphysema and wish to God you'd never started.'

Faye was on a roll, screaming as she bounced from one argument to the next, desperate for them to see what they were doing. While she ranted she glanced down and saw a packet of Rizlas and a yellow and green packet of Virginia tobacco, her blood boiling and her face turning a shade of purple. She wanted to grab Declan's collar, moved forward towards him like a bird of prey waiting to attack the boy who had clearly led her son into smoking.

'It's my choice.' Declan whimpered.

'Your choice. Oh shut up. Your choice. You're 16 years old. You don't have choices. It's illegal till you're 18. What you have isn't choice it's ignorance. You're an ignorant little boy that doesn't know any better.'

Faye swept from the room, banging the door, her heart slamming in her chest, angry. She was surprised at how she had fired off, the need to protect her son so strong, so passionate.

༺༻

It was the day after the discovery of tobacco and Faye was at home supervising a man visiting to do an annual inspection on her Dyson. He was on the landing emptying the contents of the Dyson onto a mat, changing the filter.

'The hoover's having to work very hard. We can supply you with a better head that will pick up more fluff.' Faye had heard this sales patter before. £15 for a vacuum cleaner service had seemed too good to be true. He was here to sell more products. That annoyed her and she told him so.

'No. Don't worry. I won't demonstrate any products. I don't want customers to think I'm only here to sell.' He sounded wounded and Faye felt guilty.

177

'Oh go on then show me how it works. I'm not saying I'll buy it though. I'm happy with the parts I've got thank you.'

'I'll just show you in this room shall I?' He asked.

The door to Tim's room was wide open. The man peered in, obviously clocking the carpet covered in biscuit crumbs, pencil shavings and chewing gum wrappers, pleased that it was a good carpet to test his wares on.

'A boy? I remember those days well. My mum could never get me to tidy my room either.' He gave a light laugh, took the liberty of glancing at the posters on the wall. 'How many kids have you got?'

'Twins. One of each and a girl. She's the spare.' Faye let a light laugh tinkle into the room.

His eyes were fixed on the posters adorning Tim's room as he flipped the head off, opened a packet, attached the new one to the Dyson.

'He's been taking drugs.' Faye's words stumbled into the room, unplanned.

'Walter White. I am the one who knocks. Remember my name. Heisenberg. That's a Goorin.' He was reading the words from each of the yellow posters lining Tim's walls.

'Teenagers ah?' Faye smiled. 'I'm damned if I understand how they tick. At least not this one anyway.'

The man rubbed his chin, frowned, as if he was about to deliver a profound statement.

'The key to understanding a teenager is in the music they like. Music is transforming, soul giving, all consuming. It's the start. It's the end. We find ourselves in music. We search for who we are in the lyrics, the image, the beat. That's how you're going to understand who he is. In the music he listens to.'

Faye looked down at the Dyson, his bag of tools and wondered how this thoughtful and analytical man had ended up doing a physical, menial job.

It was as if he had read her mind.

'I could have gone to university but cannabis really messed me up. I got into it at 14 and it took a few years to come out of it. I wasted the most critical time of my life.' He opened up.

He pointed to the poster of Walter White from Breaking Bad. 'Crystal meth... It's nasty stuff. You don't come out at the end. It's end game.' He looked at Faye. 'If that's what he's into - then it's very bad news. If you look at the images of guys that have taken that they look emaciated.'

They both stood looking at the posters in silence for a moment or two.

'It slowly kills.' He finally said. 'You're kids doing drugs. Be one step ahead, at all times and when you go to war take all the weapons with you.'

It was the statement again that she'd heard somewhere else. Faye had a helpless look on her face.

'Research. You need to know what you're up against. At the moment he knows more than you. You need to turn the situation around.'

And with that he turned his attention back to the hoover, dismantling parts, explaining what he was doing.

Faye was desperate to pull the conversation back. The hoover was an irrelevance; like a beer mat twirling on a pub table as two people conversed.

'The professionals don't do much.' She sighed, trying not to show any emotion. She didn't want to make a show of herself.

'They can only guide. *You're* his only hope.' He looked up at her; screw driver in hand. 'He's looking to *you* for help. You have two choices. You can give up or you can fight his cause.' Faye let the words gently filter; words which would resonate for many months to come. But it didn't feel as if Tim was looking to her for help. Outwardly he was looking to friends, a youth culture, a music culture. But inside maybe something different was happening. A boy lost in a haze of hormones, identity issues, struggling for security in a world that presented so many challenges and maybe struggling within his own family for recognition and love; the oldest need of all. And this was where Faye was failing. She couldn't be both parents, yet had to be. If he had problems she also had problems. She was trying to identify what his problems were and put them right but he wasn't trying to work out what her problems were for it didn't work like that. The child parent relationship was an unequal one; had always been. The child attacked the adult for everything they said and did, sapping their energy, reducing them to tears, making them question themselves and their role as parent and all in the name of unconditional love.

Faye didn't have a faith but all at once she found herself visualizing Mary at the cross watching Jesus die; the ultimate pain and sacrifice any mother had endured and from Mary down - every mother had experienced some degree of pain and anguish to varying degrees. For the first time she could understand why Catholics revered Mary so much.

'Looking back what do you think your parents should have done differently?' She asked the man as she watched him pulling fluff from the hoover head.

'There were lots of arguments. Bad arguments. They didn't understand. They should have diverted me to other friends and got together with the other parents. Your lad will be in a group who are all taking it. Work out a joint strategy. Pull them apart from within. Don't tell him he can't see them anymore. That's the worst thing you can do. I wanted my parents to praise me more and encourage me take up some new interests. Or maybe that's what I would have wanted them to do– in hindsight. Hindsight is a wonderful thing isn't it?' He smiled.

Faye was listening, taking it all in but feeling the huge weight of the task he was setting.

'He needs a man in his life. All boys need a man. A man that's going to understand what he's going through.' He looked around and Faye knew he had guessed she was a single mother.

'Unfortunately his dad died when he was five years old.'
'Sorry to hear that.'
'Oh God we all carry shit from the past.' She sighed.
'We carry it for as long as we want to carry it. It's easy to blame the things that have happened to us but at some point we have to take responsibility; take control of our lives.

And you know the scout leaders, the church leaders – they're all great, do a great job for kids – but they're labeled paedophile and one to one relationships with them are not encouraged and that's a great shame because many could help. A couple of years ago I watched a six year old girl fall to her death because I was wary of rushing to help for fear of being accused.'

This terrible story didn't hit Faye until later as she went over everything he had said. For now all she wanted was answers, for herself, for Tim.

The conversation paused, turned back to the hoover as he showed her how the new head worked and she agreed to buy one.

He started to gather his tools, putting them back into the bag. He got up from the floor, pulling his jeans back up to his waist and she followed him downstairs where he pulled out some paper work to sign. Faye didn't want him to go, but he had work to do. She couldn't suggest a coffee, a longer chat.

'Ring the army.' He suddenly suggested when she passed the pen back. 'Don't suggest to him he could join the TA but *they* could help. An army officer demonstrating the role he does might inspire him.' The man suggested. What a good idea Faye thought to herself. Years ago as a younger boy Tim had shown an interest in the army - watching soldiers in Iraq on TV. It was definitely an idea she could pursue. This man's visit had been more worthwhile than any of the appointments with professionals.

'Also speak to his Chemistry teacher. Get him on board. Maybe he could inspire in some way. He could have a great career in chemistry.' These were all great ideas, made a lot of sense but it wasn't going to be easy. Despite Tim's plan to make a class A drug he wasn't interested in Chemistry lessons at school. Maybe the teaching wasn't inspiring, maybe everything was very regimented, following the rigid structure of the National Curriculum the teachers had to tick boxes and in ticking those boxes he'd maybe lost the ability to inspire. But Faye was stabbing in the dark. She didn't know. All she was doing was drawing her own conclusions.

'He probably feels worthless but give him the odd *well done;* don't go overboard because he'll see through that and think *fuck off.* Let him come to you. Always have an open door policy. Don't force conversations.'

Again he had read her mind.

'All the best counseling is through silence – that's how you break people. Take him to Cliveden, for a walk round the gardens. But don't speak – let him talk and he *will* eventually because he'll have to ask *where are we going? Why are we here?* Have you seen the film Good Will Hunting? Watch it. You'll see how it's done.'

The man was making it sound easy; formulaic and prescriptive but the leaden weight was descending as her head spun a yarn of excuses and reasons that she knew would paralyse her in the mission to help Tim.

As she opened the door to this man; a guardian angel sent to help she asked him something she hadn't planned to ask. But the words had escaped and there was no pulling them back. Embarrassment thickened, her face a shade of beetroot.

'Would you come round and speak to him? Tell him about your experience of cannabis?' But then she tried to gather the words up in a string of apologies. He smiled. Looked towards the ceiling as he considered the question.

'I don't know how it would look.' He frowned. Mild amusement in his eyes.

More apologies from Faye.

'Yes. Yes I will.' Then he looked at her straight, the amusement in his eyes replaced by the gravity of the situation and how he could help.

Faye wanted to pin him to a day, a time but he said he'd call later in the week. She feared he'd forget.

As she said goodbye she made up her mind that it was time to confront Darius; the man who she believed - through his own depression and attempt on his own life while she had lived with him - had planted Tim's suicidal thoughts in his mind. It certainly seemed to be that way.

22
Faye

October 2014

Her heart was already racing as she gathered her bag, keys, headed for the car. Maybe it was through fear; not knowing how he would be after so long; or maybe it was the anticipation, the excitement of seeing him again. She waved the latter away, chastising herself for the thought.

It had been three years since she'd last seen Darius. She wondered if there was someone new in his life. Faye thought about all the pain in Darius' life, cascading from childhood: the abuse he had suffered at the hands of a priest, growing up in Liverpool and how this had impacted upon their sexual relationship. Their lives had moved on. Yet the past was now calling and she was ignoring the warning bell in her head telling her to forget the past for the past had nothing new to say. Yet it was colliding with the present and she was stuck in a labyrinth that involved the past. Her worries about Tim concerned the time they had lived with Darius. And so she decided, perhaps against her better judgment to contact him, to arrange to meet for a chat to discuss something important. It would have been all too easy to tell him over the phone and that would have ended the conversation in under a minute. He would have said *what the fuck has this got to do with me?* and *Faye we've been over a long time I'm trying to get on with my life.* She didn't want to admit to herself that she wanted to see him. She couldn't believe that she was actually thinking, feeling this way; especially after the way he had treated her and her kids all that time ago. She knew she was looking at the past through crystal glasses, remembering only the sparkles and everything that had been good.

The arguments with Darius now paled into insignificance as she remembered his deep blue eyes and the creases around his eyes as he laughed. She could hear his voice and the Scouse lilt that had never quite disappeared in all the time he had lived in the South. In her lonely moments at night when she woke worrying about Tim she imagined his big hand on her breast, his breath at her neck and she warmed at the thought of him wrapping his arms around her, nestling into his chest and looking up to his face for security and love.

Since their parting there had been fleeting relationships, none had taken off. There had been a mixed bag of odds and sods: 'laundry man;' so named because they'd met in the launderette. He'd lived in a converted lorry, which he parked up in various different places and he washed at the local leisure centre. Then there was 'salad bowl man' who had a fetish for bright green frilly, silky knickers and insisted she wear a whole salad bowl of coloured undies: carrot orange bras, tomato leaf nipple tassles and red onion socks. He'd raided La Senza during a three for two offer on emerald green knickers. Her pudenda had resembled an Iceberg lettuce. But that was the aim. He'd wanted to devour the crispness of her fanny in one big bite. Then there was 'sock man' who had to remove one of her socks at the end of each date, taking it as a gift to add to his collection. She later found out he liked to wank inside women's socks. And top of the pile – quite literally – had been 'Tip Man' who worked at the local amenity tip, pouncing on her one day offering to help her unload her car. Friends had warned her not to go on a date. He'll only *dump* you. It could be a *rubbish* date. He'll treat you like *trash*. Bet he won't *tip* the waiter. You could end up *tipsy* on a date with him. Bet he likes a *tipple*. The jokes went on. But after two dates she *dumped* him.

She'd found fault with each man. Again and again her thoughts returned to Darius. Despite his nasty streak he was irreplaceable; one of a kind. She loved the way he could weave words, the way he could inspire. He was knowledgeable on so many different areas of life but most of all she missed his dark humour. Her friends would have dismissed her feelings if she'd told them, telling her to move on; there were so many other nice men out there. But she hadn't met any.

As Faye drove over to Slough she thought of all the emotions Maria, his mother would have experienced in losing Kathleen and longing for her return. And for the first time she knew just how she would have felt. *Every family has one. A fallen one. A black sheep.* Maria, Darius and Kathleen's mother had told her once. She'd never understood the concept until now; until everything that had happened with Tim. But now she felt Maria's pain as if it were her own; the crushing weight of what it must have been like to discover her 14 year old daughter pregnant, not knowing who'd made your daughter pregnant; always wondering, speculating and fearing the worse. And trying to reconcile all the conflicting emotions; fear for her daughter's future, a future ruined, the love for her daughter, wanting to protect, to guide, to be there for her but all the time fighting her faith and what she believed God wanted her to do. No mother will ever be free, Faye told herself. Free of the pain, free of the responsibility of motherhood. And every mother, she believed, experienced their child's pain as if it were their own, sharp, tangible and raw. Maria had felt Kathleen's pain; even years later, just as she, Faye was experiencing Tim's pain now even though she couldn't see what was going on in his head. The pain of motherhood went back to the folds of soft flesh, the downy scalp, the sweet milky smell, the warmth of holding their babies for the first time.

That first memory never went away. It lived with you as motherhood progressed and in the darkest hours when the challenges were greatest it was a memory every mother returned to. That was just how motherhood was. Nothing would, could change. It was a state of mind, a bond that could never be broken.

Maria hadn't really meant for Kathleen to toughen up; face a cruel and heartless world. It had been her religion speaking within her, but not her soul. The Church had been her guiding light, her golden parachute. But as the years had gone on the grip of the Church had lessened; the lessons softer with time. Faye felt sure of that even though she'd never asked Maria how she felt.

With all of these thoughts and wondering if Maria was still alive Faye walked into Sid's Bakers where they had arranged to meet. She was half an hour early, headed straight up the aisle to the toilet with nervous tummy cramps, weaving between prams, Iceland shopping bags and zimmer frames. Several women in baggy tracky bottoms and cheap clumpy trainers were stuffing their faces with sugary doughnuts, wiping the remains from their cheeks with their grubby sleeves. Her stomach heaved. There was nothing in this bakery that was remotely fresh and colourful or anything that crunched; apart from the hard corners of a Cornish pasty under foot.

As she opened the toilet door she suddenly remembered a quote from Jacque Chirac, the former French President commenting at the G8 summit several years back: *one cannot trust people whose cuisine is so bad. After Finland Britain is the country with the worst food.*

She checked her watch, took a cold vinyl seat at the back, nerves jangling. His office, next to a big warehouse was a short walk away. While she waited she took out some paper and penned Katie a quick letter.

Dear Katie,

I must be mad. I'm meeting Darius for coffee. You met him once. You got on well, I seem to remember. But sometime after that you and I drifted apart. I don't know what I said, what I did to you. It was probably nothing. I hope Darius hadn't offended you.

You were like it with everyone. Nobody knew where they stood with you. Everyone expect Tim. You never gave up on him. I'm glad you didn't even though you gave up on me. He liked spending time at your house. I'm grateful. Really, I am.

You were hard to understand at times Katie. One minute you were flamboyant, fun and the best company ever, welcoming us all round for Earl Grey and tea cakes on a fine bone china cake stand and then it was all change; like Mary Poppins when the wind changed... and you'd spend weeks sitting in your house with the curtains drawn, avoiding the phone, not returning messages, only leaving the house to do the school run, in pajamas and dark sunglasses, whatever the time of year. You were like a celebrity ducking from the paparazzi waiting at the bottom of your drive with their long -range cameras. But you were hiding from us, your friends and everyone else you knew. In truth you didn't need to drive Ed to school. The school was only a two minute walk away. Ed wanted to walk for goodness sake. That boy had no exercise. You ferried him everywhere. Then you had a go at me because I allowed Tim to walk home alone. You can't molly coddle kids forever. You could have stayed in bed all day like Howard Hughes, the wealthy American recluse did and let Ed have his freedom.

Shit. I can see Darius in the distance. He looks slimmer. His jeans seem to fit better. I'll keep you posted.

Love Faye.

⁓

Faye pretended she hadn't seen Darius walk through the entrance. Suddenly she was aware of his shadow casting over her table. Her head was bent low as she folded the letter to Katie and put it in an envelope. She looked up, fear making her heart leap to her mouth.

Every Family Has One

'Alright?' His voice was flat. A small smile tried to light his face but it was a smile with reticence behind it. He didn't want to be there. His face and the pain etched through every line and crease around his eyes and mouth were those of the actor Bill Nighy. He was still wearing the Donald Trump wig; still too afraid or vain to reveal the truth underneath. He was a marked man: a man who had been abused at the hands of his schizophrenic wife, viciously wielding a metal coathanger leaving him with a pattern of scars across his head rather like Harry Potter's scar but much worse. Faye shuddered as she remembered his story. The soft shades of his grey wig glinted under the harshness of the spotlights above.

The familiar creak of his heavy black leather jacket as he took it off made her regret all at once having come.

'You?' She weakly offered in response. The tension was building in her neck. She stretched an arm round to rub it. Where to begin?

'Let's cut to the chase Faye. What's this about? You said it was important.' His brusque question cut through. His eyes, normally a warming blue had turned to cold pewter. He was out of breath and flushed.

Before she'd had a chance to hesitate she tumbled everything out, from start to finish. As she spoke, in fits and starts, nerves getting the better of her there was a stomach lurching feeling of vertigo. Her head was screaming *this is wrong. I shouldn't be here.*

When she finished they faced each other in limbo. His eyes narrowed and with one hand he pulled his face, as if kneading the tension, gave a heavy sigh that told her he really didn't need to hear all this. He didn't speak; got up to get a coffee, returned five minutes later.

'Jesus, Mary and Joseph.' The words, although predictable, came without warning - sudden and forceful. She flinched.

'Exactly.' She said.

'Our relationship Faye was like a leg that got gangrenous. We had to be severed. Now *what* do you want from me?' His eyes were cold.

189

'I don't know. Sorry. I thought I knew. There's no one to talk to.' A vision of Katie flitted before her eyes. Tears pricked. Embarrassed, she fought them, didn't want him to see her reduced to this sorry state.

'I thought maybe you'd understand. Suicide. Your half attempt, remember?' She continued. It was the big 'S' word. The ultimate stopper of conversations and she hadn't intended to use it but it was out, big and brash before them. It had become a word that she used only in her head and saying it now made her reassess everything that was going on with Tim. This was serious stuff. A real game changer.

'Well you've got to do something Faye.' And now he was doing what every man had ever done throughout her life. He was dictating, telling her off, making the assumption that she wasn't already doing something.

'Get him counseling. You have to. I know you're a tight bitch and don't like spending money. But this is your son. You have to get him help.'

He had turned her water works on. Big blobs were forming. She sniffed them back. Took a napkin, blotted her eyes.

'That's easy for you to say. I don't earn much.' She whimpered.

'Oh so that's what this is about.' His voice had risen, as he sang the words. Heads were turning to look.

'Attach the blame to me because the kid happens to have some sicko Face Book page devoted to *Darius the hero* then pull the emotional blackmail cord. I'm not falling for it so you can go fuck yourself.' He spat.

Faye pushed her chair back, now starting to shake, a mortified look across her face as she stifled the gulps forming in her throat. He wasn't going to do this to her.

As she stood up, inching to the side of the table to leave he suddenly grabbed her arm, tightening his grip. As she looked down she caught the fear that radiated from the tiny spider tattoo on his neck. She remembered him saying on their first date that is served as a warning to all not to mess with him. *Make an enemy of me,* he'd said. *And you'll never forget.*

'Sit.' He ordered like the Gestapo.

They didn't speak. She hovered on the edge of the seat, ready to escape. His hand was still gripping her arm, like a parent stopping a child from running into the road. The expression on his face had softened. His eyes looked a shade warmer; almost cornflower blue. Even the Bill Nighy creases around his mouth were beginning to soften.

His hand loosened its' grip. And then the next thing he did took her by complete surprise.

He reached out and covered her hands with his, like a dog placing its' paws on its' master's knees. All at once she felt the warmth, the familiarity and the security of his large hands. His touch burned through her like electricity. This was her first human contact in a while. She tried to bury her emotions, starting to bubble under the surface. She longed for a hug.

'You're like an abused dog that keeps returning.' An amused grin played on his lips.

'It's not like that.' She said, affronted. Then tried to prise her hands from under his.

'Isn't it?' He asked. Her words were the touch paper that lit the amusement in his eyes.

'Our lives have moved on.' She tried to sound cold. It wouldn't pay to melt in front of him.

'Really? Is that so? Tell me you don't miss me Faye.' He challenged.

Again she tried to prise her hands away. But the grip tightened. His eyes looked hypnotic. A bedroom look she recognized was creeping across his face.

She looked beyond him, bristling, refusing to meet his doe eyes.

'I thought as much.' He laughed, lifted his hand to pull her chin towards him. 'Of course you miss me.' He chuckled, looked victorious.

A flicker of a smile passed over her face as she began to relax. She found herself imagining plucking the wiry runaway hairs shooting from his nostrils, like weeds through a crack in a pavement. She stole a glance to the opening in his black shirt, enticing grey strands escaping. Briefly she imagined unbuttoning his shirt and feeling the warmth of his chest, then snapped her mind back.

'Maybe I do think of you. From time to time. But let's not be deluded and go re writing history in our heads. We were like a piece of chewing gum that kept stretching and stretching and eventually it stretched too far.' She sat up on the lino seat trying to regain her resolve not to get sucked into anything.

For a time their hands remained locks as they bowed their heads and stared at the flock vinyl tablecloth with its' faint smear of ketchup and coffee ring marks. She savoured the moment; the warmth of his hands, the physical connection and the empathy of another human being.

'Maybe we could have rolled it back into a putty and put it back into our mouths.' It was more a question than a statement.

'Nah. I don't think we could have done. You didn't like my kids.'

'They didn't like me.' Came his limp answer.

Here they were again, several years later on trampled ground. It was a cul-de-sac conversation she knew well.

'You on your own? Still enjoying the imprisonment of single motherdom?' He asked with sarcasm.

'Yeah. And you?'

'I'm a clapped out Morris Minor. In any case women are all takers. They treat me like a piggy bank. You lot were Greece. I was Germany. And I'd had enough. Who'd have me anyway?'

And in her head she found herself screaming *me. I'd have you.* But the voice was slayed in an instant, didn't see the light of day as logic took control. She had moved on. Made a life for herself. Was stronger without him.

'You still renting or did you manage to buy a house in the end?' She asked.

The waitress was busy behind them, folding napkins. Clean cutlery clattered into pots.

'That part of my life has worked out as it happens. 'Dough News' was bought out by a large firm in Vancouver. It made a lot of sense. We're now working for them. There are ten of us. I'm the boss. And I got a huge pay out from Vancouver. Stroke of luck... my former marital home in Nettlebed was on the market so I bought it back. I'm back where I belong, minus that bitch that ruined me.'

Faye winced at the reference to his ex wife.

'Wow. So you've got a swimming pool, tennis court and the rolling hills of the Chilterns on your back door. Bet Sam is chuffed to bits.'

'Yeah he can bring all his cocaine sniffing poofter friends over.'

'At some point you need to accept he's gay.' Faye said.

'I do. Mainly. But it's kind of hard to accept when you've got childhood memories of a kiddy fiddly priest, so it is. It doesn't sit easy with me. Makes me feel defensive. I still have a pop about it. But maybe less these days.'

He began to play with her fingers, making a cat's cradle and she didn't pull them away, enjoying the attention.

'What happened about Kathleen? How's your mum?'

'Oh God Faye it's been so long. So much has happened. I miss you. You silly cow.' He looked at her wide eyed and this time their eyes connected and held for a few moments and she knew without a shadow of a doubt that she missed him, longed for him and slowly that iron resolve that she thought wouldn't let her down was beginning to fracture.

'Let's go for a walk. There's nowhere to walk to. It's a shitty area but it's a nice day for a walk.' She suggested, gathering her bag.

⁂

Soon they were walking along the pavement past an ugly 1950s office block with blue paneling and a warehouse with corrugated roofing. A lorry thundered by. Somewhere in this locality she remembered that the scenes featured in the opening sequences in David Brent's 'The Office' TV series were filmed here. In the distance two industrial chimneys marked the power station. Faye inwardly groaned at how ugly it all was and smiled with the thought of John Betjeman writing his poem 'Come friendly bombs and fall on Slough it isn't fit for humans now!' She wondered how Darius coped with this daily miserable scene, especially when the clouds were grey above.

They walked a fair distance, past several car parks, eventually finding a verge of green by a wall to sit on. Partly from the chill air, partly because it felt natural she huddled in and before long he had his arm around her to keep her warm as he reminded her that he *had* found Kathleen through appearing on an audience participation TV show in Dublin about finding missing families and Kathleen had written to them, via his mother's solicitors but hadn't wanted to meet. He had never found out why she wouldn't meet but soon after that his mother had died, never having had the chance to tell her daughter how sorry she was. After her death the estate had gone to Kathleen. His mother Maria had changed her will, out of guilt Darius suspected. He could understand. It was her redress for everything that had happened. She couldn't take away the pain that Kathleen had experienced, the terrible life she must have had in the Magdalene laundry but she could pass on the gift of inheritance. Money didn't make up for sadness but it went a long way.

'I refused to be a vulture circling round over the Serengeti,' he said. 'It was a parting gift to express the love she wished she had been able to show Kathleen.' The change of will didn't seem to bother Darius. Faye was surprised. He'd made a packet through the sale of the business, still keeping his job as manager and had, in his words come up smelling of roses.

They sat in silence for a few moments. His hand rested on her leg and she was rubbing his hand.

'I feel sad you didn't have the Gatwick style reunion with Kathleen. I always imagined that. A happy ending. It's what we all want.' Faye smiled.

'Ah Faye.' He looked at her. Their faces were inches apart, lips drawing closer. They hovered there for a while.

'You thought you were getting Mr. Darcy but what you got was Mr. Fucking Arsey.' Their eyes locked. He took a strand of her hair entwining it with one finger and a tenderness seemed to pass over him.

'Mr. Arsey; bad tempered who could bring you down like a lift but the highs were like a bad drug. What you need is a substitute dad for those kids. A man to sort Tim out. Put him on the right road. But don't look at me because you're looking at a dying man. I wasn't the right spec' for you. I'm not up to much these days Faye. My hemorrhoids are bigger than my balls. We were the Eurozone in crisis and the currency of sex held no value.' He said.

Maybe she was misinterpreting his gestures. Her heart dropped.

'I didn't come here looking to rejuvenate things. I told you that.' Faye felt affronted -not for the first time - then wondered how he was enjoying his swimming pool and tennis court alone. It didn't seem much of a life.

'Every family has a fallen one. In your family I sensed that would be Tim. It was something about the kid. He was a shadow around everyone else's life. Silence is dangerous. More dangerous than a kid that shouts and screams. But while he's falling there's someone to help him back up, show him the way. And that's you. He needs your hand to guide him to stop him falling further. Nobody needs to falls to the ground. Not if they have someone who loves them. Maybe that's through counseling, maybe through a new interest or a part time job. Have you... told him you love him? He needs to hear it Faye.'

'You know I can't. I just can't.' Faye snapped. She was sick of everyone telling her that she was Tim's only hope. She felt crushed from all directions, Tim's problems weighing on her shoulders.

'It's weird not to. I don't understand you. How can you *not* tell your children you love them?' He wanted to know.

'He's too old to be told that. I shouldn't need to tell him. It's a given.' She explained.

'How can you say that?' He asked.

They looked down at their hands, tightly clasped and although she knew his hand was only there for a short while she felt it's warmth, it's strength. She wished there was a hand for her; somebody to carry her across the hot coals.

'That's why we have hands. To help others. Don't give up on him. He needs his mum. We all do. Even my mum, despite her pious ways putting God first hadn't quite given up on Kathleen, despite the intervening years.' He said comparing Kathleen's plight with Tim's.

'This doesn't sound like the Darius I used to know. What's happened to you? There's a calmness about you that was never there before.' She smiled, studying his face for the answer.

'Oh I don't know. Maybe it's age. Wisdom. I've fought too many battles Faye. I can't keep fighting. Hands fight too of course. And they abuse.' He looked up and away to the clouds, pain again etched across his face.

'I'm surprised you didn't think of bringing that priest to justice. Especially in the wake of the Jimmy Saville scandal and Operation Yewtree. You were always a very litigious person.' She said.

'I've been in therapy actually. I didn't want to go on some poxy *healing journey*. That's what they call it. It was all a bit Freudian. We were taught to befriend the shadow. Spooky ah? But it helped Faye. I can no longer knock the work of therapists. For so long the abuse defined who I was. I was building my life on the influence of the abuse and it was slowly dragging me down. I couldn't let it drag me down anymore. I made three attempts on my life. All cries for help, in hindsight. I can't forgive that bastard but I can accept that it's happened and I can either let it destroy me or live and go on. Tennis has helped. And in terms of getting me fit again. The physical action of swiping the hand and hitting the ball is very therapeutic. You see it's the hand again. The hand is an abuser, a healer, a helper, a fighter. It's all things to all men.'

They sat for a moment in their own thoughts, the silence between them comforting rather than awkward. She looked at his stomach. He was certainly a lot trimmer. The exercise was doing him good. He had changed. She wondered if he thought she had changed too but didn't ask, fearing a negative answer.

Then he asked what she was up to, workwise. She took a deep breath. She'd been waiting for that question, didn't relish having to answer it.

'You don't wanna know. Believe me.'

'Go on...'

'I'm an operative at the recycling plant, sorting rubbish. There. You did ask. And yes it is horrible. Hot, noisy and working at great speed. Oh and minimum wage. She stared at the tarmac, heart in mouth, dreading the harsh words that were sure to follow.

'F-u-c-k-i-n-g hell. You have got to be joking. But you've got a degree in English. What the hell's wrong with you? You're dragging those kids down. No wonder this has happened to Tim. Why do you always sink to the lowest common denominator Faye? Why?' His ranting went on. The expletives were tumbling like the rubbish she was used to seeing night after night at the factory. Chimneys spewed smoke and Darius spewed expletives. He was ahead of her now, his hands raised, clasped on top of his head.

'I was doing private tuition for kids but I couldn't find enough work. That was on top of working for a flaming care agency that should have been struck off. We weren't paid for travelling between each client which meant we were actually earning below the minimum wage. One old lady fell over and I had to call an ambulance. I rang the office to tell the agency I would be late for the next appointment and they told me to leave her door open for the ambulance crew and to go to my next appointment. Do you think I enjoyed doing that? It was shocking Darius.' She shouted at him as the memory still angered her.

'Oh don't give me that. There's plenty of work about.'

'Really. That's not what you used to say. You used to blame immigrants for the lack of work.' Faye tutted, looking away.

He stopped. Turned to face her. Grabbed her shoulders.

'What the fuck are you doing?' He screamed in her face.

'Now that's more like the Darius I remember.' She laughed sarcastically.

'Did you report that care agency to the Care Quality Commission? I hope you did.' He spat, alarm coursing through his features.

'How could I? I needed the job. Did you ever report the priest that molested you when you were young?' She challenged him.

'That was different. I couldn't re-live the experience. Faye...come and work for me.' His words were impulsive. His arms flew in the air.

'Wha'?'

'You heard.'

'I'd be crap in your office. I don't have experience. I can't. You're an ex. We'd clash.'

'Oh well, suit yourself. The offer's there if you want it. But it would be nice to see you again. For a drink, a meal maybe?'

This was the last thing Faye had expected – the suggestion of a date. She didn't know what to say. Maybe she would meet him again. What did she have to lose after all?

⸙

They began to walk back towards her car, laughing against the strength of the wind that had suddenly picked up, battering against them as they shared snippets from their lives. Passing an alleyway between two buildings Darius tugged on her arm, pulled her out of the wind, pinning her against the damp wall, sending an old bike clattering to the ground and a coke can spinning along the tarmac. He turned to her. For a moment they just looked at each other, out of breath, inches apart, studying each other's faces. And then her hands were pressing his back pulling him towards her frantically; the familiar and reassuring heady mix of his woody scent, the creak of his leather jacket and coffee breath sending shock waves across her body. The terrible visions of all the awful men she'd dated over the past few years melted away as she sought the reassurance of his warm arms and everything he could offer her.

'We could have a Quadrophenia moment.' He whispered seductively.

'Here in Slough? On an industrial estate. I don't think so.' She laughed.

She had never seen his murky blue eyes so soft, sketching every inch of her face with longing. The corner of his mouth curled into a faint smile and in that moment she knew he had never stopped loving her and she had never stopped loving him. She felt intoxicated and light on her feet as she reached to grab his neck planting furious kisses on his lips. The past had vanished, swept away in the moment and the future was yet to come as waves of suppressed love ripped through her, sending her senses spiraling. And in her heady state the problems at home melted away in the moment and she knew that what she needed, in the midst of all that was going on at home was intimacy with another human being but a relationship with Darius would be toxic.

23
Faye

November 2014

Faye was sitting opposite Darius in the Cafe Nero in Slough. It was a week later. He'd suggested a coffee.

The hot lights above, warm as incubator lights spread like a circuit board across the ceiling dazzling Faye's eyes. The cafe was noisier than a turkey farm. Babies screaming, toddlers kicking off, the clatter of cutlery, tinkle of cups and a giant coffee machine whirling, spluttering and hissing like a steam engine from a former age. Not a great choice for a meet up Darius commented, but convenient.

It was now four years on from when they had parted. He had talked a lot about retiring, or wanting to retire and she was surprised he was still working, especially given that he had sold the business on, managing to buy the Nettlebed home with money left over. But a part of her wasn't surprised. She always imagined he would be one of those 'work till you drop' types that talked and talked about retirement, but not having the courage to make that final break. But four years was a long time and in the wider society politicians were now talking about the death of retirement and how the next generation would be working well beyond 65, making use of those 'autumn' years but fundamentally it was about cutting back on state pensions in the age of austerity. She dreaded the thought of another Conservative Government, dragging them all further down with more cutbacks. The election wasn't far off.

They were quiet for a while and Faye's mind wandered to the General Election wondering who would be in power after May. Her hot topic was drugs and protecting the country's youth from the growing drug problem that Britain seemed to have. Decriminalisation wasn't the answer for her, but neither was convicting everyone. The key it seemed was to tackle things higher up the ladder but also to crack down on legal highs, a growing issue. Thankfully she didn't think Tim had dabbled in legal highs but this was an area of drug use that scared her.

She found herself fleetingly thinking about Tim's pizza ridden face and his battle with acne and wondered, not for the first time whether the acne drug was a contributory factor to his low moods.

'How are things at home?' He asked.

'Not great. It's so difficult when it comes to money. Tim needs money to go out but how can I trust that he won't spend it on drugs or fags. And if I don't give him any he could get into debt with dealers. I expect they give it free to school kids as a sweetener, to build up their customer base but getting into debt with a dealer isn't a great idea and my biggest fear is the dealer offering him other things. Like heroin.' Faye shuddered, her thoughts now miles away.

'He needs to get a Saturday job but yes the danger is more money in his pocket more drugs and fags.' Darius replied, understanding the issues she was facing.

'Quite.' Faye said. It was a catch twenty two situation. 'I want to find out who his dealer is. I want to confront him.'

'Don't play with fire. You might make things worse for Tim. Even dangerous.'

Faye hadn't thought of that but she still felt determined to find out who was selling her son drugs.

24
Faye

December 2014

Faye couldn't sleep. She glanced at her bedside clock. It was past midnight. The house was quiet. She glanced out onto the landing. Tim's light was still on. A rectangle of yellow fringed the door frame. She yawned. Her sheets, pillows beckoned. A hot water bottle gently warmed the bed. She had had enough of Tim sneaking out at nighttime. She wanted to see where he went and if he met anyone. Her curiosity was mounting.

She waited, now dressed, sitting on the side of her bed in dark coat and shoes, keys in pocket. Maybe he wouldn't go out tonight, maybe this was a waste of time, she thought to herself but if he did she was ready to follow, fired up, needed answers and needed to understand the process of what was happening. She had to find out who was supplying him. Anger burned dangerously inside her, like a towering inferno that couldn't be extinguished. She wouldn't rest until she'd confronted this nasty man that preyed on kids. And she didn't feel scared; jungle strength grew inside cushioning her fear.

Faye held back shrinking from the beam of street lighting. Most of the houses along Adastra Avenue were fringed with a variety of tall, unruly hedges, trees and walls, perfect for hiding behind. Faye dodged her way along the street between each bush and hedge careful not to be seen. At first she felt sheepish but as they came to the end of the road a wide bridge went over a steep railway embankment, flanked on both sides by a high wire mesh and barbed wire. The bridge led into a dark wood. Suddenly Faye was consumed by a deep sense of fear and unease. Tim however seemed to possess no fear, striding on in confidence, his trainers squelching in the sodden brown leaves that had fallen with the first storm of early December. She wanted to call out to him, the vulnerable son who to her was still a small child, drag him back to safety, guide him home. But part of her also wanted to lift him up and hand him away to a fairy godmother whose sole purpose was to make things right, to bring him back as he was before: the son who always had filthy finger nails and messy hair, who wiped his nose with the back of his hand and stowed Wagon Wheels under the bed. It was as if he were possessed, in a trance, heading onward into a world that seemed mystical and forbidden, knowing the dangers but unwilling to stop. For the first time in motherhood she didn't have the skills to help him face this cruel world or to bring him back.

He was her baby, trailing in his own unique and curious scent and yet he was the map that she had created. He was a piece of herself now separate and apart like a piece of flesh dangling in the mouth after drinking a hot drink. It had happened. The separation was complete and she had no idea how she was going to pull him back.

He stopped under a street lamp, a pool of orange illuminating his lanky physique. A train thundered under the bridge, sending tremours across the tarmac. From behind a tree she watched, her nails clawing into the bark in frustration, as a man approached from within the depths of the wood, pulling something from his pocket in exchange for money. *Goddam it where did you get that money?* She wanted to scream out. But she knew the answer because earlier on Chrissie had said money had gone missing once again from her ballerina jewellery box. She remained crouched, crumpling inside, her cheeks burning, her heart in her throat.

She jolted, shivering frantically. Shock swept across her body as she suddenly realized who this man was. She recognized his picture. Had met him. Slowly the pieces of the puzzle were slotting into place. Even in the half - light she could see the face of the man who didn't care. So his life had gone off course? He'd turned to drugs, then ended up dealing, she guessed. Part of her felt pleased that his life hadn't worked out. He deserved all he got but had got off scott free.

It all seemed so unfair. *You get off the hook for the crime you committed and now you're seeking to ruin my son's life? Bastard* hissed Faye into the night air.

Tim was just another punter. Fresh meat. His health, his future meant nothing to him. Life was cheap. In all probability this man had a hard exterior, didn't feel the pain he was causing. He'd learned to toughen up in order to play the game. This was about survival of the fittest in a town that probably had many dealers all in competition, protecting their patch, encroaching on other patches.

Anger burned like a funeral pyre. She backed up into the bushes, pressing her body against a wall, then crept away before there was a chance they would discover her, crouched in the shadows and as she did so she was determined, fired up inside. She would confront this evil man. Why should she, mother of a vulnerable boy stand by and accept her son's fate? Especially after what he had done several years ago.

But before she confronted him she needed to know where he lived. She had an idea that he lived along Canada Drive, at the back of the Seven to Eleven but it was a long road and maybe, since the accident he had moved. But she knew of somebody who could help in her search. A friend she hadn't seen in a while.

25
Faye

January 2015

Canada Drive was one of those roads with a 'reputation.' Every town had one; the road where trouble happened: fights after pub chuck out, brawls between neighbours and domestics late at night; the occasional ambulance drawing up. Kids played on bicycles in the street, weaving between parked cars, often knocking off wing mirrors. Police cars did random drive bys.

Faye had known Rhea when they had both lived in a nearby town years ago and Faye had only recently discovered Rhea living nearby and they had become friends again. Rhea existed on the periphery of Faye's friendship circle and had only recently moved to Canada Drive. Rhea didn't know everything about Faye's past and didn't know about Katie for example.

At one point they had seen each other every weekend, following a visit to Slough psychic festival where they had met an old Gypsy Lee who told them they were going to meet a man by some water. Following this palm reading they went to the sea, they picnicked by the Thames, they looked for reservoirs, lakes and finally stood in a puddle but not a single suitor appeared.

Faye didn't like visiting Rhea. It was easier to meet in Costa or Nero. She worried about parking her car, returning to a key scratch along the side. But for many people Canada Drive meant a happy community; some families had lived there for many years and never experienced trouble, said the houses were 'good and solid', built to last and with lovely long gardens; the only downside to the houses being the bathrooms, located next to the kitchens.

As soon as the friends greeted Faye sensed that there was a new man in Rhea's life. She looked more relaxed. Her face glowed. Faye hoped it wasn't another married man; was used to Rhea sleeping around with married men but her behaviour never ceased to shock. Rhea was like a flame licking over a dry piece of paper. There would be no smoke without fire. Every affair had ended in tears, then months of recovery and 'rehab.' Faye wondered why Rhea kept putting herself through the charade. She was beautiful and didn't need to steal women's husbands but it was useless telling her that.

They hugged and Faye breathed Rhea's familiar floral scent as Rhea headed for the kitchenette to crack open a Bulmer's Bold Cherry Black Cider.

'Drink?' She asked stretching for a glass.

'Nah. Can't stay long. I need your help with something.'

Rhea ignored Faye.

'Or just a tea?'

'Ok. Just a tea.' Faye wondered which chipped, stained mug she would be offered and braced herself for the first glug of cheap value tea.

Faye noticed dark circles around Rhea's eyes as she bent to sit in the dimly lit lounge. Her skin looked paler and pastier than normal as the light from the table lamp illuminated her face; a sure sign she'd had some recent late nights. She saw scratched flecks of dark in her eyes as they briefly met hers. Rhea picked the cat up and brushed its black hair from the settee then guided it towards the cat flap.

207

'You're seeing someone aren't you?' Faye nudged Rhea laughing.

'Is it that obvious?' Rhea lifted her mane of long ringlets to waft the cool around her neck and gave Faye a slow post coital sleepy smile, then a wide carefree yawn.

'Spill the beans then.' Faye checked the time on her watch.

'Well...he lives next door and yes he's married. But they don't get on. I hear them arguing all the time.'

'Nice catch. And right on your doorstep.' Faye tutted. 'Go on...'

'We were having a communal barbecue. We were the last ones in the garden, sharing a spliff, just chatting.'

'I thought you didn't touch that stuff anymore?' All that effort coming off.'

Rhea ignored her, swiped the back of her hand over her nose – her way of avoiding tricky subjects. Faye wanted to tell her to use a bloody hanky.

'It's hard sometimes to function without it. It explodes the brain. In the same way sex does. Makes me talk more. Gives me crazy random thoughts. It's like being without tea or coffee. The first puff of a joint, after abstinence is incredible. It's pretty harmless.'

Faye wondered whether she was trying to convince her or convince herself and remembered her saying a while back that when she was taking weed she felt like she was on the parameter of normal life; isolated, on the fringes, turning her inward gazing, Boyfriends, or men she slept with had become her suppliers. And it was convenient for the suppliers too; getting sex in return for a spliff. It was an unofficial loose arrangement that worked.

'I invited him up to finish the wine, the spliffs. I hadn't planned to sleep with him but it was amazing sex and now I want more.'

'Course you do.' Faye chuckled noticing Rhea's pupils growing larger with the memory.

Rhea held out a box of half eaten Lidl's marzipans even though she knew Faye hated them.

'I've got a picture of him.' Rhea was picking up her Samsung and scrolling through. Faye hoped it wasn't a naked shot. She took the phone, zoomed in, gasped, clapping her hand to her mouth and froze; cold tendrils weaving up her body.

'Wha'?' Do you know him?' Rhea leaned in.

'He's the reason I came round tonight. Shit. Greg Atkins.'

'No. His name's Jacko.'

'He must have changed his name. A new start. Something happened to him in the past. He needed to protect himself.'

'He's taking me to the Travelodge in Slough for a romantic night.'

'Nice. The Travelodge in Slough. I can't think of anywhere more romantic. You know how to pick 'em Rhea, for sure. Make sure he treats you to the buffet breakfast. Oh and you knows he sells drugs to kids I'm sure? He's selling to Tim. I saw them the other night.'

'No he wouldn't do that. He's a nice bloke. A few things happened to him in the past leading him into drug dealing but deep down he's ok.'

'You're not bloody listening to me Rhea. I saw him selling to Tim in the woods. It was him. Definitely him. Ok? That bastard...' Faye stabbed the phone. 'You're shag buddy is supplying my son.' Faye's voice was jumpy and disjointed as she tried to control her emotions.

'They do know each other, I expect. I've seen Tim and a couple of others from Rydon go into his flat to see his stepson - Darren. But he wouldn't supply to kids. He does have morals.' Rhea said casually, waving away her concern. 'So shall I go to the Travelodge? What if his wife finds out?' She asked trying to steer the conversation back to the Travel Lodge in Slough.

'To hell with the Travelodge. Darren?' Faye's mind was whirring. Darren, Darren. She was sure that Tim had mentioned that name before, in passing. Somebody in his class, or his tutor group, she wondered.

'Come on Faye. Get with it. Don't you know who your own son hangs out with?' Rhea mocked, as if reading Faye's mind.

'And did you know Jacko killed? He was driving.'

'No I didn't know that.'

'It was an accident. But nevertheless...'

A sickness swept over Faye as she recalled the fateful night several years back. She didn't want to tell Rhea who he had killed. She could still see the chilling picture of Greg Atkins in the local paper. Wondered why Rhea didn't know his face, although sometimes people forgot events with time. But for Faye the accident would be etched across her mind forever in the same way that the picture of Myra Hindley, the 1960s Moors Murderer was.

Faye's mind misted over. She couldn't think. The conversation buckled to silence and she made an excuse to go.

Faye sat on the settee for about ten minutes staring at the wall. All she could see was the headlines of the newspaper in her head and a picture of the bend in the road. A tree. The house. The full page spread. He was here. And had entered her son's life. One life ruined. He wasn't going to ruin another. Not her sons. She'd make sure of that. But with the revelation out in the open Faye knew, as clear as day what she had to do.

But before that opportunity came something else was soon to happen and things were about to take a turn for the worst for Tim.

26
Faye

January 2015

About to head off for work Faye felt the vibration of her phone in her pocket and pulling it out she saw it was the school.

'It's pretty serious this time Mrs. Denton. He's really put two fingers up to the establishment this time. You need to get over here. We're issuing a five day exclusion. He's very lucky it's not a permanent exclusion.' Mr. Richard's voice was brusque; the sympathy back in September gone.

Her head began to prick and thump. What could be more serious than the news they had broken back in September, Faye wondered.

At the back of her mind she had worked it out. But when she arrived at the school, ushered once more into Mr. Richard's office she could not possibly have guessed the enormity of what had actually happened or been prepared for the magnitude of embarrassment about to engulf her.

'I don't know whether you've heard what's been going on in all the schools across the town lately? We've had several boys at this school defecate on the floor in the boys' toilets.'

The wheel began to turn in Faye's head but the cogs weren't engaging.

'What's this got to do with Tim?'

He made steeples with his hands; his chin now resting on the cathedral of his fingers.

' This morning Tim defecated in the middle of the boys' changing area in the PE block.'

Time stood still, the smoke from this latest bombshell hung thick in the air as she struggled to process. And then doubt slithered into the picture.

'You must have the wrong boy.' But her words were weak.

'He was crouching in full view of the CCTV camera.' *Begging to be spotted.* Faye mentally finished his sentence, in disbelief.

A montage of images floated through her head of Tim when he was younger, in a desperate attempt to understand who or what he had become.

What on earth would Katie say? Was Faye's overriding thought.

Whatever she was about to say to Mr. Richards died on her lips as she gathered up the embarrassment and shame that she suspected Tim wasn't feeling. A series of questions scudded through her mind. Did he clear it up? What did he say? Did he laugh? Did he cry? What did the teachers say? But every question she had seemed irrelevant, trivial, and the truth was she wanted to close her eyes and pretend this wasn't happening.

'That's not all I'm afraid.' Mr. Richard's face was solemn. This was deja vu. He'd said something similar back in September. She braced herself.

'He was waving cannabis around in front of the camera. He's been very cooperative. He allowed us to search his bag. We found a small quantity and a grinder. Obviously if there had been a bigger quantity

Every Family Has One

and money on him this would indicate dealing. And dealing on school property...' He let the words trail into the air. Faye's mind hooked on the word *cooperative*.

'What now?'

'Take him home and bring him back in five days time. We will provide all the work he needs for the exclusion and then you will be required to attend a meeting at 8.15am on the day he returns. And during the entire exclusion he must be kept at home under supervision during school hours.'

'But all the work is on computer.'

'That shouldn't be a problem apart from 'My Maths.' We also took his phone away.' He slide the phone across the table and Faye put it into her bag determined that she was going to get the password from him, read his messages, find out other things that might be going on in his life.

∽∂

The short journey home in the car with Tim was made in silence and was reminiscent of the day in September when they had asked her to take him immediately to the doctor. Car journeys were an opportunity to talk, a captive place he couldn't escape from but Faye always found journeys with Tim difficult. She tried her best, asking questions, commenting on the traffic and scenery around them but still he said little. She was painfully aware that nothing had changed. Things were now worse. She was floundering, pulling information from every source she could but the direction was not clear and there was no recognized standardized pathway to follow.

'Why?' The wobble in her voice betrayed her.

'It was just a prank. I'm a prankster.' His hands descended into his pockets defensively. She noticed his legs stiffen. Caught a glimpse of his face pinking as her hands tightened their grip around the steering wheel as if it were a stress ball.

'What you did was absolutely disgusting. Filthy. Horrible.' But the words needed a beef injection.

'It wasn't just me. Other people are doing it. It's what cool boys do these days.'

Tiny bubbles of anger were popping in Faye's head. Was he insane? The conversation - like many before - felt surreal.

'You're not getting your phone back or your computer for the next week. You'll have to do your work from books.'

'Whatever. I just won't do any work.' He stretched the sentence for effect as if it were a piece of chewing gum.

If his words were chosen to provoke they were working. Anger rose like a small fountain. And now - from within - Faye had found the emotion to match the words.

'You stupid, stupid boy. What the hell are you doing? Where is your bloody life going? I'm taking your phone and I'm going to find out who is supplying you. What's the password? I'm going to meet whoever it is that's ruining my son's life.'

'I'm not telling you.' And then a light laugh escaped his lips. 'You think a dealer is going to meet you? What are you going to do? Wave your big finger in his face and tell him not to be naughty?' He asked and although her eyes were on the road ahead she knew he was wrinkling his nose mocking her.

'Fine. You just won't get it back again.' She sniffed.

'I'll save up for a better one.' He was quick to outwit.

'What with? Why don't you get a Saturday job like Meg? Earn some money.' She screamed. But the truth was she didn't want him to get a Saturday job or a paper round because money in the pocket meant drugs or fags.

'I will.' He muttered.

Faye's eyes were filling, her face flushed. She wanted to pull her words back, start the conversation again but new words hadn't formed and at the back of her mind snagged the word *suicide*, looming large, a warning cloud hovering. It seemed that she was saying everything that could so easily rattle the cage that contained the beast with the name of *suicide*.

༺༻

It was early evening and Faye had removed the computer once more and the other gadgets that Tim possessed as an exclusion punishment. It was becoming quite a charade; the toys emptied once more from the pram in the hope of change.

Meg stood in Tim's doorway, arms folded demanding answers.

'What the hell did you shit in the changing rooms for? Are you mental?' She was wearing a black crop top and blotches of red heat were multiplying across her chest as fury began to take hold.

'It's a prank. Some kids go to Syria to join the jihad. Which would you rather?'

'You're a complete prat. I hope they got you to clear it up.' She inched up to him shrieking in his face.

'They've got cleaners to do that.' Tim said dismissively. 'I wasn't given any gloves.'

'Oh for God's sake. Did you hear that Motheroon? He didn't have to clear it up.' She shouted in disbelief.

'What were you hoping to achieve? To get chucked out of school, then end up in the doorway of the Poundstretcher?'

'I'm going to Canada to be a lumberjack and chop trees all day. I'll buy a pet mousse and wear one of those nifty checked shirts. I might even take your head off with my chain saw.'

'Don't be stupid. What gave you the idea to be a lumberjack?'

'I saw a tree.'

'You're just a classic idiot.' Meg snorted then retreated back to her room and ginseng tea.

༺༻

Tim had refused to give her the password to his phone and so the following day, with Tim at home on his first day of exclusion from school she nipped into a mobile phone repair shop to ask them to crack into Tim's phone and find out if there was any information to indicate what drugs he was ordering and from whom. The school had told her that Tim had to be supervised on exclusion during school hours and was not to leave the house. Faye thought this was ludicrous. She had to go to work.

The men in the repair shop looked like Tweedle Dum and Tweedle Dee. Both in their early twenties they exchanged suspicious looks and when she explained her purpose they both frowned and asked what school he went to and what his name was. Faye wondered why they wanted to know. It seemed a very nosey question, as if they might be dealers themselves, keen to sell to him.

Later on she returned to pick it up and because it was an iphone they couldn't get into the security.

⁓

During Tim's exclusion Faye bumped into the hoover man in town. She told him about the exclusion and they made an arrangement for him to drop by. Events had moved on, she told him and he'd happily agreed that coming over would be a good thing. Tim had objected, raising his eyes to the ceiling and screwing his nose up in dismissal but she had insisted that he had no choice, almost pleading with him to at least listen to what he had to say.

It felt odd to invite him in, offer a beer for she barely knew him but in some ways this was a good thing. She placed a bowl of peanuts and a couple of beers on the kitchen table and while they chatted she flitted around the house doing jobs, pausing to listen at the kitchen door every now and again.

She caught his words while hovering in the hall straining to hear above the flings of Chrissie in the lounge bouncing on the trampoline in her *Frozen* nighty and X Factor on the TV.

'You're young enough to get out of drugs while you can mate. It's not real. It messes with the head. I think of all the things I could have done with my life and I'm nearly 30 and repairing hoovers. Friends would say let's go out. But if they had no weed I wouldn't go. Without weed I couldn't function. I was on the outside and everyone else was getting on with normal life. In the end you start to hang out only with those who can supply you or smoke with you. It's a bit like being Jewish and being restricted by a kosher diet. You can't integrate. You don't want to integrate. You seek out your own kind. And it goes from there. But Tim they weren't real friends. Most were dysfunctional individuals, struggling with life, with issues, propped up with weed.'

Every so often Tim grunted. But he listened. Or at least Faye assumed he was.

'It only takes a few smokes to get hooked. Some can take it or leave it. Some wake up the next day ok. But if I had it I'd be thinking about it the next day and when I took it oh God it was fantastic. I had an explosion of thought. Ridiculous thoughts. Creative, imaginative thoughts. When I was high I could be anyone, do anything. It was a mental race. But everyone's different. It made me want to talk to anyone. It gave me the confidence I lacked. It was crazily random. I couldn't walk past it and say no. But there came a time when I had to. It was fucking my life up.'

They were silent for a time. Faye dabbed her fingers on a towel, in the cloakroom, waited.

'Go back to a point in your life when everything was going well.'

There was pause. Tim offered no answer. Faye wondered what Tim was thinking; what that time would be.

'Your mum told me your work experience went well. She told me you were doing the Duke of Edinburgh and walked a section of the Thames last year. They're all things to be proud of mate. That's the point in your life to think *I'm a clever guy*. You know I could so easily pull out a spliff, share it with you but it's a crutch. You are your own super hero. You don't need that shit to feel invincible. In the beginning it's good. Your mind is sharp but over time it fucks with your memory. It makes you inwardly gazing. You create a bubble around yourself and nothing else matters. It's a lazy brained existence. My mum and dad are still supporting me. It's not right at my age. I should have done something with my life.'

'It's not too late.' This was the first thing Tim said.

'Maybe not. But it gets more difficult with each passing year. Your opportunities are there now Tim. Don't miss out.'

'Well it's my choice to take it. And I'm not hooked. It's not a problem for me.'

Faye's heart sank. The man's words had been spot on. Brilliantly said. But they had fallen on deaf ears. At least that's what she thought. Maybe he was digesting small snippets of information from all sources. Maybe there was still hope. But what was it going to take for Tim to come off cannabis she wondered.

༄

It was the last day of Tim's five day exclusion. In the early hours of the morning an uncomfortable thought had started to worm its' way into Faye's head. She would book an appointment to see the doctor. There were questions that needed answering.

Faye was slotted in at the end of day, arriving to a packed waiting room, two overweight receptionists with crimson slashed lips and bold statement glasses; finally seen two hours later at the end of the session – confirmation she thought - of the media stories about the NHS in crisis.

'And how are *you*?' The doctor's hands were resting on his head as he listened.

It was a floodgate opening question.

'I feel isolated, alone. You'll have me in tears.' She smiled but inside she quelled the tears.

'It's ok I've got plenty of tissues.' He furled his hands like a flamenco dancer and pointed to the rescue box of man-sized tissues.

'I'm sick of the blase attitude of people out there –from professionals down to parents -telling me it's just a phase, he'll come out of it, it will be ok in the end, they're all doing drugs. And even if they are all doing drugs - which I'm sure they're not - it doesn't make it right. I was shocked when the school police officer told me a good number had taken cannabis in year 11.'

'There are facts and there are facts. They may have tried it just once. Eliminate those kids and you have maybe 20% regularly taking it and out of that 20% maybe 10% will carry on using it. It's not the majority. It's still not the norm to smoke weed but *yes* this area does have a significant drug problem. Of my patients eleven are heroin users – just to give you an idea.'

'Here in Trentum? That's hard to believe. It's such a middle class area.'

The doctor swiveled his eyes in a look that said don't make assumptions based on class.

'If he was at one of the public schools it would be cocaine you'd be fighting.' He smiled gravely.

'I see your point...But what can I do? How can I help him to come off it?'

He turned to the computer. 'Have you looked at Frank. Frank has all the answers. He typed it into Google. 'There are support groups, live chats, the chance to ask questions.'

'I'm quite conservative. I would rather we had a zero tolerance approach to drugs.'

He looked back at Faye, reassurance etched across his face. 'I take it seriously.' He said emphasizing the I. 'I'm often laughed at for that.' He gave her a warm smile and in that moment she felt a strong doctor-patient bond that made her want to reach over and hug him. He was a gem.

'As a doctor what symptoms do you see in cannabis users?' She managed to ask.

'Anxiety, paranoia. I've had cannabis users who have developed schizophrenia and categorically denied the link.'

'Why is everyone so blasé about cannabis? I don't understand.'

'Maybe they don't know what to do. They pretend it's not happening.'

'Please tell me you do see plenty of parents like me, distraught, tearful, anxious.'

'Sadly I see too many who are the other way - parents who have good memories of using cannabis at university and so they think their kids will be ok. They don't see the harm. But the fact is it's much stronger now than it was in the past. And most cannabis is skunk. You don't know what you're getting into. The THC levels are much higher - that's the biggest issue.' He said, explaining what THC was although she had recently watched a Channel 4 documentary in which several well-known figures – including Jennie Bond and Jon Snow were filmed taking skunk with various tests to establish the effect of skunk on their memory, appreciation of music and paranoia levels. The results had been shocking. Jon Snow had described the experience as worse than being in a war zone. The programme reported that two million people in the UK smoke cannabis according in an 'industry' worth £6 billion. One young lad on the programme said initially cannabis had made him feel good but after persistent use it made him paranoid. He thought people were after him. He had hallucinations, felt suicidal, had to be sectioned and mugged to feed his habit. (see footnote below 4)

'The reason why I came to see you...' and she then filled him in on the events at school and the exclusion.

'And in light of all of that I'm now beginning to wonder whether this whole suicide thing is just made up so that he can claim the sympathy vote; a big distraction to what is really going on; ie the drug use. It all seems a bit convenient to my mind. All the time I think he's at risk of topping himself it stops me coming down hard on him. I'm side stepping around the elephant in the room. Suicide is the end of everything; an obliteration and too enormous to contemplate.

⁴Should he carry on with the Prozac? Nobody has told me. And we haven't been offered counseling yet. The Child Mental Team were crap by the way.'

'Is he any better on it? And he's stopped taking Ruaccutane I hope? As I explained before there is a very small link to low mood in some people?'

'Yes the therapist at the hospital wanted him to come off it immediately. Of course he's not very happy about that. Worried his acne will flare back up.'

'Maybe too early to tell with the changes in medication.'

The doctor looked at his notes, trying to establish Tim's mood from previous meetings.

'It's all so confidential. It doesn't help me - the parent - because at the end of the day it's me trying to help him.'

She sensed a calculation as she looked at his face.

'I'll let you read these notes.' He turned the screen towards her. 'I'm not supposed to show you.' A shadow moved across his face.

'Thank you.' Faye quickly read the notes; anxious as she read the words *making serious plans to end his life* and *planning to jump in front of train on way to school*. She looked away in the same way someone might turn from vomit. Her body rigid, bile rising in her throat, she didn't want to read anymore. Her doubts were confirmed. She needed to take this more seriously and keep a careful eye on Tim.

But something was soon to happen. Faye thought she was one step ahead of Tim's problem but she was soon to find out that this wasn't the case.

⁂

---

⁴ This was broadcast in February 2015. See www.channel4.com

Many of Faye's thoughts came in the night; jumbled, haywire licking over the anxiety that threaded its' way through her sleeping mind. As she gradually woke the anger popped and a burning desire to do something - for the community, for the country - to tackle the drug problem started to form. By morning she was fired up, ready to go. But where? She didn't know. Could she set up a parent support group? Could she hold a public meeting and gather the community leaders, the parents? But the more she considered the issues involved, the opposition she might face to labelling the town *a town with a significant drug problem* – the professional's words not hers and the exposure to Tim and her family and all the related implications - it was easier to sit back and do nothing.

Drugs, like sex were a taboo subject and despite this being 2015 they were still taboo. But ignorance abounded and she was painfully aware that she was also one of the ignorant ones. Remaining ignorant had it's price tag because all the time it abounded drugs were creeping into every community across the country, ruining lives, staining communities, bringing crime, wrecking families while too little collectively, at ground level was being done. It seemed that everybody - from the community leaders to the parents to the kids themselves - was burying their heads in the sand either accepting of the situation or waiting for the problem to pass.

A cold lump of steel twisted in her gut. At the very least she could fire off a letter to her local MP.

25 Swallow Walk
Trentum

Dear Sir Andrew,
    Here in Trentum we as parents are confronted with a growing drug problem. I am told by my local GP that the area now has a SIGNIFICANT drug problem; the police officer at Rydon High School says that a GOOD number of pupils

have tried cannabis but out here in the community I continually hear so much apathy. One of the doctors at the child mental health team at Nettle Rise Hospital told me 'many of them are taking it.' There seems to be an acceptance of the problem yet on all fronts a lack of a willingness to do anything to fight the problem. Parents who say 'well what can we do?' 'They're all at it,' 'It's just a teenager phase, it will pass' and even 'it may not be that harmful it's a natural plant.' But none of them have answers.

I am astounded at the lack of knowledge out there; the misconceptions, the variety of opinions and the acute apathy. I am a single parent struggling to cope. I have a very bright 16 year old son, polite, a lovely boy who used to have many interests and now he is telling me 'I need cannabis. It's my choice.' Back in September I discovered he was buying chemicals and items over the internet to make and sell a psychoactive substance. He had also found a way into the dark web, TOR. I took the items straight to the police. The substance misuse officer had never heard of the drug he was planning to make. He also said 'just between you and me skunk isn't as potent as the press make out. I won't be able to stop your son taking cannabis but I might be able to help him manage his use.' Not exactly what I wanted to hear. I had pinned more hope on Government Services but so far nobody has delivered. My son had never before been in any trouble at school. This was a huge shock to me.

We, as parents no longer have control over what our children are doing on the internet. They have too many devices.

My doctor says the problem is stemming from our country's drug laws. I don't know enough to comment on this. How can you as an MP help? What are you doing in the town to try to fight this problem? The school tell me there's only so much they can do without it looking to parents as if the school has a big drug problem and creating an adverse image.

I would strongly urge you to address this problem in our community.

Yours faithfully
Faye Denton.

༄

Several weeks later came a reply saying how sorry her MP was to hear of her son's experience and that on her behalf he had made representations to the Minister of State for Crime Prevention and to the county's police team. He also enclosed a written ministerial statement on the Government's 'Drug's Policy' and informed her that he intended to meet with a member of the neighbouring policing team to discuss the matter further. He thanked her for contacting him about such an important matter.

And a couple of days on came an email reply from the local Police Station forwarded on to her from Sir Andrew.

Several key sentences caught Faye's eyes sending a chill through her body.

I would respond quite candidly by agreeing that the number of young people misusing cannabis in and around Trentum is a significant cause for concern.

It is my observation that that there is a poor understanding of the long- term dangers of cannabis misuse amongst young people who are taught by their peers that the drug is harmless. In a low-crime area such as ours parents are often niave as to the actual dangers and are therefore ill-equipped to support their children...'

'The refusal of some schools to address the problem...'

'The links to family conflict and dysfunction as cannabis use increases...'

For Faye this was the final acknowledgement she needed. A *significant* problem the letter had said. And *ill-equipped* parents. She desperately wanted to do something to help the police in their 'war' on drugs but she was just one parent and she had her own corner to fight. A corner that she felt she was rapidly losing.

27
Faye

February 2015

It was now February. Faye was firing up her laptop. The kids were at school.

After going round in circles for so long Faye felt she was finally beginning to make some headway having discovered a youth support group run by the council and wondered why no doctor had suggested dropping along to this group. In the face of the Government's austerity programme this vital service was still running but yet not being promoted by the professionals who could have been promoting it.

She spoke to a man on the phone at the youth support team who promised to refer him for counseling and so one evening Faye took him along with a couple of his druggy friends in tow. She was amazed that they had readily agreed to go but the man had enticed them saying they were having a barbecue and there would be other teenagers there too.

On the way home after the barbecue they passed a variety of leaflets to each other, laughing at the wording on the leaflets.

'Look at this one Tim. *You may feel frightened after taking cannabis.*' His friend mocked.

'*Drugs: a course we don't recommend.*' Tim jested back. 'Colorado recommend it though. It's legal there.' Tim was quick to remind his friend. Tim was leaving her in the dark and there was only so much she could do. But what she didn't realise was that she was about to find something in Tim's bedroom – something she had been looking for, for a very long time – and this finding was to directly led her to the root of Tim's problems.

༺༻

It was the day after the support group. It was a Saturday and everyone was late getting up. Rushing to put a washer load of laundry in the machine Faye stopped in her tracks as she picked Tim's pillow up. She turned to Tim, on Facebook at his desk.

'What's this?' Her voice was weak, the blood draining from her face. She already knew the answer. She slumped to the bed, unable to stand as reality slowly hit and the enormity of what she had found.

'It's Mr. Daddy. Don't throw him away.'

'Wha?'

'He keeps me company in the darkest hours of the night.'

Faye smiled at his wit, still intact.

'Someone gave you this when you were born but I don't remember who it was and...'

'Katie gave it to me.'

'I've never seen him under your pillow before.' Faye was confused.

'He slips behind the bed sometimes.'

'Hidden behind all your junk no doubt. Katie... you sure?'

Faye frowned, turning the cloth gingerbread man around, examining the fine stitching, looking at the familiar fabric design. She raised it to her face breathing in the smell.

'Why do you have to smell everything?'

'I was just thinking...' Faye was miles away.

227

'You're weird. When I used to stay over with Ed two, Katie would tuck Mr. Daddy and Mrs. Mummy in bed beside us and make up stories. She'd sit at the end of the bed, Mr. Daddy in one hand, Mrs. Mummy in the other, two puppets. Ed and I made up stories too. They were good at burping and farting and doing big poos.' Faye raised an eyebrow, shook her head. Some things never changed.

'Then she'd fly them through the air singing *twist me, turn me, kiss me, miss me.*'

'Miss me...' Faye repeated softly, the words slicing the air, lingering like heavy mist between them. A solitary tear formed in her eye. She looked at Tim. A shadow had crept across his face and discomfort over hers; this was something she didn't want to confront. They had never talked about Katie's death.

'She used to put a CD on of a song that reminded her of her dad, killed during the Troubles in Northern Ireland.' Tim said.

'Really? She never mentioned her dad in all the time we were friends... What song?' Faye asked, her heart leaping to her throat as she began to put two and two together coming up with five. Surely... she wondered. This was just a coincidence? It wasn't possible...

'Luther Vandross, Dance With My Father.' Tim was quick to remember the song.

Faye suddenly felt chilled. The song was one of the most beautiful ever made; a fitting tribute to Katie's father.

⁓⊃

A portcullis was rising again and so when Tim's manner changed, asking her to *go away now* she was quick to get up, take her exit, clutching Mr. Daddy, ready to show him to Darius the next time they met. But something was about to happen, the following day to prevent her from doing this. Events were moving fast. The roots of Tim's problems were starting to make sense; like looking through a kaleidoscope the view was slotting into place. And recalling 'Dance With My Father,' she hadn't realized, had stoked a deep well of painful emotions in Tim; emotions which were about to erupt and stain the course of their lives.

28
Faye

February 2015

It was late evening. Faye had been to see Fifty Shades of Grey. She climbed the stairs, light headed, shot through with the happy warmth of whisky. A glow of light rimmed the frame of Tim's bedroom door. She poked her head round the door to say goodnight. A woody pungent aroma competed with body odour and computer heat. It was too late for another battle but in the morning she planned to challenge him yet again about smoking weed.

'Come on, bed. School tomorrow.' He was hunched at his desk, playing a computer game. Or so she thought but he was in fact about to play 'Dance With My Father' for the umpteenth time that evening. She didn't see his face. Had she seen it the events that were about to enfold might never have happened.

She was becoming familiar with the pungent smell from several nights back when Meg had come rushing into her room shouting that he was smoking cannabis in his bedroom and for her to do something. Meg had taken him by the shoulders of his new turtleneck jumper and yanked him back and forth like a rag doll, just as she had when they were toddlers.

Getting into bed she chuckled to herself as she recalled how the cinema auditorium had been full of cackling women clutching dustbin sized buckets of popcorn, cheering each time Jamie Dornan whipped Dakota Johnson, shouting out obscenities such as *give her one* and at the back two token middle aged men in zipped up ancient army green anoraks who looked like train spotters, ogled eyed throughout the showing.

In her heavy sleep she was vaguely aware of Tim going up and down the stairs several times. This wasn't unusual. She was used to him grazing on endless nighttime snacks. She couldn't bring herself to call the snacks *munchies* because of the connection between a raging appetite and cannabis use. But this time - unknown to Faye - he wasn't going downstairs for snacks. What he was doing was much more serious.

She couldn't keep up with the amount of food he was now consuming and no sooner had she filled the fridge with mini sausages, scotch eggs and pork pies and woof it was all gone. She had found new places to hide biscuits and cakes: in the craft cupboard or an empty flour bag in her baking cupboard or inside the packet of a cereal box such as Shredded Wheat or All Bran knowing nobody would touch it.

She drifted to sleep.

༄

It was three in the morning when the landline startled Faye. With scrunched eyes and a foggy head she glanced at her radio alarm.

'Mrs. Denton? Sorry to wake you. It's Father Ian from St. Agnes.'

'Wha'?' This had to be a prank. She hit the red button, put the phone back on its' cradle and crashed back onto the pillow her heart in her throat.

But she was now awake and her brain in gear. Who the hell was it?

The phone rang again.

'Mrs. Denton I'm ringing from an ambulance. I found your son nearly unconscious in the graveyard of my church. St. Agnes Catholic Church.' His voice rose at the end of the sentence; an assumption being made that she knew the church well.

In her confusion and still convinced this was a prank she asked to speak to a member of the ambulance crew.

'Your son was found by the priest in his graveyard. He says he's taken several packets of painkillers and we found an empty bottle of vodka next to the bench. We're on our way to hospital. Can you get there?'

'What's going on? I don't understand. He's in bed. I know he's in bed. Who are you?' Faye screamed into the mouthpiece, a twisted knot of anxiety tightening its' grip in her stomach. She stood up, the room swimming, her blood cold as ice as shiver after shiver came in waves, her mind on lock down. And then she was in his room, still clutching the phone staring at the empty bed, the pillow where his head should have been sleeping, the duvet that should have been wrapped around him, the towels, the crisp wrappers, the pile of dirty clothes strewn across the floor. His computer was still on. She touched it and it sprung to life. She saw the red You Tube icon and the song 'Dance With My Father' on the screen. Her heart sank.

'Where? Why? When? What?' Questions with no endings fired like bullets and answers she couldn't process.

Back in her room she cursed over and over *Tim what the hell have you done? You stupid, stupid boy, what have you done? What the fuck have you done?*

The phone returned to the cradle she pulled off her nighty as quickly as she could, searching for clothes to put on, eyes darting all over the room rather than at the chair where yesterday's clothes lay; the cylinders in her brain unable to fire and function normally or at the speed she wanted.

Now dressed, bag, keys in hand ready to get into the car, make the short trip to the hospital she paused in the doorway of Tim's room. Darius' words a few weeks ago hit her now like meteors scudding through the dark sky. Fear started to prickle and bile rose in her throat.

He's been a fading light within your family for a very long time. A waning candle in a darkened room and little by little he's slowly removed himself and

Every Family Has One

suicide - just to warn you - is the final extinguisher. I of all people know that. You need to find a way to reignite the flame before it's too late.

༺༻

When she arrived at A&E she half expected to be told she'd dreamt the whole thing and to go home. But as she flew through the automatic doors, trainers squeaking on the polished vinyl, ahead she could see him; her son whom she no longer recognized, changed so much and a priest sitting with him who seemed to know him well. The priest's arm was draped around him. All at once she thought about Darius and the abuse of his childhood at the hands of a priest.

Their lives were sliding away into a place she didn't understand.

What had he been doing in the graveyard she wanted to know and who was this priest?

As she drew closer, her trainers screeching to a halt, the weeping of someone nearby became in that moment her own private lonely weeping inside. She embraced the vision of Tim huddled on a plastic chair, so far away from her in every conceivable way and yet so near, touchable yet untouchable. Her hand went instinctively to her mouth. She wanted to recoil. Wanted to run; be anywhere but here. This wasn't happening. This was Trevor all over again. History repeated. And not for the first time she also wondered if Katie had stepped in front of the coach deliberately or had it really been an accident? Had she been so depressed, so mixed up that she had felt suicidal, taken the step that very few have the courage to take?

This was too big to happen, too big to deal with. She tried to focus, forced herself to look at him; to his eyes, those of a wild cat on a wilderness trail, redder than she had ever seen them before. It was as if they were about to pop and there was something deeply troubling radiating from his eyes - the windows to the soul – they were glass-like and fragile. She looked at his lips; black, sooty and cracked with dryness. Flecks of black vomit dribbled down his chin, onto his beige turtleneck. What on earth was it?

From behind her members of the ambulance crew were adjusting bags of equipment onto their shoulders, preparing to leave, job done; another night completed.

'Why's his mouth black? Oh my God Tim what have you done?' Tears were threatening but Faye kept her composure, somehow removed from the situation as if watching the scene from above. It didn't occur to her to embrace him or offer sweet words of kindness. She was strangely detached yet didn't want to be.

What was she supposed to say to her child who had just attempted to take his life? There was no book to consult. And why was she feeling anger and despair rather than rushing to tell him she loved him?

She didn't know what she felt other than an overriding fear on every level.

The ambulance crew explained that they had given him a charcoal drink to bring up the contents of his stomach and instructed her that she needed to get him across to the county children's hospital and then they left, leaving her to cope alone once more.

Except that she wasn't alone. Father Ian was still sitting next to him, looking from face to face as if biding his time, waiting for an opening. With the crew gone the atmosphere buckled to a silence. He smiled up at her; a smile which didn't reach his eyes. There was something about him that unnerved her. Maybe it was his dog collar, black clothing or his raven eyes. Whatever it was he didn't belong on a hospital ward. He looked out of place - like finding a mermaid in a supermarket - but the ease with which he sat next to Tim suggested he did belong: very much so. She knew in an instant that a bond had developed between her son and this man and yet again this was a part of his life that didn't include her.

But now didn't seem the time to find out what had happened and why he'd been in the graveyard. Suddenly she snapped into action. She had to rush him over to the other hospital as instructed.

'I guess I'd better get him over there.' She looked directly at the priest. 'Hopefully it will be signposted and the parking not too difficult or expensive.'

'At some point Faye we need to talk.' The priest's words cut into the night, his tone deep and grave.

Faye looked at him. She had never met him and yet he knew more about her family than she cared for him to know or cared to admit. She could no longer hide behind the letters to Katie, hide in the bubble that she had created for herself; a bubble that dealt with her grief; the letters a channel for her grief but also a painful act of denial. The letters had maintained the cocoon of warmth and friendship with Katie that she imagined would carry on through to eternity. As long as she had the will to keep writing, she reasoned. But in writing she had been excluding Tim; squeezing him out, protecting herself from her own grief and denying him a channel for his grief.

The reality of the situation was that the priest was the only one reading her letters because she had addressed them to the churchyard and never putting her own address on the letters. All she had been doing was opening her soul to the priest, unknowingly and maybe through him to God - if God existed - for as the priest he was God's representative on earth.

Piece by piece things were starting to make sense. Nothing had made sense for a very long time; not until the discovery of the gingerbread toy under Tim's pillow and tonight's events at Katie's grave. Why hadn't she seen this coming? Knowing how close he had been to Katie; all the times he had stayed over at her house with Ed while she was working night shifts at various care homes, supermarkets and depots why did she imagine he wasn't also suffering from grief? What had given her the right to deny the existence of his grief? This was his loss too. He hadn't cried. He hadn't made a fuss. He'd remained strong. Got on with life around a family who were all busy finding their way and fundamentally a mother busy working, supporting a family on her own but also searching for love on the internet after things had fallen apart with Shayne.

What made her think that children didn't suffer grief? She asked herself over and over.

And maybe it was time to start talking about Trevor. No longer present in a physical sense there was no reason why he couldn't build a relationship with his father based upon her memories, her stories. Deep down she knew it was ridiculous that she'd never showed the twins pictures of their father or the stacks of videos she had tucked away under her bed. The twins had been so tiny; too tiny to remember.

Faye's head was spinning with so many *what ifs* in her head, tripping over each other, knocking each other down like a row of dominoes as she guided Tim to the car.

29
Katie

October 2012

Dear Michael,
    I've been waiting all week for today. Friday October 12th 2012. The day Ed gets back from the Isle of Wight. But now that today has finally arrived and I can breathe a sigh of relief and look forward to his return I don't feel elation. In fact I feel an intense fear.
    The silence in the house these past few days has helped me see how things really are. I've sat in bed all week, thinking, crying and all the time feeling numb. Ed doesn't need me, you don't need me. And although my baby died she wouldn't have needed me either. Would have been whisked away to America to be brought up by a rich and capable couple. But you don't know any of that. God knows though it's been hard keeping it all to myself. For years I felt like a dirty little slut. I was a bad person; maybe I still am. I was a Magdalene. I am a Magdalene and as long as I live I'll be a Magdalene. That's why I can't go on. It's just the way it is, the way I feel and nothing will change.
    Maybe I provoked the priest with the skimpy clothes I was wearing. What would you have thought if I'd told you?

My greatest fear was you pressurizing me to report him and being dragged through a big court fight with all the press coverage and the humiliation and stress that would have caused. It was easier for me to turn my back on the past. And the longer I didn't tell a soul the harder it became to open up.

You have another week in the Far East. Faye can look after Ed until you get back. I've done enough for her over the years. It's her turn to help. But I expect you'll return as soon as you get the call. Remove yourself from her bed. She won't be so keen when it's just you and Ed and she has a moody teenager vying for your time.

I can't go on Michael. I suppose I've always known that. Parenting is too hard. It's quite literally killing me, eating away at my soul. Now I know how my mother felt. No wonder she never came for me.

Parenting Ed can only get worse; there'll be more things to worry about. Always things to worry about. The worry feasts on me, destroys me. In no time at all he'll be driving on our mad roads. He'll be going to late night parties where there are drugs and copious quantities of alcohol; because let's face it kids today binge and some end up in hospital, their livers damaged. I can't face that fear. You and everyone else will tell me he'll be fine, he's a good kid and I'm worrying unnecessarily and yet again I'll feel like a freak, a killjoy. I'll be expected to kiss him goodbye and wish him a good time. How can I though knowing there are so many dangers out there?

You don't know just how bad my nightmares are. I see her in the mesh bin in the corner of the room drenched in blood and thick gloopy vernix with the gelatinous umblical cord trailing around the room, crawling up my bed, pulsing, slithering then coiling around my neck, tightening...and then I scream. Sometimes I see her face. I never saw her face. Can you imagine what that was like for me? To create another human being but not to see your baby's face? Was she beautiful? Or would she have reminded me of him? In my nightmare I see her face and it's twisted and scarred and her eyes have been pecked out by the sister's fingernails and left out on the windowsill for the birds to feast upon.

When you are here you're a good dad. You're not a good husband though, because you won't give her up. But I don't blame you for that. I didn't enjoy our lovemaking. I think you picked up on that. I think you guessed when I faked. How could I possibly enjoy it after what had happened to me? It was easy, to begin with to refuse you. I blamed it on thrush, cystitis, vaginitis. Anything to get me off the hook. To begin with you were patient. You loved me. But how long could I keep denying you? My own husband? It wasn't fair.

Ed misses you. Boys need their dads. You only have to look at Tim to see that. Of course in an ideal world kids need two parents but one functioning parent is better than two non-functioning parents and at the moment that's us. That situation needs to change.

Please understand.
Love Katie. (Kathleen in a former life)

⁓

It was dark outside and a wind was kicking up as Katie stood at the window looking out over the rain-drenched lawn; the moon hidden by the dense inky clouds; an ideal night, she thought to herself. She folded the paper trying to decide whether to leave it by her bedside in an envelope addressed to Michael. After a few moments she folded it again then tore it into tiny pieces, opened the window and watched the pieces lift into the wind then begin their descent into the darkness.

She walked around the house, looking in every room, lingering in Ed's bedroom, her eyes casting over his Doctor Who duvet, his teddy tucked in, his collection of books and the tatty, now very old Action Man wallpaper that she had been meaning to replace for so long. She wouldn't be here to watch the next phrase of his life; the scariest phase of all. She closed the door, walked downstairs without putting the light on, then headed to the coat stand to put her long black cape on.

A text pinged through startling her. The school coach would be late. A further text would follow on its' arrival at school.

There was still time she thought to herself. Still time to escape all this. Soon it would all be over.

She opened the door feeling the gush of wind slap her face. Clusters of sodden leaves were gathering around the tree. She waited by the roadside until she could hear an approaching vehicle. She heard the sound in the distance - a gentle sound like a tumbling waterfall, then an orchestrated symphony; a laboring vehicle trundling now up the hill, groaning and changing down in gear. She saw the lights as it turned the corner piercing the darkness, blinding her and then she stepped out...

30
Faye

February 2015

They arrived in the nearby town. Tim was in the back of the car. The signposting for the hospital was poor. All the signs pointing to the visitor car park were hidden by goods vans and trucks parked precariously across pavements. The hospital was in the centre of the town; a rabbit warren of haphazard buildings from different eras of ad hoc development. In the face of this - which was of complete irrelevance given the nature of their visit – Faye's stress levels and impatience began to rise. She slammed to a halt on a zebra crossing under a walkway linking two parts of the hospital. She banged her fists on the steering wheel swearing for England, throwing questions to the silence in the car. It was, as ever, the silence of disappearance - a suffocating and strangulating silence.

'Where the fuck is the car park? Where the fuck is the entrance to this bloody place?' She got out, slammed the door, left the car running. The air was dank, the sky now a paler ink as light began to force its' way through to another day. There was no one to ask and several doors with no signage. Which one to choose, she didn't know.

And in her confusion, cursing, hands flapping and now tears of frustration Tim was crouching by the roadside vomiting. She could see his temple throb. Vomit frothing at the corners of his mouth and the look of disgust on his face. At first she wondered what the vomit was laced with then remembered the priest's words. *He's taken some painkillers.* Her eyes moved away, it was an image she didn't want to store, grabbed his sleeve walking him fast in the direction of the nearest door; saw a nurse in the corridor and screamed for her to take him, check him in. She'd be back soon; had to park.

In the hours that followed different nurses, doctors, auxillaries came and went, clutching clipboards, asking robotic questions, ticking boxes, filling in charts, faces that expressed nothing other than complete professionalism; all wearing *happy to help* Asda style badges; psychological cosh with heavily accented voices. The engine was in motion; the trail of paperwork weaving its' way around the issues. Blood tests, blood pressure and more blood tests because the blood had coagulated. She stroked Tim's face offering him the love she hadn't shown in so long. But he flinched and frowned and after a time she sat and watched him instead.

They were put in a room with a sign near the door saying 'short stay' as if it was a car park for people dropping off relatives at Heathrow. In effect it was a holding bay, more like a small terminal lounge at an airport. But this wasn't British Airways. It was the NHS. And on the news that morning a Labour politician had warned that *the NHS is deteriorating in a way not seen since the early 1990s.* But in the centre of this monolith all she could think was that they were asking too many questions and following the standard procedures in a mechanical and clunky way. But that was what the NHS to her mind had become; unwieldy and clunky but delivering very little.

Faye looked at the cardboard bowl beside his bed filled with more black vomit and then at his face, yellow and clammy and wondered how they had arrived at this.

When the bloods came back the doctor explained that Tim's liver function was slightly damaged and in order to protect his liver they needed to put a drip up for around twenty hours and then when he was deemed to be fit a social worker and a member of the child mental health team would visit to establish whether he was ok to go home.

༄

Faye stood at the window of the ward studying the changing clouds and symphony of golds and reds of the scenery below. She studied the pastel shades of the Lego bricks of the town's houses and buildings and over to the rolling Chilterns peppered with tiny hamlets and the many fond memories of walks with Katie and the kids admiring the flora of the changing seasons: blissful picnics in flowery meadows, finding rare purple gentians growing around tussocky anthills and sheltering under an ancient oak when it suddenly rained. Faye's breath was upon the glass, her eyes focused on a distant spot and the memories started to scud through her head. Katie had loved the great outdoors. She hadn't liked the kids to be indoors on computers, watching TV. She'd always said it was something to do with her own childhood: long hours spent within walls, not allowed to go out. And now she understood where these walls were. She'd seen the walls for herself: the oppressive walls of The Weeping Lady Magdalene Laundry and maybe if she had been searching for Katie and not Kathleen she might have felt differently about the whole Magdalene experience – angry, disgusted – for Katie was her friend, her best friend and although she was then and still was Darius' sister it was vastly different. Faye was still struggling to believe the coincidence – Kathleen was her friend Katie. It all seemed incredible. Searching for Kathleen had been a futile exercise. Something she had just gone along with because she was dating Darius. In truth Kathleen had been nobody to her.

If only Faye had known. But how could she not have known? The pictures of the young Kathleen looked nothing like Katie. She couldn't have guessed based on photos alone. Katie had lost her Liverpudlian accent and so that link hadn't been there either. She had a posh southern accent. She had never talked of her past. And while she had been with Darius she hadn't seen much of Katie; too wrapped up in her relationship and travel. She was certain she had discussed Kathleen with Katie. Why hadn't Katie said anything? It was bizarre; as if she didn't want to be recognized, identified and her past uncovered, wanting a fresh start, a chance to move on. She had rebranded herself. And she had achieved that, to a large extent because no one would have guessed. Not even Darius. Fuck. Faye suddenly thought. Darius had even met Katie on one occasion and still the penny hadn't dropped. How could a sister and brother meet, chat over lunch and not even recognise each other?

But the tragic thing was that Kathleen had carried the demons of the past into the present in the way she had over protected Ed and the post natal depression she must have suffered from. And now Katie was dead. It was too late.

Faye's interest in the Magdalenes had been shameful when she looked back; the interest of a journalist or a ghoul looking for an intriguing story about pain and heartbreak. She needed to speak to the priest.

Katie had lived in Ireland for a time, she'd told Faye, but she had never elaborated and Faye hadn't asked but in Ireland Katie had learned to love the green fields, the fresh air and the rain falling on her face and the smell of peat moving like dust on the wind. When she had talked about Ireland's countryside she hadn't used the sentimental phrases of poets. There were snippets of information that filtered into conversations; hedges growing above your head, walls of peat, the sweet smell of pine sap, the gnarled roots of oak trees like elderly hands and she said you could stand at the foot of a tree and almost feel its pulse.

The word freedom was never far from her vocabulary. Until now Faye had never really understood why the concept of freedom had meant so much to her. Sadness tugged at Faye -for Katie and all that she had been through - and sadness because Tim had lost a truly great person who seemed to be in touch with emotion like no other friend she'd ever met. Katie had been the missing ingredient that it was hard to find in friendship; the nutmeg that made the friendship special. Maybe this was the Irish influence or maybe the label Darius had given her - *the fallen sister* - changing her into someone who was in touch with feelings, sincere and above all deeply loving.

She looked back at Tim. *Life begins and ends within these sterile hospital walls*, she thought to herself and everything else happened out there in the maze called life.

༄

The priest had asked Faye to visit him. It was the day after Tim had been admitted and the glucose drip was helping his liver to recover. Before driving back to the hospital she decided to nip over to chat with Father Ian before driving on to the hospital.

'I saw the lad several times in the graveyard, just wandering around looking at the headstones; always on his own. It was as if he was contemplating something, always deep in thought. Sometimes the gardener would have a brief chat with him. He told him about Katie. I saw them sitting on a bench together, back in the summer. Jim the gardener was eating his lunch, his fork resting against the bench.' The priest pointed across to a bench next to a hawthorn hedge that ran along the side of the graveyard disappearing into an apple orchard beyond. 'It's a peaceful place to come I suppose. To contemplate. Be at one with God or if you don't have a faith just to be at one with nature. I always wondered what was on his mind. I never asked Jim. I thought it was best not to. Sometimes people want privacy, to offload to a stranger.

But then, the other night I had to return to the vestry to pick up some papers. I couldn't sleep. It was horribly late. So I took my torch and came down here. From behind the yews I could hear someone crying. I waited; the sharp intoxicating fragrance of the yew in the shadowy air filling my nostrils. At first I thought it was foxes mating, then my mind was racing with ridiculous thoughts of the dead coming back to haunt. I thought I was about to see a ghost rise from a grave.' He paused to chuckle. 'So I crept round the yew, my feet cracking on the dry blanket of brown needles underfoot. And then I saw him, splayed out on the bench next to Katie's plot. The headstone will soon be erected. They cost the earth. It's taken a while for her husband to save the money. And it won't say Katie Smith. She always wanted to revert to her maiden name and proper Christian name to re connect with her past.'

' What was her real name Father?' Faye wanted this confirmed. She waited, her heart banging in her chest.

'Kathleen O'Brien. Although on her marriage certificate it looks like the vicar misspelt her maiden name because he wrote O'Breen. I think she liked it that way. It suited her from what I could gather. She said it would prove impossible for her mother and brother to find where she was living, track her down. She wanted to forget the past. She said something happened a long time ago, in Liverpool where she grew up and she'd had to tuck the pain away into a box and try to forgive and forget. I shouldn't be telling you of this. She told me in confidence. Please keep it to yourself.'

Faye suddenly felt woozy. The vicar was just chatting, pleasantries to him, filling her in on the headstone he was about to erect, blissfully unaware of the enormity, to Faye of what he was saying, as piece by piece the puzzle slowly slotted together: the huge coincidence of everything. Faye looked up to the pastel sky; a ploughed field of white tracks and suddenly, as the events of the past six years flashed before her eyes like a visual diary the world seemed a very small place. The long search for Kathleen was over. The reasons why they hadn't found her had been due to a simple penned mistake. Kathleen's soul rested now, in peace, in a better place. And Kathleen's mother Maria, resting in a graveyard at the opposite end of the country, not even reunited in death; her mother's dying wish unaccomplished.

The vicar was talking but his words were carried away in the gentle breeze as so many sensations flooded her. And then her mind snapped back to the present, to the reason why she was here, to find out the story of how Tim had ended up in hospital.

'You were saying... Tim... splayed out on the bench.'

'You were miles away.' The vicar laughed. 'I thought you weren't listening. 'There was an empty bottle of vodka lying beside the bench. Packets of aspirin, paracetomol. He was out of it. I flashed the torch into his eyes. They were a deep shade of red. I thought he was going to pass out. This was your son but he looked like a wino, a tramp sleeping rough on a bench. I immediately fumbled for my phone.'

'Thank you. I'm really grateful. I don't know what would have happened if you hadn't been there. It doesn't bear worth thinking.' The image of Tim, a tramp on a bench appeared in her mind with clarity but she tried to reject the image, wondered if there was a filter in her mind. It was one of those images she knew would never be erased and a memory that would always make her well up.

The priest stood up. She thought she could hear his bones cracking as he unstiffened his body. She looked up at him, smiled and he smiled warmly back and she thought how like a tiny, brittle leopard he was, vulnerable yet worldly, carrying so many secrets for so many folk.

And now, as she said goodbye she wondered what Darius' reaction to the news would be. She couldn't wait to tell him.

31
Faye

February 2015

Darius was on the phone, leaning back in his leather recliner, feet on desk when she walked into his office. Laughing into the mouthpiece he looked up as Faye stood in front of his desk holding the soft toy up to him. It was hard to imagine, she thought, that in a former life he'd been a headmaster, many moons ago, back in Liverpool where he'd grown up.

She watched his relaxed look turn a shade of grey as shock shimmied across his face. He sat up, removed his feet from the desk and stared. In a few hurried pleasantries he made an excuse and ended the call.

Neither spoke for several seconds. His hand was squeezing his face; it was what he did when overwhelmed by news he couldn't digest.

• 'Fuck. How? Where? When?' A splurge of questions fired from his mouth and then he yanked the bottom drawer of his desk, the metal runners clanking as he fumbled, pulling out the matching toy, holding it up for Faye to see. Faye put Mr. Daddy onto a pile of invoices and Darius laid the other one next to it.

'It turned up under Tim's pillow. He said Katie had given it to him a long time ago. My friend Katie. You met her once? I just don't remember her giving it to him but he said she used to make them on an old Singer sewing machine and when he went to stay there, while I was working nights she would sing. Mr. *Daddy eating spaghetti, twisting turning...* and play Luther Vandross 'Dance With My Father.' Tim couldn't remember the rest. Something about a spaghetti night with musical instruments.'

His eyes had turned a misty pewter as if he were remembering something from a long time ago. A stunned silence filled the desk between them. She could see his mind reeling back and she remembered their first date, walking along Brighton Pier singing Ferry Across The Mersey, Darius reminiscing about the fun spaghetti musical nights his dad would arrange; a happy and powerful memory she knew Darius hadn't forgotten; a memory Katie had never forgotten and it transcended all the darker memories that floated across their minds.

And then, as swift as a storm cloud a change came over Darius. The haunted expression on his face eased away, replaced by dismissal and disinterest. He leaned forward, pushed the toys in her direction, telling her to take them away, get rid of them.

'It's a coincidence Faye. Didn't all you women sew in those days? There must be tons of these soft toys out there. It doesn't mean anything more.'

'You met her. You had lunch with her. Remember? For Christ sake.' Faye screamed. 'Look... here's her photo.' Faye thrust a picture in front of him but his face remained blank.

'It's not her. Katie isn't Kathleen. She would have recognized me even if I didn't recognise her. Mind you I've changed a lot in forty years.'

'Exactly. It was so long ago. You wouldn't necessarily recognise each other. And it wasn't as if either of you talked about Liverpool. If you had then maybe the conversation would have led you there.' Faye shot.

She picked the toys up, waved them in his face.

'Coincidence? Look at the stitching. Look at the eyes. Now tell me it's too much of a coincidence.' A tremour had crept into Faye's voice as she carried on making her case, waving Mr. Daddy around and telling him about Tim and the grave and the conversation with the priest of the church where Katie was buried. She was finding it hard to comprehend the fact that he had searched for her - for so long - and all along she had been living just a few miles away. It was tragic.

'You saw the painting of this toy on the side of your auntie's old house in the Falls Area. She lived in Belfast with your auntie for a while. That much we've established even though your aunt died leaving no other clues. The painting was even entitled Mr.Daddy. It was a tribute to your father, Paddy who died in the Troubles. We've been over all this Darius when we were in Belfast.' She pleaded.

Faye had started to shriek now, pacing up and down the office, her face turning red.

'This is ridiculous Faye. Jesus, Mary and Joseph.' He replied, rising to his feet as he began to rub his forehead.

'Is it so ridiculous? It's not a coincidence at all. Think about it... She found out where you were both living and settled just miles away. She wanted to be close to you. I think she was building herself up to coming back into your life.'

The truth sat between them and yet he was doing his best to deny it. She watched a melancholy creep over his face. Was he thinking about the priest she wondered or the general sadness of so many lost years of a relationship with his sister that he could have had. Going through his mother's last years alone and the journey of divorce without family support; someone there that might have understood and offered help. It was the combined grief of everything that might have been that wasn't. Everything he hadn't had but had longed for. And it was the pain of his youth; the abuse that he couldn't share with anyone in his family because of fear and shame. She didn't need to ask; didn't need to pry, she didn't want to pick the flesh of his open wounds. Instead she offered him the soothing gift of silence. He closed his eyes and as she watched him slowly come to terms with the truth tiny glistening tears started to form in the corner of his eyes.

A pained frown appeared on his forehead, he bit his lips, opened his eyes then swiveled the chair to look at her again.

'Katie... Kathleen... she even changed her name so we wouldn't find her.' He huffed, stared through her. 'What happened to her? I remember when you took me round there for lunch to meet her. Her eyes looked familiar but I would never have guessed it was her. She had changed so much. I wonder if she recognized me? Was that why you fell out with her? Was she avoiding you Faye?'

There was so much he wanted to know.

'It was just the way she was. She was such fun. A flamboyant, wonderful person but suffered from depression. We wouldn't see her for weeks. I never knew why she suffered. Now I do.'

Faye went to stand at the window, arms folded, her back to Darius as she looked out over the warehouses and tall chimneys, the scene over Slough's industrial park that she had grown to know.

Tears were forming in her eyes. She pulled a tissue from her sleeve bracing herself as she prepared to tell him what had happened to Katie.

'She died. In October 2012. I'll take you to her grave. The priest said the gravestone – soon to be erected - will say her real name; Kathleen O'Brien not her new name; Katie Smith. Your mother had a dying wish: to find Kathleen and ask for her forgiveness in sending her to a laundry. And Katie's dying wish must have been to return to her old name. The name she was given in Liverpool, her roots. She never forgot her roots after all Darius.' Faye wiped a tear away. She was getting emotional again, thinking of Katie's death.

She took a deep breath, didn't want to go on but knew she had to. One way or another he would find out the truth.

'A coach ploughed into her but it wasn't the driver's fault. She was standing in the road, daft cow dressed in black. He didn't see her. She was waiting for her son to return from the Isle of Wight. She hadn't wanted him to go. She was a protective mother. Never let him out of sight. Even at 12. She was terrified of him going on the school trip. She stayed in bed the entire week the kids were gone while the rest of us went to the wine bar each evening, enjoying our freedom... I miss her so much.'

She turned to look at Darius, the sun behind hair; the warm shade of an Autumn maple tree. She thought about telling him about Jacko but as she went to open her mouth to speak she decided that some things were best left.

'October 2012 you say. Several month's after mum's death and a year before...oh my God. Jesus Mary and Joseph.'

A terrible sadness swept his face as he spoke and Faye knew exactly what he was referring to. They had talked about the momentous milestone that happened on the 19th February 2013 when the Irish head of government - their Taoiseach -Enda Kenny gave a landmark speech and apologized in the Dail Eireann to the women who had been incarcerated in Ireland's Magdalene laundries. Kenny had promised to put a scheme of compensation in place. 'From this day on' he had said 'you need carry your story alone no more because today we acknowledge the role of the state in your ordeal.' He believed the women and not the nuns. This had been a sobering moment for everyone present that day in the Dail. The women were heroes of the hour, having achieved something miraculous.

Faye sat down next to Darius and they embraced in a hug sharing their sorrow. Soon tears were coursing down their faces as they rocked back and forth in each other's arms, united in their grief. Through their loss; Katie to Faye, Kathleen to Darius – the same woman in different time zones - their relationship was now changed forever, bonding them, giving them the glue they had never had; for her death, her life had revealed so much. They didn't need to spell out the deep sadness they both felt for the fact that Kathleen had not been in the Dail that day to hear those words 'sorry,' sharing the achievement for justice with the other Magdalene survivors; feeling the hope and the triumph with all the women who had suffered together, broken as individuals yet coming through at the end; stronger women who had been determined not to give up.

After several moments they loosened their grip and looked deep into each others' eyes. Through the sadness there was joy for although Kathleen hadn't wanted to meet her mum, Maria again, she had seen Darius on the TV show about the Magdalenes, back in January 2012 and heard his words directed to her. 'Please Kathleen mum wants to ask your forgiveness for sending you to a laundry. Please get in touch.' And the final seal - acknowledging the pain she had caused – came through the money Maria had left Kathleen in her will. 'Money to right the wrongs of the past,' her will had said.

'I write to her Darius. Addressed to the churchyard. It's my way of coping. If I write to her I believe she's still here, in the next room. It's as if she's never gone away but as soon as I've posted the letter the reality hits and I know she's gone forever.'

Darius listened, saying nothing, taking it all in. Then he spoke.

'What was she interested in?' He asked tentatively. 'Tell me all about her.'

'Well... she was always talking about the wildlife and the plants in Ireland. The strawberry trees in Killarney. Of course I didn't, at that time put two and two together. Why would I? But the pieces are all slowly slotting together now.'

And so they chatted for the rest of the afternoon, Faye pouring everything out, filling him in and at the end of the afternoon he asked the question that she knew he most wanted to know.

'Was she raped by the priest?'

Faye sat quietly for a moment or two, staring at the carpet.

'I don't know Darius.' Came her flat response.

Darius sighed; buried his face in his hands. Faye knew how important it had been for him to discover the truth; to find out whether Kathleen had suffered the same fate as him. Finding out, for him meant closure but Faye doubted that would happen. If anything it would stoke his anger more if he had discovered that she too had suffered at the hands of the priest.

'Some secrets are best taken to the grave and some are safer told to strangers. I hope, whatever trauma she went through that she was able to unburden to someone.'

'We could ask her husband?' Darius wasn't going to drop it.

'No. I think if we were meant to know we'd know.' Faye whispered.

Faye looked at him and took his hands in hers and as their eyes met she knew that he was thinking of his meadow – the place where he had gone to purge his mind of the secrets he carried, coming to terms with them; releasing them into the gentle breeze. She imagined him lying on the soft bed of grass under the Summer sky, breathing in the air, his legs and arms wide like a snow angel.

32
Faye

February 2015

It was Tim's last day in hospital. The treatment had finished and the results had shown that his liver had recovered, with miniscule damage. An Indian doctor appeared at his bedside his head wobbling from side to side.

'God has been kind to you but if you want to be treated like an adult you must act like an adult.' He sniggered and it was as if he had been telling Tim off for dropping litter in the street. Faye was surprised he mentioned God; didn't think it politically correct.

An hour after the Indian doctor's discharge the social worker and a member of the child mental health team emerged. When they were in a side room away from the bustling ward the social worker looked at him and asked the uncomfortable question Faye knew she could never ask but wanted to know.

'Did you intend to end your life?'

Faye had been wondering if it had been a premeditated act or an impulsive one. A successful suicide needed careful planning, a cool head and a strong nerve but what he'd done had none of these ingredients. It had been a reckless, emotive, spontaneous act. She could see that. Maybe it had been a cry for help. But a cry in whose direction?

255

Not hers, that was for sure. He never turned to her. Even when he was young it was Katie he'd turned to. And Faye could see why. Katie was a tea and sympathy friend, a dab and wipe mum.

Tim shrugged his answer.

'How were you feeling in the hours before you took the pills?'

'Sad.' Another shrug.

'Can you explain?' She spoke in a careful neutral tone as if negotiating the release of a hostage from a mad terrorist.

'I was playing a Luther Vandross song. It made me think of Katie and daddy.'

His words were the hot sting of a jellyfish in Faye's face. Faye gaped in silent shock.

'So you thought you'd drown your sadness in pills and alcohol?' The woman smiled gently.

'I guess so.'

The words further impaled Faye.

'What did you take?'

'Everything I could find and there was a newsagent open. The one on the corner near St. Agnes.'

The social worker was taking notes, furiously scribbling. She paused to laugh about how she could never remember how to spell Ibrubopen.'

'I understand you were on Isotretinoin. It's a great drug for treating acne and its use is soaring. It's been a real breakthrough in acne treatment. Although it is rare - the manufacturers say — there is a very small link to depression and suicidal thoughts. There have been several high profile cases recently in the news. I don't know if you were aware of this small risk and what your thoughts are?' She looked at Faye for the answers.

'I'm not sure the doctors properly warned him of this or whether he just didn't tell the doctor at his check ups. What did you tell the doctor Tim?'

'Don't know.' He shrugged.

'I don't think you were telling the doctor. Come on. Be honest.'

'I wanted to stay on it because it was clearing my skin up.'

The social worker, the mental health worker and Faye looked at each other, eyes rising as they shared a knowing look.

'Can I go now?'

'Well we need to be certain that you are safe to go home. What is the likelihood of you doing this again?' What a ridiculous question Faye thought to herself. They wanted boxes ticked and Tim wanted to get home, back to the virtual world. The meeting had been emotionally and physically draining. They had covered his computer use, his school life, his friends, home.

'I guess I don't want to kill myself.' He smiled, raised his shoulders. This was the answer the social worker wanted. Tim was playing the game but heat was pricking under Faye's clothing; the issues were simply being passed back to her to resolve.

'Coming to hospital for three days was an inconvenience then? Took you away from your friends?'

'I guess.'

⁓

Faye and Tim arrived at the acute mental health unit at Nettle Rise Hospital for a further appointment; a hospital discharge appointment a week later. A new unit, light and airy it still smelled of fresh calming blue paint and around a semi circle reception area glass cases housed an array of children's art projects. Faye fixed her eyes on the energy certificate on the wall, focusing on what might be said in the meeting but half listening to the conversation of the three receptionists. They were talking about music and one was saying that her sister had been the Berkshire Beatles Fan Club Secretary back in the 60s.

Faye was relieved. They weren't going to see the crusty man with the hearing aids and tweed jacket. A short, fat lady with limp black hair in her early 40s came to collect them; a warm smile on her face. They followed her down the corridor, lined with bespoke wallpaper owned by the hospital; according to the lady. As Faye enjoyed the country scene of deers and trees her head chanted *Berkshire Beatles, Berkshire Beatles*; words fixing like araldite in her head for the day.

Looking around the clean modern consulting room Faye thought the news that morning had been dramatic, sensationalized. *The NHS is deteriorating at an alarming rate.* Was this true or were things being dramatized she wondered in a pre-election bonanza? But from personal experience with Tim's problems she had come to the conclusion that the number of children suffering from mental related issues - was on the rise - and that if parents needed swift help they had to pay for it.

The lady adjusted her clipboard on her fat legs and smiled warmly from Tim to Faye, back to Tim where her eyes settled. Even before she spoke Faye knew she was kindly, motherly and would say all the right things.

'So what brings you here Tim?' As if she'd met him in a foreign country on vacation.

'I guess because I was in hospital.'

'And what happened?'

'I took lots of pills.' He said with a rising cadence.

'And a bottle of alcohol.' Faye added.

'How long were you in hospital for?'

'Two days.'

'And did being in hospital help you to reflect on things? Or are things the same? Is your mood still low?'

'Not sure.' Tim shrugged.

'My concern now... to be honest is his use of cannabis.' Faye said, trying to steer the conversation onto the issues that most concerned her.

The lady looked at Tim with an encouraging smile.

'I have to agree with mum on this one Tim. I know it sounds very old fashioned and not what you want to hear. In my work I've seen young people ruin their lives to cannabis. Some can cope using it. Many can't. I know of one young man, Jim. He's lethargic, has suffered bouts of depression due to sustained cannabis use. He's nice but dim Jim. That's what they call him. At your age you're brain is still developing and like mum says the cannabis on the streets today is much stronger than it used to be. There can be damage to the brain. Your cognitive abilities. I would hate to see that happen to you. How often do you take it?'

' I don't have a set timetable.' He quipped.

Faye stifled a smile. She wondered where he'd stolen the line or had it just rolled from his tongue? A dry wit Shayne had called him years back. He was the boy who would watch a clown at a birthday party then copy the banter. She remembered him asking another child fifty times over what their name was and then said *but you've told me that about fifty times.*

'Where do you get it?' The lady asked but Faye knew he wasn't going to reply.

'There are people.'

'Well if you are wanting to quit the Substance Misuse Service can provide help.'

'He's already seeing a lady from that service. She comes round now once a week but she said to me she can't stop him she can only help him manage his use which is all a bit ridiculous. He's young. He hasn't been taking it long. He's not hooked so it can be nipped in the bud quickly but I don't think she's even trying to do that.'

'Well she can't make him do anything he doesn't want to do.' The lady smiled, understanding Faye's frustration.

Faye sighed.

'So far all we've done is fill in forms.' Tim said.

'What are you good at Tim? You're about to take your exams?'

Faye interjected, using the opportunity to sing his praises; something she didn't always think to do, telling the lady that he was a good all rounder, loved languages, History, Geography and the lady responded by asking if he'd been watching all about the burial of Richard III and what he thought about that.

'I wish we could go back to the days when everyone sat in the lounge watching things on the TV together. We could watch the general election coverage, the political debates coming up. Like we used to watch Eastenders and Coronation Street together years ago.' Faye said sadly.

And the lady just smiled and Faye knew there wasn't much she could do to turn the tide, for the tide could not be turned. Gone were the days of cosy nights around the TV, everyone squabbling for the remote, squashing up along the settee, cups of tea during adverts. Suddenly a crushing feeling of loss and nostalgia for the recent past washed over Faye. Life was moving on, changing. She thought of every era in the past. How the Victorians had played the piano in the front parlour; families in the mid 70s playing cards under candlelight during the power cuts of Heath's Government. She remembered how TV had been blamed for destroying conversation. But now Smart phones were the new evil.

~

They walked back to the car in silence. Faye asked Tim what his thoughts were about the meeting and whether it had been useful.

'I don't want to go there again. I would rather eat my right leg than go again.'

Faye was taken aback. She had thought the meeting was productive and the lady had been very kind with a gentle manner.

'That's a bit harsh. Any particular reason?' Faye wanted to know.

'I don't need to go. And I don't want to see the substance misuse woman either. Most of her drug users take crack and cocaine. I'm not one of them.'

Faye took a deep breath, acutely aware that she had to be careful how she responded. It was like carefully stepping around eggshells. But words were snagging in her mind as she tried to form an answer.

'No one is making you go. I only want to help. But if it's not helping it's your choice whether you go or not... but my worry is that today it's cannabis but tomorrow it could so easily be cocaine.'

'Why would it?' He looked at her with a twisted face, as if she were stupid and not for the first time Faye felt out of her depth.

'You're dealing with...' She struggled to find the words. Tactful, calm words that weren't going to inflame, exaggerate the situation or turn it into a melodrama. '...Something that's illegal, not without risks and all of these people are making sure you're kept safe and that you aren't out of your depth, I suppose.' She finished, feeling proud that she had chosen careful words.

But Tim wasn't listening. He was starting to head in the opposite direction to the car.

'Where are you going?' She called after him.

'For a walk. I'll be back later.'

Faye sighed. That would be another meal in the bin. Despite everything that had happened she knew he was off to buy more cannabis. She reached the car, leaning against the door to fumble for her keys in her bag and began to cry with frustration as she watched his lanky figure disappear into the distance.

And as she turned the key in the ignition she decided it was time to visit Jacko.

33
Faye

March 2015

Faye had been biding her time. Over a number of weeks Faye mustered the courage and strength she needed to confront Jacko. She kept telling herself *drug dealer or not he doesn't scare me. He's just a piece of shit*. The more she repeated those words the stronger she felt until she was finally ready to visit his flat. It was just a case of choosing a suitable time.

It was getting late. Tim was out. She had sent him a text to ask where he was but as usual he hadn't answered. What was the point, she wondered in paying for a mobile for him never to answer her texts? And as she passed his room to go downstairs while she waited for her heated rollers to set her hair under a net she saw Meg crouched over his computer looking at something.

'What are you doing?' She asked surprised to see her crashing into his computer.

'Oh my God.' Meg's voice was quiet, controlled, as she sat at Tim's desk, dressed in a leopard print onesie with a tail sprouting from her bottom. Faye sensed this was the lull before the storm. The shrieking would soon begin. It was rare for Meg to swear -at least in front of her mother. It was inevitable that she was about to erupt like Vesuvius.

This was Meg after all. Faye waited with bated breath. She was scrolling up and down on Facebook, reading private messages.

'Tim's still logged into Facebook. Look. Oh my God. No.'

Faye glanced over Meg's shoulder breathing in the fragrance from the bath she's just had. Tim's face filled the screen. Faye was drawn immediately to his eyes and there was a look in those eyes she never wanted to see again. They were murky pools on a downcast day. His skin was mottled, pasty. His dark curls tumbled across a cushion she didn't recognise; a selfie taken at someone's house. And then she looked to his dry, parched lips, unable to avoid looking at the ragged spiff in his mouth and the rising plume of smoke. She looked away. He could have been having sex with a girl; for the impact on Faye was exactly the same. She turned to the bathroom, clutching her stomach ready to heave its' contents into the toilet bowl. This was a vision that would remain in her head forever. Her son stoned. What had happened to him? Why was he like this? Why was he doing this?

'You haven't read the caption Motheroon.' Meg turned to look at her; her face a thick white pancake dotted with oatmeal, gently exfoliating. But Faye was too busy throwing up. 'It says *my cool mate Jacko has given me a 4 gram joint for free.*'

'Do you know who Jacko is Meg? He's not a kid in Tim's class. He's the father of Tim's friend. A boy I've never heard him mention before. Darren. The step father of Darren is supplying Tim. And probably all the other boys that are involved.' Faye's blood was boiling once more.

'How long have you known this? For God sake you have to do something.' Meg was flashing her teeth now, arms waving around as she began to work up into a Meg style frenzy.

'I was working out what to do.' Faye defended.

'Listen to this. It's a thread with friends.' Meg had turned back to the computer, reading a private conversation. 'It's between Darren, Matt and Jez. Have you heard of these boy's names before because I haven't? They must be his druggy friends. The ones he keeps secret from us. Oh my God...' She read in silence and then began to read out loud snippets of the conversation from different boys, Tim included.

I can bring some alcohol, you bring some Benjamin Franklins. Can you find some in your house? Raid your mum's purse, kitchen drawer maybe? My step dad will provide as much gear as we want. Mater will be out on her night shift. You stow the goods. Made any bit coins lately on porn images of your body? We'll have a big blaze lads!

'Porn. Oh Meg what is going on? They're selling pictures of their naked bodies on the internet to feed their addiction. This just gets worse.' Faye flew from the room, threw up again.

Wiping her mouth she returned to Tim's room.

'And I wasn't just imagining that my bottles of rum and whisky were being depleted.' Faye said, feeling suddenly used and stupid that she hadn't put two and two together. He'd never shown any interest in alcohol before. This was news to her. He only ever wanted her to buy cola. She thought he hated the taste of all alcohol and now he was going on alcohol fuelled binges with friends she'd never met. Suddenly she remembered Darius telling her a long time ago that she should have a controlled drinking session in the house supervised in a safe environment so that the twins could learn about alcohol and the effects before they encountered it with friends. She wished she had taken his advice. But now it seemed everything was out of her control. He was experiencing alcohol to excess without any lead up or real knowledge of its' dangers.

Meg was still oh my godding, her head swinging around in every direction like a puppet on a string as she became more and more worked up. Faye began to explain who Jacko really was and with that revelation and the fact that a grown man had been supplying her twin brother she couldn't contain herself any longer. She fled to her room to get her flowery crocs, running back down the stairs to join Faye.

'I'm going over there. To his flat. He lives opposite your slaggy friend Rhea did you say?' Grabbing her coat she headed for the door forgetting to remove the Boots face mask.

'No Meg. The man could be dangerous. You can't go.'

'You're not going to stop me Motheroon. We can't let him get away with this. We just can't.' She had started to pull Faye's jumper, shaking her back and forth like a wild cat.

'Wait. I'll come with you.' And with that they both left the house; ten minutes later arriving outside a run down sixties block of flats on Canada Drive. There didn't appear to be an entrance system, which was perfect Faye thought. They would soon be outside his door, on the top floor causing a commotion. Inside the hall flyers and leaflets from every estate agent and takeaway in the town littered the entrance, leading to a clanky metal staircase. There was no hiding their presence: Meg in her onesie, tail trailing behind, Faye in her curlers and hair net clattering up the staircase in flowery crocs and spotted red wellies. The clatter sounded like a heavy metal band gone wrong. At the very worst she knew that Rhea would be in to call the police if things turned nasty. Adrenaline pumped, they were both psyched up and ready but as they pounded on the door fear began to weave its' tendrils around Faye's stomach and from the look on Meg's face she knew that she was feeling the same. Faye suddenly felt like a helpless mermaid flung ashore on a dessert island. And when the door opened and they saw Jacko's face hard rasps of jungle panic ripped at Faye's chest. Was she going to turn back? Fight or flight? What was her body about to do?

34
Faye

March 2015

But Meg didn't melt with fear. She placed her foot into the doorway, pushed past him. Faye followed, hiding behind her daughter. Jacko stood dumbstruck in his entrance hall, mouth gaping as he tried to understand what the woman in the hair net and the girl in the onesie complete with trailing tail were shrieking about. But soon everything slotted into place and the man whose face and hair reminded Faye of Iggy Pop was pinning Meg to the wall shouting venom into her face. She watched the pulse in his neck pumping, a cold look in his eyes. Rooted to the spot, too terrified, unable to move, unable to speak, Faye couldn't process a single thought. She could see the boys; Tim, Darren and someone else gathered in the lounge at the bottom of the hall, sniggering, watching and all the time she felt as if her body had left her and she was now floating on the ceiling looking down on this terrible scene unfolding. She sketched a gesture across the hall to Tim but it didn't feel like her arm, it felt like a limp appendage that didn't belong to her body.

She could feel the satisfaction tucked into Jacko's deep voice and from her malaise she began to hear what Jacko was saying about Meg.

'Don't you come barging into my flat, you stupid little bitch. I've heard a lot about you. Eating your acai berries to help your brain function, green tea and bloody ginseng infusions. Miss Lar-Di-Dar thinks she knows it all and aiming for bloody Oxford University to join the bunch of privileged champagne-quaffing tossers. Well you don't look like a great candidate for starring in Brideshead Revisited.' He sneered, casting an eye of malice up and down Meg.

'I bet neither of you have even tried weed. You can't condemn what you've never tried. It's his choice to smoke it. You and your mother aren't going to stop him. All you're doing is driving him away. Is that what you want? At least I know what he's getting. Do you think I'd give my step son here a pile of shit to fry his brain?' Jacko turned to look at Tim and Darren who were watching, through sniggers, the scene unfolding like a stage play and for the first time Faye noticed the ridiculous thing that Tim was wearing on the top of his head.

'What the hell are you wearing Tim? Why are wearing a piece of rag on the top of your head? Looks like you're trying to look like a black person. You look really stupid.' Meg asked, laughing, crying and shaking nervously at the same time, across at the two boys who were wearing black durags.

'It's what all the cool boys are wearing.' Tim called back, turning beetroot.

Then Meg turned to Jacko addressing his last point.

'And who sells to you? How would you know what you're getting?' She braved back. 'And the person that sold to him?'

'They're all trusted people. And if they're not well that's a good case to decriminalize.' He said.

Meg sneered in his face, undefeated, laughing at his twisted logic.

'You're to blame for him turning to weed to cope with life.' Jacko said with a sense that he'd lost the argument with Meg, turning his attention to Faye, splattering her with accusations and recriminations; his eyes cutting through her. He wiped his brow. Faye slowly inched backwards towards the front door, her back jabbing into the metal handle. As Jacko crept towards Faye she could smell the ghastly sweet sickly smell of burned leaves in an autumn garden mingled with a splash of cheap aftershave and for the third time that evening she wanted to vomit.

'I've heard all about you.' He said wagging his finger in Faye's face. Bile rose to her throat. Meg was screaming in the background for him to shut up, her eyes pools of water on a lunar landscape of crusting face pack. 'Treating your son like a complete baby. Talking to him like he's a baby. *Little Timmy Tankers*. He's a six foot lad now for Christ's sake. And you've always treated him differently. Making him eat up the broccoli stalks but not his sisters. You dozy bitch treating him like a two year old in a high chair. You embarrass him. In fact at times he's ashamed to call you his mother.' He mocked, spittle forming at the corners of his mouth.

Tears started to well at the back of Faye's eyes. She was too stunned to speak. She gulped back the tears, a chill cooling her body as she mustered the strength to fight his crushing words.

'And I've heard all about you. Yes...' She stepped closer, courage mounting as she served the last trump card. 'And I know exactly who *you* are.' Her finger was in his face now, a violent flare in her eyes. 'And what you *did*. Greg Atkins.' She stretched out his real name.

The atmosphere froze, buckling to silence, the shock registering in Jacko's face, the satanic look now gone, distress misting his eyes, his feet cemented to the spot. They held each other's gaze for a few moments.

'You were the woman that visited me in hosoital.' Jacko studied Faye's face. ' Oh Just get out. Get out of my flat.' The thaw had begun. The violence in his eyes had returned, this time mixed with fear and a hint of sadness.

'Oh don't worry. We're going alright. I wouldn't want to be in the same house as a murderer. Come on Tim. This man killed Katie. Did you know that? Bet he didn't tell you that one? Time to get home.' She snapped, keen now to get out before her anger showed itself in a physical way.

Jacko called to Tim, with the same words for him to go, clearly now keen to get rid of him, not wanting him or Darren to hear the details of what he'd done in the past.

'There are always two sides to a story. That's your first lesson on life. And you were saying drug dealers aren't evil creatures...well this one certainly is.'

With Tim at the door it was time to challenge Tim again Faye thought.

'Of course when he told you he'd had an accident, gone for counseling, found consolation in cannabis rather than in cognitive behaviour therapy you fell for it, hook line and sinker. Well there are always two sides to a story. That's your first lesson on life. And you were saying drug dealers aren't evil creatures...well this one certainly is.'

Faye could see a change come over Tim's face. The bravado had gone. A deep sadness clouded his eyes as tears began to form.

With the door open, nobody saying a word, Faye's eyes met Jacko's. 'She was my friend Greg. My best friend. Katie was. And now she's gone. And not a day goes by when I don't miss her.'

Jacko looked down now, at the floor, unable to look up and meet her eyes and with the good sense not to answer back.

Jacko rubbed his forehead, sighed then slumped to the ground and began to sob while Faye looked on, incredulous.

'I'm sorry.' He sobbed. 'If it's any consolation that accident fucked my life up. I thought I was a careful driver. How could I trust myself on the road after that? Who would it be next? A small child? I haven't worked since. I lost my confidence. I couldn't go on. I still see her face in my nightmares. I still hear her scream. And the children' screams. I think of her son and it kills me to know what I've done. A child without a mother because of me. Without weed I can't sleep. And coke helps me forget.' Jacko buried his face in his hands and momentarily Faye felt his pain.

'But look what you're doing now Jacko.' She suddenly jolted back to the present. 'You're still ruining lives. My son's life for one.'

'But they'd get it from somewhere. Don't you see that? Drugs are everywhere. There are some nasty dealers out there. I'd rather they came to me than someone else. My cuts are clean. I won't beat them up if they get into debt.'

Faye looked over at Tim, whose eyes were misting over, the tone in Tim's face sinking like a soufflé. She hovered, her hand on the open door wondering how to reply and unable to think they turned to go.

All the way home Meg was *oh-my-godding* and Tim sat in the back in silence. Faye caught his eye in the mirror, told Meg to shut up, sensing that for once Tim had something he wanted to say.

'Why did he have to stay in the area, after the accident? He should have made a life somewhere else.' Tim said, his voice muffled as if they were underwater, trying to reach her through blurry waves.

'That's what any sensitive person would have done Tim. Out of respect. For Katie and for all the kids on the coach that witnessed her death that evening.'

'He was just Jacko. Darren's dad to me.' Tim replied, sadness etched in his tone.

'You didn't know who he was. Like the drugs he dishes out, you never quite knew what you were getting.' Faye said, in a soft voice.

She smiled at Tim in the car mirror and knew in that moment a change was beginning to take place in their relationship and felt more hopeful than she had felt in a long time.

35
Faye

March 2015

Faye hadn't seen Tim all day. It was four in the afternoon and she wondered if he was still in bed, after bringing him home from Jacko's - half drunk and stinking of weed the previous evening. She wondered what he was thinking and what effect finding out about who Jacko really was and what he had done had had on him. The Jacko he thought he knew – turning to cannabis to dull his pain – had killed a very dear friend of theirs; someone Faye and Tim both loved. In Faye's mind Jacko, or Greg Atkins would always be the dangerous, careless driver. Maybe the revelation would make no difference to Tim, or maybe he had thought things over, during the night.

Faye went in to check on him; found his room empty, his duvet folded back, fresh pajamas on the plumped up pillow; the way she'd left it the previous day having changed his sheets. The window was still open, the curtains flapping in the gentle spring breeze bringing fresh air to the dense fug that normally pervaded the room. She sniffed the air; detected the lingering aroma of whatever scent the Everglade spray was that she had used.

'Meg. Shit. I think Tim went out again last night after we brought him back. He's not slept in his room.'

Meg came rushing up from the kitchen looking alarmed.

'It's ok. I'm going out to look for him. I've got a good idea where I think he is.' Faye said looking at the empty pillow where she had remembered putting Mr. Daddy the previous day.

⁓

Walking under the wooden lychgate and the canopy of yews she saw him splayed out on the wooden bench next to Katie's grave. He was asleep, his arms resting under his head. Her step was light on the spongy brown needles and he didn't stir until she sat, jolting the bench. She looked down at him, his eyes red and startled to see her, long lashes flickering against the light, hair disheveled. He muttered something, quickly sat up, coughing, hands straight to pockets.

'You couldn't sleep then?' She asked. They stared ahead at the black granite before them, knowing the reason he was here.

Neither spoke for a while, their eyes fixed on Katie's new headstone which read:

Kathleen O'Brien.

Gone but not forgotten

True words, Faye thought. True words.

And then she looked around, out towards the allotments and the hawthorn running down the side of the graveyard. But her eyes fell upon the explosion of pink; cherry blossoms in full riotous bloom. A sprinkling of fringed pink petals – like toppings on a cupcake -some swirling, performed a graceful and dainty dance in the breeze. Others had drifted with the larger waxy petals of a nearby Magnolia to rest on the plots, their presence almost ethereal. They represented hope and peace, yet they filled the air with a sense of melancholy she couldn't explain. Shafts of pink sky speared the late afternoon sky and with it the promise of another beautiful day in the morning to look forward to and with it a fresh start for them both.

Faye wondered how to begin talking to Tim, as she had wondered so many times over the past months. Words didn't come easily. She thought about telling him that this Spring had seen the best cherry blossom in five years - according to experts - due to the combination of sunny days and cold nights. But for Tim that was old lady natter; not the sort of thing that would interest a 16 year old boy.

But finally it was Tim who broke the silence; his words taking her by surprise yet saddening her at the same time.

'Every family has a fallen one. One who stumbles, loses the plot, messes their life up. Katie used to talk about the fallen one. She said she was the faller in her family. And I'm the fallen one in this family.'

Faye gulped back the tears beginning to form in her eyes and the stab of his words and inched closer to him, their hips now touching.

'You only fall as far as you want to fall and there's always a hand to help you back up.' She said gently.

She looked down at his hand and swallowing her pride took it in hers and gave it a rub. Her hand had always been there and maybe he had known that all along or maybe he was waiting until he couldn't fall any further.

'We all need help to get up again. That's what family is for. And maybe we only stumble when we can't see the road ahead. Maybe there's destruction in every teenage... to some extent. But there's always a destruct override button.' She said still rubbing his hand.

'I can't see a road ahead. I miss her. I miss how things were. And I miss the dad I never had.' His eyes were fixed on the gravestone.

'I know Tim. So do I.' But Faye was thinking not just of Katie or Trevor. She was thinking of the young Tim whom she missed so much: Tim the toddler; the cheeky grin, the dimple on the chin, the sweet innocence, his laughter.

'I can't believe you didn't tell us what happened to Dad.'

Faye's heart jumped.

273

'I'm sorry.' Her voice was jittery. 'I should have told you years ago. But I didn't want you to blame yourselves. At the end of the day your Dad was in control of his own destiny. We all are Tim.'

And then they were looking at each other, the reflection of sun and blossom dancing in their eyes as they both reached out to each other in a tight embrace. From deep within his tears came, soft at first, then great gulping waves as she clung tighter to him.

'All the tears in the world won't drown the pain of grief. You just somehow learn to live with it and surround yourself with people who care.' Faye whispered.

'Mum.'

'Yeah?'

'Can you stop calling me Timmy Tankard?'

She looked at him, smiled.

'Yep. I can stop calling you Timmy Tankard.' She resisted a chuckle.

'And Timmy Tonkers. Timmy Tinkers and Little Timmy Tarkers? And can you make an effort to come to the next parent meeting?'

She rubbed his knee; her way of saying yes.

'Can I dye my hair pink?' He asked.

She laughed, looked at him with soft eyes.

'Yeah. You can dye your hair pink. If you must.' She said. She gave his knee a friendly pat.

'It's what all the cool kids are doing.'

She smiled. Put her arm loosely around his shoulder. And then without giving the words a moment's thought she said:

'I love you Tim. You funny boy.'

'Love you too Mum.' Came his whispered reply and hearing those words made her heart lurch.

The End

Author's Note

Thank you for purchasing Every Family Has One, which I hope you enjoyed. If you did then maybe this will inspire you to read The Catholic Woman's Dying Wish; about the search for Kathleen and the relationship between Faye and Darius.

Here is the link:

http://www.amazon.co.uk/Catholic-Womans-Dying-Wish-Things/dp/1511936703/ref=sr_1_2?ie=UTF8&qid=1441187121&sr=8-2&keywords=joanna+Warrington

Also, if you have a moment please would you kindly post a short review on Amazon – reviews are the lifeblood of authors and always appreciated.

You can also visit my website at http://joannawarringtonauthor-allthingsd.co.uk with links to social networking pages where I post articles from time to time on subjects in the news beginning with the letter D. Subjects covered include depression, dementia, diabetes, dating, divorce, driving, drink, dieting and much more.

Made in the USA
Charleston, SC
22 September 2015